Praise for *Ghost Planet*

"A won't-let-you-go story...hooked me right up front and kept on twisting and turning all the way to the satisfying end. Fantastic...a wonderful read!" —Kat Richardson, national bestselling author of the Greywalker paranormal detective novels

"An absorbing and exciting story full of science, sex, and intriguing plot twists." —*Publishers Weekly* on *Ghost Planet*

"Fisher's SF romance debut thoroughly impresses. In Elizabeth's struggle to reconcile the mystery of her existence as a ghost, Fisher offers a pitch-perfect balance of a cohesive scientific vision with poignant, naked emotion." —*RT Book Reviews*

Praise for *The Ophelia Prophecy*

"An immediately likeable heroine, a gorgeously layered world, rich supporting characters, and a powerfully exotic hero in a heady blend of high-stakes adventure, sexual tension, philosophy, and high-concept SF—superbly written and thrilling to read." —Skyler White, coauthor of *The Incrementalists*

"With the elegant pen and graceful hand of a master storyteller, Sharon Lynn Fisher lures us into a world where adventure lurks in every corner and nothing is quite what it seems. Exotic and powerful, *The Ophelia Prophecy* is absolutely captivating. SF romance at its finest. This book is a rare and delicious treat!" —Darynda Jones, *New York Times* bestselling author of the Charley Davidson series

"Fisher, whose last novel was the superb *Ghost Planet,* returns with a sexy, irresistible take on the enemies-to-lovers trope. Asha is an independent and resourceful heroine, whose internal struggle of competing loyalties makes her a compelling lead. While Pax's mating instincts provide a convenient excuse for him to feel unusually protective of—and warm toward—Asha, Fisher's light touch guarantees that the development of this slow-burn romance feels authentic, organic, and totally satisfying." —*RT Book Reviews*

TOR BOOKS BY SHARON LYNN FISHER

Ghost Planet
The Ophelia Prophecy

ECHO 8

SHARON LYNN FISHER

A TOM DOHERTY ASSOCIATES BOOK
NEW YORK

ECHO 8

A Tor Book
Published by Tom Doherty Associates, LLC
175 Fifth Avenue
New York, NY 10010

www.tor-forge.com

Tor® is a registered trademark of Tom Doherty Associates, LLC.

The Library of Congress Cataloging-in-Publication Data
is available upon request.

ISBN 978-0-7653-7637-4 (trade paperback)
ISBN 978-1-4668-5120-7 (e-book)

Tor books may be purchased for educational, business, or promotional use.
For information on bulk purchases, please contact the Macmillan Corporate
and Premium Sales Department at 1-800-221-7945, extension 5442,
or write to specialmarkets@macmillan.com.

First Edition: February 2015

Printed in the United States of America

0 9 8 7 6 5 4 3 2 1

For ADELAIDE BEBB—died June 23, 1940, on the Seattle ferry *Kalakala*—who "found life too beautiful and at once too difficult."*

And for JASON, who finds all of life beautiful, even the difficult.
You are an inspiration.

* "*Kalakala*'s Table Set for Unseen Guest,"
Seattle Post-Intelligencer, February 13, 2002;
Bremerton News-Searchlight, June 24, 1940.

Quantum theory successfully describes physical behavior from the atomic to cosmological domains. . . . It would be astonishingly unlikely to find that one small domain, the one that our bodies and minds happen to inhabit, are somehow *not* best described as quantum objects.

—Dean Radin, Ph.D., *Entangled Minds*

Every atom of your flesh is as dear to me as my own.

—Charlotte Brontë, *Jane Eyre*

ECHO 8

BEYOND HELP

But a stranger in a strange land, he is no one.

—Bram Stoker, *Dracula*

Seattle Psi Training Institute—August 10, 2018

T HE MAN on the floor was transparent.

He tracked Tess as she crossed the room, stopping a couple meters away from him. He studied her, and she knew he was trying to understand. Trying to remember.

Her heart ached for him. He was human, after all. At least he had been.

"How do you feel?" Tess asked, taking another step toward him.

"Close enough, Doctor." The low, cautioning voice came not from the fading visitor, but from the FBI agent who'd moved to stand behind her. Tess did what she usually did when Ross McGinnis spoke to her in that tone. She ignored him.

"Where . . . am . . . I?" The visitor's voice scraped like dry leaves blowing across pavement. "Who are you?"

"I can answer those questions for you, but . . ." Tess swallowed. "It's going to come as a shock."

He blinked at her, and his gaze slid around the lab. The equipment had been removed, leaving nothing to look at but the exposed brick walls, painted ductwork, and gleaming hardwood floors.

"Where am I?" he repeated.

There was no time to make him understand. He had maybe an hour to live. But he deserved what little explanation she could offer.

"You've come here from a different Earth." His gaze snapped back to her face, and she could imagine what he was thinking. "There was a catastrophic impact event—an asteroid. The destruction knocked some of you loose from your own reality. Brought you to ours. We don't know how or why."

He stared at her, long and hard.

"Who are you?" His voice was stronger now, more insistent. But it still had a hollow, echoing quality.

"My name is Tess. I'm a parapsychologist."

One corner of his mouth twisted. Tess started to ask if he was in pain—but then realized the half-dead transparent man was smirking at her.

"This is a joke, right?"

She frowned. "I'm sorry. No."

Tess debated about how much to tell him. Compassion for the dying man warred with her sense of duty. She had a responsibility to glean as much information as she could from him. The lives of people on her own Earth depended on it.

"What's your name?" she asked as he continued to study her.

"Jake."

"Jake, I'd like to ask you some questions."

"How about you answer a few first. Like why do I feel like a pile of grated cheese?"

"That's complicated." She knelt on the floor so he wouldn't

have to look up at her. "Your dislocation left you unable to sustain life energy."

"What does that mean exactly?"

"I'm afraid I don't have a more scientific explanation for you. The impact somehow relaxed the laws of physics as we understand them. Weakened boundaries between our universes, which allowed some of you to pass through to our Earth."

"I got a D in high school physics," said Jake, "but I'm thinking that shouldn't be possible."

"Some scientists believe we might one day be able to communicate with parallel worlds, and communication is just an exchange of energy. But the short answer is since you're here, it's possible. And without the connection to your own world, well . . . you're broken, for lack of a better word."

"Yeah, I noticed that." His eyes searched around the room. "There are others like me?"

"We know of as many as twenty. And more keep popping up."

"Where are they?"

She studied his face, which was little more than a ghostly residue. "They died, Jake."

"I'm dying too."

"Without a transfusion of energy, yes."

He gave her a tired smile. "I don't think my insurance covers that."

"I'd help you if I could. Unfortunately the effects of—"

"Doctor," interrupted the agent, "I think you've told him enough."

The Echo's ticking clock, and her compassion for his situation, shaved a slice off her already thin tolerance for the Bureau's interference. Glancing up she said, "Agent McGinnis, please do your job and allow me to do mine."

The agent's dark eyes registered no surprise. From their first handshake—months ago at the International Echo Summit in Washington, D.C.—they'd generated neon sparks of animosity that had singed anyone within a three-meter radius.

As she glared at him, his gaze cut back to Jake. The agent frowned. "Doctor..."

She returned her attention to her subject—or to the spot on the floor where he had been.

"No," she groaned. She stepped toward the empty corner, kneeling.

"Careful, Doctor," warned the agent.

A dead bulb in the overhead light flickered on, and she jumped. Glancing down at the floor she noticed something that looked like chalk dust. She reached out and touched it with the tip of a finger.

"Tess!" the agent shouted. But it was too late.

White heat seared up her arm, and she screamed.

Sharp pains slashed down her body, a riptide of razors. Tess's life gushed out of her and into Jake, who rematerialized before her eyes. He gave a long, low moan, and Tess felt him strengthening, pulsing with her energy.

He rose to his knees as she fell back onto the floor, head striking the hardwood. He crouched over her, hands sliding up the outsides of her thighs. She gave another cry of agony.

From far away she could hear Agent McGinnis shouting. But Jake's arms coiled round her like serpents, and Tess knew she was beyond help.

The Messenger

Though they have proven malignant thus far, I'm convinced they are not *malign*. They are not murderous by nature. As with any predator, we're dealing with a survival instinct.
—Professor Alexi Goff,
University of Edinburgh, *Echo Dossier*

One week earlier

Tess walked slowly to the conference room, dreading the impromptu meeting with her supervisor, Seattle Psi Training Institute director Abigail Carmichael.

Tess knew Abby had just received notification about Tess's appointment to the Echo Task Force. She would almost certainly try to talk Tess out of the post, despite the fact Tess had been nominated by a man they both respected—Tess's mentor, Professor Alexi Goff.

The post was dangerous, and Tess was young—the youngest task force member by a decade. But the White House had approved the appointment, and Tess had accepted. Everything was official now.

Opening the door to the conference room, Tess was surprised to find two people waiting for her. The unexpected—and familiar—face scrambled the mental notecards she'd assembled for her anticipated argument with Abby.

Black hair and a suit to match, accented with a vividly blue tie. Handsome and clean-shaven, with eyes that might be blue or gray—the only thing indecisive about him, in her experience.

He took a few steps toward her, and she glimpsed a shoulder holster as he offered to shake her hand.

"Tess," began Abby, "I believe you've met Special Agent Ross McGinnis."

"Yes," replied Tess, taking his hand.

She'd never understood why the Bureau had sent this man to the summit. He was clearly hostile to the sort of work she did. She was used to skeptics. To rigid, fear-based ideas about science that hardened even the highly educated in the face of compelling evidence. But someone like him didn't belong at a summit created to address a very real international threat. Dozens had died at the hands of Echoes. Many more might if they couldn't find a way to stop them. This was no pseudoscientific woo-woo.

She supposed he'd had similar reservations about her—a young postdoc rubbing shoulders with the world's greatest minds. She questioned it herself daily. But Goff was in the thick of it, and her collaboration with him—albeit long-distance—had rendered her more qualified than even the Nobel laureates in attendance.

"What brings you to Seattle, Agent McGinnis?" She offered him a chilly smile.

He exchanged a glance with Abby, and the tiny gesture of uncertainty—of deference—caused her heart to jump into her throat.

"What's happened?"

Abby came a step closer, fingers brushing Tess's arm. "Agent McGinnis has brought some news about Professor Goff."

Tess backed away, bracing a hand against the conference room table. "He's dead."

She didn't need confirmation; she felt the truth of it in her gut. Might have felt it before, had she not been preoccupied with the appointment.

She sank onto the edge of the table, and Abby moved to sit beside her. They both glanced at the agent.

Nodding, he said, "Six hours ago. The fade attacked him."

Tess closed her eyes. Echo 7, the only one currently in confinement. "Are you sure about this?"

"I spoke to the SAS agent assigned to Goff. I'm sorry, Dr. Caufield."

Goff was thorough and methodical. He had taken every precaution. Tess knew because she'd been videoconferencing with him since 7 was picked up by the SAS. Before that, in fact—after his interviews with 5 and 6. But 7 was almost gone when they got him—hadn't fed in days. Had Goff seen the window of opportunity closing and started taking risks? Until someone could discover a nonlethal way of sustaining Echoes—of conducting energy transfers without killing the donor—the current shoot-on-sight policy would stand. That was an escalating tragedy neither she nor Goff could stomach. Because anyone who spent five minutes with one could see they weren't monsters.

Yet Goff was dead.

Abby slipped an arm around Tess, and she realized she'd begun to tremble. "I want you to take a couple of weeks off. Fly to Scotland for the service. You can decide about the appointment later."

Tess glanced again at Agent McGinnis, who stood waiting and watching. She didn't want him here. She could feel the cracks in her composure forking and expanding, and she didn't want him reporting back to his superiors how the new task force member had gone to pieces when she heard the news.

"Why did they send you?" she asked.

He was a cool customer. No hint of emotion.

"I've been assigned to you," he replied.

Tess gripped the edge of the table, lips arcing down. "What do you mean 'assigned to me'?"

"Assigned to protect you."

"Protect me from . . . ?" But she knew where this was going.

"No one wants to see what happened to Goff happen to you. There's growing evidence the Echoes are drawn to members of the task force. I thought you were aware."

Tess was aware. Goff wasn't the first to die. He'd hypothesized there was some kind of entanglement involved—in the quantum sense, where entangled particles were able to share information across distances without contact. "Spooky action at a distance," Einstein had called it. It was like the Echoes knew where to go for help, at least on a subconscious level.

Though as of yet they hadn't managed to help a single one.

Despite all this, she didn't quite buy the agent's explanation. It felt like interference. Like they weren't sure whether they could trust her to do her job. Goff had openly disapproved of the FBI's policy regarding Echoes, and Tess suspected the disapproval ran both ways.

"You don't have to do this," interrupted Abby. "Not for Goff, not for anyone. Tess . . ." Abby's voice deepened. "I'm asking you *not* to do this."

Abby had complete authority over Tess in her role at the institute, but she could do nothing to stop this appointment, and both of them knew it. She was the only maternal figure in Tess's life, however, and Tess appreciated her protective impulses.

"Goff was the only one who understood," Tess said simply. "Now it's just me."

She *did* have to do this. She had believed in Goff, and his efforts had cost him his life. She couldn't let that be for nothing. And she still believed it was the right thing to do.

The director rose and turned from her, toward the window, resting her hands on her hips.

Tess slipped off the edge of the table and glanced at her new colleague. "Welcome to Seattle, Agent McGinnis. If you'll excuse me . . ."

Tess was barely out the door when the first sob heaved out of her. She hurried down the corridor and up the central stairway toward her apartment.

Footsteps sounded on the stairs behind her.

"Doctor, wait . . . I need to talk to you about—"

She rounded on him, startled to find him close behind her. "Later, Agent McGinnis," she snapped, her voice raw with grief.

He sank backward a step, and the controlled lines of his face loosened. "I'm sorry. I didn't realize—"

She turned and ran up to her apartment, closing and locking the door behind her.

—the two of you were so close.

Ross felt like an ass. He turned and headed back down the stairs.

They'd gotten off on the wrong foot now. Though really that had happened at their first meeting in D.C. On orders from the Bureau's director, Ross had been seated next to her at the summit's opening dinner. She'd taken an immediate dislike to him.

I'm sure it had nothing to do with questioning the validity of her life's work. Asking her how it was possible to train people in a skill that had never been scientifically validated had probably not been his smartest move ever. Her resentment had been palpable. And her accusation that he was criticizing a field he knew nothing about had been deserved. It was a mistake someone in his position should not make. But when she'd explained her line of work to him over the bouillabaisse, she'd unknowingly pricked a nerve.

He'd been ordered to stay close to her at the summit, and it soon became clear that the assignment had been compromised. It was difficult to subtly shadow someone who was actively avoiding you.

He'd confessed his sins to Bureau Director Garcia, with far less fallout than he would have expected. He had not been reassigned. Garcia did not seem to care that Dr. Caufield hated him.

But it was going to make his job a hell of a lot harder.

She'd accepted an apology from him on the last day of the summit, but it hadn't thawed her even minutely. Now he'd brought her news of the death of her colleague. He doubted he could recover with her, but he had his orders and he had to try.

Instead of going back down to the conference room, he stopped on the second floor, where they'd assigned him the studio apartment directly below Dr. Caufield's. He tossed his bag on the bed and started transferring his clothes to the dresser and closet. The room was spare, with battered secondhand furniture, but he'd slept in far worse places.

His thoughts returned to Caufield and all he'd learned about her for this assignment. He'd scrolled through dozens of images of her on the ride to the summit location on the outskirts of the capital. As he'd studied her features, his gut had told him she was going to be difficult. His gut was hardly ever wrong.

But it was hard not to wonder whether he'd created his own reality in that hour before their first meeting. And then fulfilled his own prophecy with that barbed comment at dinner. That was his problem with psi abilities in general. How much of it was simply self-deterministic, even if on a subconscious level?

There was more to it than her being difficult, or a psi expert, though. When she'd taken her seat beside him—smiling warmly, her auburn hair wafting jasmine with every turn of her head—parts other than his gut had responded in unexpected ways. *That* was a recipe for disaster, and he had to consider the part it might have played in his antagonistic behavior.

But Ross had been a field agent for ten years. Far from his

rookie days, he was loyal to the Bureau and unfailingly professional. He could deal with one moody, sexy scientist.

For two days Tess holed up in her apartment on the third floor of the Seattle Psi building, a renovated circa-1900 elementary school. The abandoned Colman School had been slated for demolition ten years ago when the nonprofit Pacific Northwest Psi Foundation stepped in and converted it to a research and training facility, as well as onsite housing for scientists. Tess and Abby had offices on the second floor and apartments on the third. The first was reserved for meeting areas, a break room, and research space and equipment.

Agent McGinnis had been given one of the apartments used by visiting researchers, and he was far too close. Tess knew when he was showering or shaving. Videoconferencing or talking on the phone. Entering or leaving the apartment. She knew he didn't play loud music or watch TV. She heard him moving around at all hours and knew that like her he didn't sleep more than a few hours at a time.

She resented that she'd been forced to become so aware of him. But for now it was better than having to deal with him face-to-face. The loss of Professor Goff was a suffocating weight. Tess needed space to work through it, and she needed time to find her footing on her new assignment—*without* the interference of an outsider with an unknown agenda.

Thankfully she had a lot of catching up to do. The first item on the agenda: acquiring the details of Goff's death. Unfortunately that one proved easy to tick off, because the investigation ended at a file that had been sealed by SAS Special Projects, Britain's counterterrorism unit.

We'll let Agent McGinnis earn his keep on this one. She fired off an email asking him to throw his weight—and if possible, the Bureau's—behind her request to unseal the file.

After that she dove into a lifetime's worth of reading on the Echo threat. McGinnis had gotten her access to the Bureau's case files, and the University of Edinburgh, where Goff had worked as director of the Koestler Parapsychology Unit, had sent her his *Echo Dossier*, an electronic packet of research notes and video files. She was also playing catch-up on in-progress task force discussions. Grave as the situation that had led to this appointment was, it was impossible not to feel a little heady about working directly with world-renowned physicists, biologists, and psychologists.

Tess had a long-enough task list to justify holing up for a week, even considering the fact that Abby had temporarily reassigned her Seattle Psi projects to other staff members. But on the morning of the third day, having exhausted her food stores and—more critical—her coffee supply, she was forced to head down to the center's café for breakfast.

She arrived at 7 A.M., hoping to avoid chitchat with her colleagues and intending to grab coffee and a bagel before heading back upstairs. But as she scanned her meal card for the sleepy barista, Agent McGinnis appeared before her.

"Good morning, Doctor."

"Good morning."

He crossed to the dispenser for brewed coffee and picked up a mug. Tess seized the opportunity to escape.

"Could I talk to you for a minute?"

Damn. She froze in the doorway, taking a deep breath before turning. "Of course."

"Why don't we sit outside so we won't be interrupted?"

So much for hopes of being rescued by a colleague.

Tess followed him to the double doors that led out to a small patio with a cluster of tables and umbrellas. It was the first week of August, and so far this summer they'd had nothing but rain. But the sky was finally cloudless this morning, with the sun just peeking above the hill to the east.

"Will you be warm enough?" he asked, holding the door for her. If nothing else he was considerate.

She held the edges of her cardigan together with her free hand. "I'll be fine."

The patio faced the grounds that had once been a playfield for the school, now a rhododendron garden with benches and graveled walks. She sipped her latte and breathed the fresh morning air. It felt good to be outside while the rest of the world was just waking up. Almost the rest of the world. She glanced at her companion.

"I didn't know you and Goff were so close, Doctor. I'm sorry for your loss."

Tess managed a polite smile. "Thank you." No one but Abby *would* know. Goff had been more of a father to her than her real father, despite the long-distance working relationship. "What did you want to talk about, Agent McGinnis?"

"I wanted to brief you on the measures we've taken to ensure your safety." His long fingers pressed the sides of his mug, fingernails lining up in neat, clean rows. She curled her own fingers, with picked-ragged cuticles, into her palms.

"Your building has minimal security," he continued, "so I've called in agents from the Seattle Field Office to help me keep an eye on things. At least two of us will be on duty at all times. And you have my cell number—I'm here for you twenty-four-seven, Doctor. Call me about anything, anytime."

Tess lifted her eyes to his face and studied him more closely. He was as neat as his fingernails—clean-shaven, with short-cropped dark hair. The black suit deepened the overcast gray of his eyes. She'd never seen him in anything else, and she wondered if he wore it every day.

"Do you have questions for me?" he asked.

"I've been wondering what I'm supposed to do with you, Agent McGinnis."

He squinted a little and picked up his cup. "I'm not sure how to answer that."

"You said you're here to protect me. Are you going to follow me around?"

He smiled. "You're direct, aren't you?"

"It saves time. I'm busy. I work better with people who are direct with *me*."

"Noted," he said with a nod. "I'm afraid the answer is yes. We will be monitoring you, as unobtrusively as possible. In fact we have been already—I have an agent walking the upper floors day and night."

Tess raised her eyebrows. She really *had* been buried in her work. How had she failed to notice strangers pacing the creaky hallways?

"I'd also ask that you pay more attention than you normally do to your surroundings," he continued. "The fade that killed—"

"I'd prefer not to refer to them that way, if you don't mind. They're *people*. What's happened to them is not their fault."

McGinnis considered this, tapping the side of his cup. "As I understand, we don't really know why it's happening, do we, Doctor?"

"That's true," she conceded. "But I think it's dangerous to dehumanize them."

"That wasn't my intention. If you're more comfortable with the term 'Echo,' I'll use that." He sipped his coffee. "I'm sure you're aware the Echo that killed that French biophysicist two weeks ago appeared not five feet in front of him. The man never had a chance. I can't save you from that, so I need you to stay sharp. If anything odd or unexpected happens, even if it's just a funny feeling, like someone watching you, drop what you're doing and find me."

Tess suppressed a smile. One of her ongoing projects at the institute involved helping research subjects sharpen their precognitive skills. She'd become an expert on "funny feelings"—which

McGinnis had made clear during their first meeting he didn't believe in.

But she let it pass. "I understand."

"Do you have any experience with firearms?"

Her stomach clenched as she anticipated what was coming next. "I don't like guns."

"It's something we might want to consider."

"I don't see the point. When they're hungry, bullets are useless. Energy depletion affects their mass, so—"

"I'm aware, Dr. Caufield." There was a bite in his reply. She watched his features smooth, and his tone evened out as he continued. "But we've observed that some are more aggressive than others. Some will feed even when they don't need to. At those times they're vulnerable, and a gun could save you."

Tess shook her head. "I have no training. I've never even held a gun."

"That's easily remedied."

"Agent McGinnis, I don't want to shoot anyone. You're aware I was assisting Goff. He nominated me for the task force so we could collaborate more directly. I have every intention of going on with the work he was doing. I can't do that until I have a subject to study. If one lands in my lap, the *last* thing I want is to shoot him."

"I'm afraid that won't be your call to make, Doctor. I have orders to keep you alive."

Tess clenched her teeth. Arguing with him was the least productive thing she could do. But she couldn't get past resenting the fact they hadn't consulted her about sending him.

"I understand you have your orders," she conceded. "But I assume you have no authority to force me to carry a gun."

"I don't."

Relaxing at this confirmation, she continued. "I hear what you're saying, and you're right that there is some evidence Echoes are drawn to task force members. Do you suppose we could compromise? Some nonlethal device?"

His frown deepened as he considered. "We haven't tested electroshock devices against Echoes. But it's better than nothing."

Tess nodded and rose from the table. "All right. If you'll excuse me, I have a lot of work to do."

"There's one more thing, Doctor. Please." He gestured to the chair, and all the blood rushed to her face as she sat back down. Professional courtesy was important to her, but she didn't want him getting the idea he could order her around.

"You should know that the Bureau wasn't entirely on board with the research Goff was doing." *Ah, here it comes.* "Don't misunderstand. Everyone had tremendous respect for what he accomplished. For what he was able to learn about them before he died. But the Bureau is most concerned with mitigating the threat."

"Are you here to tell me how to conduct my research, Agent McGinnis?"

"Doctor, try to—"

"Yes or no?"

The agent's lips pressed into a hard line. His gaze shifted to the playfield. She could see the artery in his throat pulsing.

"I'm not a scientist. The White House has tapped your expertise, not mine. But the Bureau is taking the lead in managing this crisis, and they do expect us to work together. As for Goff's research, obviously we have no authority over how other countries choose to oversee the efforts of their task force members."

If nothing else, she had to admire his ability to evade a direct question. But the answer was clear enough.

Over the next few days Tess found it easy to return to the policy she'd adopted in D.C.—focus on the task at hand; avoid her new shadow. She didn't have cycles to spare on him.

As long as he stuck to his job and stayed out of her way, they'd get along fine. But the last words he'd said to her never completely left her thoughts: "They do expect us to work together." It was only a matter of time before their interests collided again.

But for the moment she was still playing catch-up. The other task force members from the life sciences had been happy to help her get up to speed. She was not all that surprised to find that, in true academic fashion—and in spite of the task force's stated purpose of cross-discipline collaboration—cliques had formed. Her life sciences colleagues, like herself, had been focusing on understanding the Echoes, and she got the sense their work was considered low priority—unlikely to bear fruit that would help resolve the crisis.

The physicists and cosmologists were focused on discovering the cause of the dimensional dislocations in hopes of shutting it off, and their work seemed to be most in the spotlight. They spent a lot of time debating which of the various theories regarding multiverses had been validated by the appearance of the alternate-Earth visitors.

The investigative experts had thrown all their resources at finding better ways to track Echoes. No one had any clear idea of how many were at large. The reports of mysterious deaths were edging up, but thanks to next year's U.S. presidential election and the water riots in the developing world, big media hadn't taken notice yet.

Tess wasn't political—that was Abby's job as director—but she knew the upcoming election was likely a major factor in the Bureau feeling pressured to get a handle on the Echo crisis as quickly and quietly as possible.

As the only parapsychologist on the task force, Tess struggled to find her place, especially after the loss of Goff. Welcoming as her new colleagues had been, she knew that many of them were politely masking the same prejudices McGinnis had revealed at the summit. For some people it didn't matter how many dramatic results you dumped in their laps—they simply felt too threatened to see it.

The end of the week rolled around without Tess even noticing. On Friday after the close of business, desperate for something with sugar in it, she headed down to pilfer from the kitchen. The café was run by a contractor, and the residents were supposed to stay out after it closed. Occasionally someone broke the rules and a memo would circulate, reminding the staff that the contents of the kitchen were not institute property. Tess had been one of the more persistent offenders.

She'd just poured a glass of orange juice when she heard dress shoes tapping on the hardwood floor.

"I'm afraid I'll have to report that."

Her heart jumped, and she turned to find Agent McGinnis frowning at her from the other side of the counter. "Unless you're prepared to share."

Tess suppressed a smile and got down another glass, carrying both over to the counter. "I should warn you that our deviant behavior is sure to be the subject of a sternly worded memo."

"Well, if they try to prosecute, you can blame me. I'll take the rap."

She held up her glass. "Honor among thieves?"

He clinked his against it. "Hardly. I'm trying to make you like me."

Tess chuckled, sipping her juice to cover the blush that had taken her by surprise. "I didn't realize it was—"

She broke off as she heard a rattling noise in the lobby, just on the other side of the wall from the kitchen.

McGinnis glanced at the café entrance, and the sound came again. "Someone's trying to open the front door."

Tess slipped from behind the counter, but he caught hold of her arm. "Wait, Doctor."

"Don't!" she protested, tugging her arm back. The sudden contact had jolted her, but the extremity of her reaction surprised her.

He let go and held up his hand. "Wait here until I see who it is."

"It's just the delivery guy," she said. "They forget to use the buzzer after hours."

"Doctor—"

She slipped away from him, trying to shake off both the man and the way he made her feel.

She grasped the bolt and slid it free—and gave a surprised cry as whoever was on the other side shoved the door open, *hard*. McGinnis grabbed Tess around the waist and dragged her away.

A shadow stumbled through the door. Not a shadow—an *Echo* stood gawking in the low-lit lobby, shoulders hunched, eyes raking slowly over the stairway and sparse furnishings.

"Head for the stairs," McGinnis hissed, drawing his sidearm. "Go up and get behind a door that locks."

Tess's heart pounded as he edged her toward the stairway. "We need to get him to the lab."

"Doctor, *upstairs!*"

She was scared—every bit as scared as the agent clearly thought she should be. But she had not joined the task force to run away at the first opportunity to make a real contribution.

"If we lose him he'll just end up hurting people," she reminded him. "You know you can't shoot him while he's half faded. Let me *try*."

McGinnis hesitated, gaze riveted to the visitor, who stood quiet and bemused in the entryway. Finally he let go of her, saying, "Stay close to me."

Tess took a couple steps toward the Echo, and McGinnis followed.

"Hey, you okay?" she asked.

The bearded man seemed to notice her for the first time. She watched his confusion and distress evolve into something else. He took a step, reaching for her, but she staggered backward.

"You can't touch me, okay?" she warned. "It's dangerous."

The agent's arm shot around her waist again, and he pulled her against him as he moved toward the corridor behind them.

"We want to help you," Tess called. "Follow me, okay?"

Tess and the agent backed across the floor, the Echo following, and together they slow-danced toward the lab where the scientists ran their experiments.

"What's wrong with me?" the visitor asked. His voice had a subterranean quality, like it was rising up out of a well.

"I can explain, but we need to get you someplace safe first."

"Am I . . . are you . . . *real?*"

"Yes, I'm real. So are you."

"I'm so tired. I've got this strange, sort of aching . . . *itch*. I need . . ."

He took a couple quick steps, reaching for her again, and McGinnis forced her to the floor. "*Stop!*" the agent ordered. "You can't touch her." He shoved open the lab door on his left. "You can rest in here."

One of the other agents—Perez—had appeared in the corridor and stood with her pistol at the ready. But she was as helpless as they were. All of them were at the Echo's mercy. It was up to him whether this worked or not.

The bearded man stared into the lab.

"It's okay," urged Tess, rising to her feet. He blinked at her, bewildered. "You're going to be okay."

He walked into the lab, and McGinnis closed the door behind him, locking it with a click. Through the window in the door she saw the Echo turn, startled.

Tess punched the intercom button beside the door. "The lock's just a precaution. Don't be afraid."

He glanced slowly around behind him and then moved farther into the room.

Tess turned off the intercom and sank against the door.

McGinnis blew out a long breath. "Jesus, Doctor."

He reached for her arm, but his hand hovered a moment and he gestured with his fingers instead. "Come away from the door."

Tess righted herself and turned to peer into the lab. The Echo had sunk down in a corner of the room, head resting on his folded arms. As she watched him, his form sank lower until he lay flat on his back staring at the ceiling.

"He doesn't have long," she murmured. Tess had watched Echo 6 die. One minute he'd been hungry and dangerous, pacing tiger-like in a lab much like this one, and then some kind of switch had flipped. Over the course of the next several hours he'd faded away until fatigue and paralysis set in, and then finally he just wasn't there.

This one wouldn't make it until morning.

"We can't afford to take any risks," said McGinnis. "Perez, no-tify Dr. Carmichael. We need to get any staff out of the building ASAP. Everyone but Carmichael and Caufield."

Tess pressed the intercom button again. "You okay in there?"

No reply. No sign of movement.

She turned to McGinnis. "We don't have much time. I'll watch him for an hour to be sure, but I don't think he's getting up again. If he doesn't, I want to go in."

McGinnis was shaking his head before she finished. "No. It's too risky."

"Have you been paying attention? He was more dangerous five minutes ago than he is now, and he didn't touch me."

Still he shook his head. "He tried. If you want to talk to him, do it through the door."

Tess braced a hand against the wall. "Talking to them—asking them questions about what they remember—it's all we've got right now. You understand that, right? This is my *job* now. I need to talk to him before he's gone, and it's useless to keep shouting at him through the goddamn intercom."

McGinnis raised his hand to his head, rubbing his temples.

"This is important, Agent McGinnis. I shouldn't have to tell you that."

He dropped his hand and met her gaze, his expression flat. "You win, Doctor. We'll watch him for *two* hours. Then I go in with you."

ENTANGLEMENT

British SAS in Scotland initially failed to release critical information about the death of Professor Alexi Goff. Details are enclosed, but please be advised that the Echo interaction that killed Goff occurred *post* fadeout. Access to the containment area should be restricted for at least an hour after the event.
—Echo Task Force Bulletin, August 9, 2018

Two hours later

"JAKE!" TESS shrieked as the fade pulled her close.

"Let her go!" Ross yelled, snatching his Glock from its holster. "You'll kill her!"

Sweat beaded on his forehead, and his heart thumped so hard it jeopardized his aim. Ross had to *wait* while the fade drained her enough that Ross could shoot him. Then, finally . . .

Solid as me now, asshole!

Ross jammed the gun into Jake's face, but the fade released Tess and scrambled backward against the wall.

Panting, Jake cried, "What the fuck?" He stared slack-jawed at the palms of his hands.

Burning with rage at his colossal lapse in judgment—and its tragically high cost—Ross pointed his gun at Jake's chest.

"Ross . . . don't."

Jesus Christ. It was no more than a whimper, but Tess was *alive.* No fade on record had released a victim before they were dead.

Ross's gaze darted toward the door. The agents he'd stationed outside had burst into the room when the shouting started, and now he verified they had their weapons trained on Jake. Holstering his gun, he sank beside Tess, lifting her in his arms.

"Lock him in!" Ross ordered. "Don't open the door for *anyone.*"

"What the hell just happened?" the fade demanded. "Is she okay?"

Ross ignored him as he whisked Tess out of the room.

Abigail Carmichael had exited the adjacent observation room and now hovered in the corridor.

"Oh my God, Ross!" She pressed slender fingers against Tess's pale throat.

Tess had lost consciousness and her head hung limply, arms and legs dangling. Ross adjusted his hold to better support her neck as Carmichael's hands fluttered over her face.

"Is she alive?" he asked tightly.

"I'm barely getting a pulse." Carmichael shook her head, frowning. "She's cold as ice."

He knew; she was chilling him even through his suit jacket and shirt.

"She needs a doctor," Carmichael said.

Their gazes met. The Echo threat was classified. The panic generated by going public could kill more people than the Echoes themselves. At least that had been the opinion of the dignitaries attending the summit.

Ross's heart jumped as he noticed a lock of hair on the left side of Tess's face had blanched white as snow. "Let's get her upstairs. I'll contact the Seattle Field Office and have them send someone with clearance."

For whatever good it would do. Echo attacks left no wounds. No marks. Just empty, dried-up husks. There was conceivably hope for Tess in the fact the fade had stopped before draining her completely. Whether or not a survivor's energy could recharge was a question they'd never had the opportunity to ask.

He followed Tess's supervisor down the corridor toward the central stairway.

"Your apartment," said Carmichael, reading his mind. He could have easily carried Tess up to the third floor—she felt like she weighed about twenty-five pounds—but his instincts warned him they couldn't afford to waste any time.

They exited the stairs at the second-floor landing. The setting sun glared through a window at the end of the hall, polished wood floor reflecting coppery light. It was August and far too warm up here—the building was sealed like a tomb, and the ancient ductwork circulated mysterious noises better than air. Sweat trickled between his shoulder blades, but for Tess's sake he was glad for the heat.

When they reached his apartment, Carmichael pushed open the leviathan of a door that Ross hadn't bothered to lock. The hundred-year-old hinges protested with a series of loud cracks, like rifle fire.

"Put her down on the bed," ordered Carmichael, pulling back the covers. Ross was grateful for the director's steady presence. He wasn't used to someone else calling the shots, but the situation was awkward. He barely knew the woman in his arms, but if she woke scared and confused, he knew he was the last person she would want to see.

He laid Tess gently on his bed, digging out his phone while Carmichael covered her with blankets. He had to speak to three people before he reached someone senior enough to field his request, but by the time he hung up they had reached a physician.

"She's in the north part of town," said Ross. "Twenty minutes."

Carmichael groaned. "What are we supposed to do until then?"

"Keep her warm."

The director touched the younger woman's cheek. "This isn't helping." She glanced up at him. "I think we should try the bathtub."

Ross crossed to the closet-sized bathroom, grateful for something to do. Despite the fact Tess had been the one to insist on interviewing Jake, he couldn't help feeling he'd failed her. The professional tension between them had distracted him, just like the opening night of the summit, when he'd walked both feet into his mouth.

The guy was dead. But this was no reassurance. They didn't even know what dead *meant* with these people. Apparently a dust smear on the floor was not dead enough to call it.

Shedding his jacket and loosening his tie, he rolled up his sleeves and filled the tub, testing the water temperature against his wrist.

"Ross?"

He hopped up and hurried back out to the main room. Glancing at the bed, he froze in his tracks.

Carmichael had peeled off Tess's clothes, leaving her luminous, slender body concealed by nothing but a short tank top and low-cut briefs. Dropping his gaze, he nudged himself forward and joined Carmichael. He bent and lifted Tess, breath hissing through his teeth as he felt her marble-cold skin through his shirt.

Carmichael followed him to the bathroom, and he lowered Tess into the tub. The director grabbed a towel from a shelf and eased it behind Tess's head.

"Just like Goff," she muttered. "Stay with her, Ross. I'm going upstairs for dry clothes and blankets."

She rose to her feet but hesitated in the doorway.

Ross turned partway, one arm still pinned under Tess's shoulders.

"Can I count on your help, Ross?"

He knew the director hadn't yet decided whether he was trustworthy. He couldn't blame her for that. He answered to the Bureau, not to Carmichael, and the Bureau had its own agenda. They hadn't sent Ross all the way from D.C. merely to serve as Tess's bodyguard.

"Of course," he replied.

As Carmichael left them, his gaze returned to Tess's almost translucent features. His eyes traveled the length of her body to the deep-crimson polish on her toes. He listened to her shallow breathing. He pressed the pads of his fingers to her throat and felt the weak throbbing of the artery.

The two of them were the same, really. Moving parts in a machine whose purpose had not been revealed to them. The only difference was Ross knew about the machine. He'd *signed on* to serve it without condition. But Tess . . . she was just trying to do the right thing.

Ross touched the inch-wide streak of white in her wavy auburn hair. "Come on, Doctor," he muttered. "I'm staring at your half-naked body. Wake up and tell me what an asshole I am."

The muscles in his throat hardened and he reached for the tap. The water in the tub was already cooling.

When the physician arrived, the first thing she did was order Tess out of the tub. Ross waited in the other room while the others dried her and wrapped her in blankets, and Dr. Bakshi's EMT moved her back to the bed. The physician examined Tess briefly and pronounced there was nothing more she could do unless Tess went to a hospital.

"The VA?" suggested Ross. "It's the most secure."

Dr. Bakshi shook her head. "Director Garcia has already made that call. No hospitals unless her condition deteriorates."

"If her condition deteriorates she'll be *dead*," protested Carmichael.

"I have my orders," Bakshi replied. "I'll stay until she shows improvement."

Ross studied the physician and got the feeling she was less concerned about Tess showing improvement than what would happen if she and her EMT left the facility—that Carmichael would flout the Bureau director and take Tess to the hospital.

"What should we be doing?" asked Ross, heading off more protests from Carmichael. He understood her position—was not, in fact, on board with the Bureau's long-distance pronouncement—but they were wasting time.

"She's hypothermic," replied Bakshi, her gaze resting on Carmichael. "The safest treatment is skin-to-skin contact with someone warmer. You have something else she needs too, though I don't currently have any medical understanding of it."

When both Ross and Carmichael stared at her blankly, she continued. "It's probably worth seeing whether energy can be shared along with body heat."

Carmichael was already unbuttoning her shirt.

Ross turned. "I'm going down to check on the—" Tess's request that he not use the word "fade" rose to his mind unbidden. "I'll be back."

"He's been asking for you," called Agent Perez when she saw Ross coming.

Ross moved to Jake's door, glancing through the square window. He jumped back when Jake appeared behind the glass, inches away.

Ross punched the intercom button and reached for his sidearm. "Back off."

"I want to know what's going on," demanded the fade. His eyes flitted nervously from Ross to Perez. "Where's Tess?"

The *last* thing Ross wanted was to hear her name in the fade's mouth. "Not your concern. You keep quiet in there and *maybe* no one shoots you."

Jake's features contorted in anguish. "Did I kill her? Please—I don't understand—"

The fade's head swiveled, like he'd heard something behind him. His body practically hummed with nervous energy, reminding Ross of his meth-addict brother. Except there was nothing sunken or hollow about Jake—not anymore. The bastard was bright-eyed and fully charged.

Jake's gaze anchored on Ross again. "Am I some kind of—*vampire*? I felt like I was sucking the life out of her."

"You *were*."

"Is she dead?"

Ross took in Jake's distress and allowed a pinprick of compassion. "She's not dead. Not yet."

Jake squeezed his eyes shut. "God . . . why didn't you just shoot me? Why don't you shoot me now?"

Ross studied the fade—dark-blond curls, narrow forehead, brown eyes, short beard curling over chin and jaw. He was about Ross's height but thinner and closer to Tess's age.

"You want me to shoot you," Ross replied, dubious.

"Why did you let her get so close? You're a Fed, right? You *have* to be, dressed like that. Were you supposed to be protecting her or what?"

Jesus. Ross felt like he'd been punched. He slipped his weapon back in the holster and turned to go.

"Hey!" called Jake. The intercom was still on.

Impatient to get back upstairs, Ross hesitated before turning. A part of him could empathize. What a position to suddenly find yourself in.

"What she told me," said Jake, "—the alternate universe thing—is it true?"

"Probably. It's a theory."

"Based on what? I mean, how can you know something like that?"

"We can't, not for sure. But they've questioned enough of you to piece it together."

Jake chuckled darkly. "I thought she was nuts. Or I'd wound up in some purgatory for suicides."

Ross lifted an eyebrow. "You killed yourself?"

Jake's lips set, and he glared at Ross. "I'm finished talking to you. If she lives, I'll talk to *her*. Shoot me if you want to. I don't fucking care."

When Ross entered his apartment the lights were dimmed, and he thought Carmichael and the physician had gone.

"I'm here," Carmichael called from the bed. She had her arms around Tess, pressing her head against her chest. "Dr. Bakshi went to the room next door to sleep."

"How is she?" asked Ross.

"She's still so cold. Will you throw the rest of those blankets over us?"

Ross grabbed the pile from the couch and spread them over the bed.

"Sorry about your bed," said Carmichael. "I don't think we should move her again."

"No, I agree. I can go to one of the other rooms."

"Don't do that. I might need you."

Ross breathed a little easier. He was prepared to defer to Carmichael, but he didn't want to be sent away. "Okay, Doctor."

"For God's sake, call me Abby, Ross."

He sank down on the couch and glanced at his watch: 11:15 P.M. He felt crushed and emptied. Numb and completely useless. He'd been here, what, a week? His charge was comatose, and his boss was refusing her the care she needed. He let his head fall back against the cushions and waited for Carmichael to tell him what to do.

"Ross, wake up."

He sat straight up, reaching instinctively for his weapon. How could he have fallen asleep?

Abby gripped his arms. "Easy," she hissed.

"Is she—?"

"No change. But she's freezing me. I need a hot shower." Abby's icy fingers trembled on his arms, which was bizarre. All the windows were closed, and the apartment had heated up like a furnace. His back and neck were soaked with sweat.

"Okay." He nodded, rubbing sleep from his eyes. "What do you want me to do?"

"Get in the bed with her until I warm up. Maybe let me get an hour's sleep."

He stared at Abby.

"I know it's awkward. If you're uncomfortable, maybe you could call Agent Perez—"

"No, I'll do it," he said, recovering from the initial shock of the idea. "It's just . . . well, she wouldn't like it."

The director gave him a tired smile. "It'll be fine. If she wakes up and takes a swing at you I promise to intervene."

"If she wakes up, she's welcome to beat me bloody."

Abby squeezed his arm and started for the bathroom, hugging herself for warmth.

He took a deep breath and turned his gaze on the woman in his bed. He removed his sweaty clothes and walked to the dresser, fishing out a clean T-shirt. As he settled the shirt over his shoulders, he remembered what the physician had said and pulled it off again.

He prepared himself for the saunalike bed, but as he slipped between the sheets he found they were pleasantly cool. His foot brushed Tess's leg and he swore. How could she be so cold and still alive? He gathered her against him—and felt like he'd plunged into frigid water. He drew her arm around his waist and hugged her head to his chest, as Abby had done. He wrapped one leg around both of hers.

Despite the short, strappy nightgown Abby had slipped over Tess for the sake of modesty, and despite the curvy softness pressed close against his body, his gear retracted, confused by the temperature of the creature in his arms. But that didn't last. The smell and feel of her invaded his senses, coaxing blood back into his extremities.

"Sorry, Doctor," he mumbled.

Her body gave a jerk—whether in response to his voice, he wasn't sure—and she coughed.

He eased her head back and looked at her. The lights were dimmed to the lowest setting, but bright moonlight shone through the west-facing windows, washing over the bed, and he could see her throat working.

He moved closer, listening for her breathing.

Her eyelids lifted and he froze.

She stared at him without blinking, her body resting limp in his arms. Her green eyes shone like glass, or the surface of a lake.

Oh God.

"Doctor?" He rubbed his hand up and down her arm, then over her back.

Still she didn't move.

His jaw clenched and he swallowed. His arms clutched convulsively.

He felt her hand twitch at his waist, and he drew a sharp breath as it slid slowly up his ribs. Her fingers continued to glide up to his neck, raising chill bumps on his skin, and finally threaded into his hair.

Her eyelids fluttered closed as her fingers pressed the back of his head. He shivered and let her guide him. Their lips met, and a soft moan sounded in her throat.

This was *not* what he'd been afraid of when Abby asked him to crawl into bed with Tess. It had been the furthest possibility from his mind.

It was the very last thing he should be doing.

But here she was lying against him, awake and responding to his proximity, as he had responded to hers. The woman was aggravating without a doubt, but she was also interesting and sexy. And he was no more or less than a man.

He kept as still as he could, unsure whether she was awake—not wanting to wake her by trying to extract himself.

She continued to work her lips gently against his—so soft, so *warm*. Her lips parted, her tongue probing into his mouth, and *he* moaned. Her chest expanded with deepening breaths.

Finally her lips opened and released, and her head sank onto the pillow. He could feel her skin warming, and her heart beating solidly against him.

His hand closed over her waist, and he took a slow, tremulous breath, trying to steady his own hammering heart.

Ross's eyes opened suddenly, and he found himself staring into Abby's smiling face. Her straight blond hair, free from its usual twist, tickled his bare chest.

But Abby wasn't looking at him.

Gazing down, he discovered Tess's head resting on his chest, her hand splayed across his sternum. Her fingers stretched, lifting at the tips, and she turned her face to Abby, blinking in the morning light.

Relief mingled with surprise at finding Tess curled up against him. Both of them were damp with sweat.

"Thank God," murmured Abby, touching her face.

Tess nestled against him, nose brushing his chest, and she drew in a breath through her nose, smelling him. Not exactly the reaction he'd expected. Was she really awake? Did she think he was someone else? Again he held still, afraid of what would happen if he broke the spell.

Tess gasped. She shot away from him, pressing her back against the windows next to the bed. Her eyes opened wide. He watched the rapid rise and fall of her chest, and the color stealing over her pale cheeks.

"Good morning, Doctor."

Agent McGinnis sat up and combed his hands through his dark hair. Tess's breath caught. She was sure keeping fit was some unwritten job requirement—maybe even a written one—but wow, the man was ripped. Not in a gross, exaggerated way. More of a tight, sexy, the-better-to-hold-you-with-my-dear way.

She shook her head, trying to clear the cobwebs. "What are you doing in my bed?" The throaty, morning-after timbre of her voice caused her to flush again.

She glanced around at the unfamiliar, spare furnishings and then at Abby. "Whose bed am I in?"

No one answered right away, and she looked down, noting with a hiss of alarm the low-scooped, green chemise stretching across her breasts. What had she missed? Had she and Ross . . . ? *No, not possible.*

Abby grabbed the top blanket and wrapped it around Tess's shoulders, sitting beside her.

"Do you remember what happened with the Echo? Ross got you away from him."

"No," muttered Ross. "He let her go."

Tess closed her eyes, grasping, and finally it came rushing back.

He let me go. She hadn't thought them capable of leaving a victim alive.

Her eyes snapped open. "Ross, you didn't shoot him?"

"No, Doctor. He's very much alive."

"Tess," said Abby, "we thought we were going to lose you. Ross and I have been taking care of you all night."

She read the reassurance in her supervisor's gaze. There'd been nothing compromising. No inappropriate behavior. Apparently she and Ross hadn't gotten drunk and fallen into bed together. But then why was her head pounding like a fraternity house hangover? And why wouldn't Ross look at her?

She watched him rise from the bed, boxer briefs stretching over his thighs and backside. He walked to the dresser and slipped on a pair of faded jeans and a black T-shirt. It was the first time she'd seen him in anything but a jacket and tie. The funeral director uniform suited him, but this—this was much better. He looked like a real person. Like he had a soul and a beating heart. Of course she'd heard his beating heart for herself, just moments ago.

Ross turned slowly, eyes settling on her face. He looked confused and unsure—another first. "I can make coffee," he said. His lips curved down. "Except I don't have any."

"I'll go down and borrow from the cafeteria," said Abby, rising. "I'll update Dr. Bakshi on the way."

Tess shot her a pleading look, but Abby was already on her way out the door.

Ross and Tess stared after her.

"How do you feel, Dr. Caufield?" he asked without turning.

Eyeing the slinky nightgown again, she thought about how it had felt to lie pressed against his body. Safe. Warm. *Interesting.* "I think you might as well call me Tess."

"How do you feel, *Tess?*"

"My head hurts. I feel heavy." She drooped back against the window, sighing. "I feel lucky. How is Jake?"

Ross sank down at the kitchen table, about as far away from her as he could get in the studio apartment. He stretched his legs underneath, crossing his ankles. She noticed he had long, bony feet, like hers.

"A little twitchy. Wretched about what he did to you. Wretched in general, I think, and really confused. He told me he killed himself, back on his Earth."

Tess sat up. Professor Goff's subjects had died right before the destruction too. It had seemed like too much of a coincidence not to be related somehow to their dislocation.

"At least I'll get another chance to talk to him," she said, rising from the bed and pulling the blanket around her. She scanned the room for her clothes.

"You're going now?" asked Ross.

Her gaze settled again on his face. A little of the old resentment flared, but things had changed now. She owed him her life, and she could no longer so easily dismiss him.

"After I shower and have some breakfast."

He frowned. "You're sure you're up to that?"

"Does it matter? It's my job."

Her instincts warned her not to let him see her eagerness. He wouldn't view her near-death experience as the breakthrough she did. Jake had recharged without killing her. It *was* possible. She had to find out how. And before he faded, they'd have to do it again. It was the first real hope for addressing this crisis.

Ross moved from the table to the couch and pulled on a pair of well-worn basketball sneakers. He lifted a laptop bag from the coffee table.

"We're in agreement you stay outside the lab?" He paused a beat, gripping the shoulder strap. "The agents have orders not to let anyone in."

"We're in agreement," she replied. *For now.*

He nodded. "There's something I need to do. I won't be long."

"Ross," she said, arresting his movement toward the door, "I want to thank you for getting me out of there. And for . . ." She couldn't help glancing at his pillow. "For everything you did to help."

"You don't need to thank me, Doctor. I was assigned to protect you. *It's my job.*"

There was nothing uncivil in his tone, but it dropped the temperature in the room. He left, closing the door behind him.

She rose on shaking legs and walked to the coffee table, where her clothes lay folded in a neat pile. She carried them to the bathroom, dressed, and washed her face. She was bone-tired, like she'd been down with flu. Catching a glimpse of herself in the mirror, she gasped at the stripe of white in her hair. She ran her fingers through it and tucked it behind her ear.

As she straightened, her eyes moved over Ross's things—toothbrush, shaver, hair gel.

She exited the bathroom and headed down to the lab, leaving the shower and breakfast for later. Grateful as she was for what Ross had done, she wanted some time alone with Jake.

WINDOWS

According to quantum theory and the many experiments that bear out its predictions, the quantum connection between two particles can persist *even if they are on opposite sides of the universe*. From the standpoint of their entanglement, notwithstanding the many trillions of miles of space between them, it's as if they are right on top of each other.

—Physicist Brian Greene,
"Spooky Action at a Distance," PBS.org

THE ECHO lay on the floor with his arm draped over his eyes. Tess raised her hand and tapped the window with her knuckle.

His arm dropped, and in a heartbeat he'd crossed the room to the door.

She turned on the intercom. "Are you okay?"

"Oh my God," he choked out, "are *you*?"

"I'm okay," she assured him.

"I had no idea, I swear. I never would have . . ." He shook his head. "This is insane. You're sure you're okay?"

"I'm sure. Just take it easy. It wasn't your fault."

His eyes fixed on the white at her temple. "You really shouldn't be here."

"I need to ask you some questions. But if I'm too close—if I'm making you uncomfortable—we'll figure out another way."

"Making *me* uncomfortable?" He laughed. "I'm glad to see you. I was afraid I'd killed you."

"I *should* be dead, Jake. I need to understand why I'm not."

Jake frowned, and his gaze flitted in a random, nervous way before settling again on her. "What do you want to ask me?"

"Maybe we could start with how it felt, and what you were thinking about while we were connected."

He hesitated, and more color stole into his already flushed cheeks. "I don't understand why you're bothering with this. Wouldn't it be easier to just have your bodyguard shoot me?"

She braced herself against the door. Her legs felt like dry spaghetti about to snap. "That's exactly the way we're managing you now. I'm looking for a better way. I need to understand how much choice is involved in . . . in what you do. I need to understand if it's possible to control your impulse to feed."

Jake chewed on this a moment. "Did you say you're a parapsychologist?"

"That's right."

"And that's what, exactly?"

"A scientist who studies psychic and paranormal phenomena."

"You mean like ghosts?"

"Yes, but that's not my particular specialty. I'm more interested in precognitive ability, and psychokinesis."

He eyed her like she was some kind of strange insect, which struck her as ironic. "Are you a Ph.D.?"

She nodded. "I have a doctorate in psychology. I did extra coursework in psi through the University of Edinburgh."

"So what does a parapsychologist write her thesis on?"

"I wrote a scholarly analysis of the impact of quantum physics on our understanding of psi phenomena."

Jake's eyebrows shot up. "Okay, I'm impressed."

"Tess?"

She turned from the window to see Abby headed for her,

bearing a cafeteria tray and a disapproving frown. "I knew I'd find you down here. You should be resting."

The tray was loaded with food—cereal, toast, blueberries, even a steaming mug of coffee. Tess's stomach growled. "You're an angel, Abby. I'll take a break right now."

Tess turned back to Jake. "I want to continue our conversation. I'm just going to slip across the hall and eat something first, okay?"

"Okay, Doc."

Abby followed Tess to the conference room, and they sat down at the table.

The director gave her a troubled look. "I don't know what to do about this damn board meeting."

Tess poured milk in her coffee. "What do you mean?"

"I can't leave you alone here. But I'm supposed to go in"—she glanced at her watch—"less than an hour."

Tess laughed. "Apparently you haven't noticed all the people with black suits and matching accessories wandering the halls."

"I know, but what if you need someone who's not one of *them*?"

"I'll call you." Tess eyed her over the rim of her cup. "You can't be seriously thinking about not going. This is your biggest meeting of the year. Who's going to give your funding presentation?"

"Yes, it's important. But it's *two days*, Tess. They know we're working on something classified—I'll tell them we have to reschedule."

"No, don't. It's too late for that. Some of them traveled from out of state, right?" Tess picked up a piece of toast. "I'll keep in regular contact, Abby. Go and don't worry about us."

Abby leaned back in her chair, crossing her arms. She watched Tess inhale her breakfast. Tess was careful to keep her eyes on her food, because despite the confidence with which she'd dismissed Abby's concerns, she would prefer Abby stayed, in case she needed help with the Bureau.

"Don't take unnecessary risks, Tess," Abby finally said. "Listen to Ross."

Tess groaned and rolled her eyes. "Why does everyone seem to think I need a keeper?"

Abby fixed her with a maternal glare, exasperation warring with affection. "You know that's not what I mean."

"Do I?"

"I couldn't ask for a more dedicated researcher. You put your job before everything else. That's okay—you're young. You have energy and ambition. I know what this job means to you."

"It's bigger than me and the job, Abby. It's—"

"I *know* all that. I get it." She folded her hands on the table. "God, Tess, you've learned everything from Goff—the best and the worst. You can't do your job if you follow in his footsteps."

Tess dropped her gaze to the tabletop, feeling Abby's words like a blow.

Abby covered Tess's hand with hers. "Don't try to do it all yourself. Work with the task force. Let Ross protect you. That's all I ask. Okay?"

Tess met her gaze. "Okay."

Abby rose from the table. "Check in with the doctor the Bureau sent before she leaves. She's next door to Ross. I'll see you Monday morning."

Ross had intended to leave the institute. He needed to clear his head so he could figure out exactly how much he was going to say to Director Garcia, and there was a coffee shop a couple blocks away. He'd only planned to be gone for half an hour. There was an agent on Jake, two more walking the halls, and a fourth outside on the grounds. Abby had checked the resident scientists into corporate housing for the weekend. The building was as secure as it *could* be.

But no sooner had the barista placed the circa-1950 chipped porcelain mug in front of him than he asked for a to-go cup and headed back to Seattle Psi. He carried his bagel and coffee to the observation room adjacent to the lab, where he could send his email *and* keep an eye on Jake. He avoided questioning himself too closely about what other motives might have led him there.

He sat down at a narrow desk that faced the one-way glass. Jake stood near the door on the opposite wall, and he could see Tess through its window.

Ross listened to the end of their initial exchange, and when Tess excused herself to eat breakfast, he sat deliberating about whether to make his presence known. He wanted to see what she would do if she thought she was alone. . . . But was that serving the Bureau's interests, or his own?

He swore under his breath. He wasn't used to second-guessing himself, and he couldn't afford it in a situation where he needed to stay sharp. He debated again about whether to inform Garcia about what had happened the night before, with Tess. It was his duty to do so—the assignment had been compromised.

Yet he hesitated.

Tess reappeared at the window, and Jake crossed the room and joined her, leaning on his elbow against the doorframe. Ross's hand crept to his sidearm. The glass between Jake and Tess was not reinforced—the research lab had not been designed to confine prisoners. He hoped his man in the corridor was paying attention.

"What do you say, Jake?" asked Tess.

"Okay," he agreed. "But I have some questions first."

"That's understandable. I'll do my best to answer."

"Explain again what happened to me. You said there was an asteroid?"

She nodded. "You remember nothing about that? The other Echoes we've talked to remember. It was all over the news."

"I sort of checked out for a while." Jake's voice had grown quiet, and Ross remembered what he'd said about killing himself.

"I really can't tell you much more than I did before," continued

Tess. "The impact displaced you. And the disruption of your connection with your universe—it changed you."

"I was almost dead yesterday. I'm alive again because I drained some of your energy. I'm basically an energy vampire."

Jake's fingers traced along the top of the window, and Ross squeezed the grip of his gun.

"I don't care much for that word," replied Tess. "You're not a monster. But you've got the gist of it. Over the course of a couple days, your bodies run down. You fade."

"Any guesses about why?"

Tess shifted on the other side of the door, and Ross wondered how long before her legs gave out. She must be exhausted.

"Many," she replied. "More than we have time for. But in my opinion, the hypotheses with the most merit include Schrödinger's notion of 'entanglement,' which suggests the possibility of imperceptible links between nonlocal entities."

Jake hesitated. "Um, Doctor . . ."

Ross knew what she meant but only because he'd read her doctoral thesis.

She smiled. "Sorry, it doesn't have to be that complicated. Based on this idea of links we can't see, some scientists have hypothesized that our universe and everything in it is connected—like a web, or a network. Some of us who've studied you believe that your individual energy was drawn from your universal web, and you're severed from it now."

"You're saying our batteries run down, and we can't connect to the battery charger."

"Yes, good analogy."

"But we can drain power off *your* batteries."

"Exactly."

"Which is what I did to you. But you're still alive."

"For some reason you released me before I was . . ."

"Sucked dry?"

Tess and Jake stood staring at each other. If she replied, it was too quiet for Ross to hear. Finally Jake stepped back from the window and began to pace. Ross breathed and let his hand fall away from his weapon.

"I'm sorry," said Tess, watching Jake. "I can't even imagine how you must be feeling right now."

"Did he tell you I killed myself? Your boyfriend, I mean."

Ross stiffened with surprise, and wariness. His eyes darted from the fade to Tess.

She lifted her eyebrows. "Do you mean Agent McGinnis?"

"Yeah, the Fed. Tall-Dark-and-Handsome."

"He's not . . . I'm not involved with him." Ross leaned closer to the glass. He read nothing but surprise in her face. *She doesn't remember.*

"Agent McGinnis is here to help me with my work."

Ross straightened, guilt worming through his intestines. She was partly right. The White House *did* want them to work together, but mainly so Ross could monitor her activities. Her mentor had resented the fact that the United States—and specifically the Bureau—had taken the lead in addressing the Echo threat. Professor Goff had been vocal in his disapproval of the shootings, and of the policy to keep the public in the dark about the danger. Tess and Goff were viewed as valuable resources—and security risks.

Jake stopped pacing and looked at Tess. "He's not a very *good* boyfriend, leaving you alone with a murderer."

The expression Tess now wore was all too familiar to Ross. The knit brows, with the upside-down "v" between them. The pursed lips.

"You're not a murderer, Jake. It's a survival instinct. But he did tell me that you took your own life. Do you want to tell me why?"

"No, I don't. I want to talk about *you* now."

Tess folded her arms. "I thought we had an agreement."

"We do. I'll tell you what you want to know. But apparently I'm not going to be around much longer, and I like the sound of your voice. So humor me for a minute, okay, Doctor?"

Jesus, what kind of game was this? The fade was *flirting* with her. Jake seemed like he was probably an okay guy in his former life— maybe a touch cocky and manipulative. But he was a predator now, and he was standing just a few feet from a woman who was so wrapped up in her job she seemed to forget she needed to keep breathing to do it.

"Okay," replied Tess. "What do you want to know?"

"How did you get interested in this kind of work?"

"This is not the kind of work I normally do. I spend most of my time compiling study results. Or reading other people's study results."

"But how did you get interested in psychic stuff?"

Ross closed his eyes as the tension in his gut worked its way to his chest. This was something Tess didn't want to talk about— something Jake had no business knowing, or Ross either for that matter. But Ross did know, because he'd read the Bureau's file on her.

Tess grew very quiet, and Jake waited.

"My mother had precognitive ability."

"You mean she knew things before they happened?"

Tess nodded. "She was always predicting things. Small things. Not like natural disasters. Like my grandmother was going to call, or a friend was going to turn out to be pregnant. My aunt called them 'little prophecies.'"

The shrinks had hardly been able to get Tess to talk about her mother, yet here she was, opening up to Jake. There was no reason Ross should be annoyed, but he was.

"Was she always right?" asked Jake.

"She was. At least that's what I remember. One time she knew my hamster was going to die, and she made sure I was gone the day it happened."

Ross smiled, and so did Tess. But she wasn't smiling at him. . . . She was smiling at Jake.

"Was it weird growing up with that?"

"Not at all." Tess laughed. "I thought everyone's mom could do it."

Jake's hands slipped into the back pockets of his jeans, and he stepped closer to the door. "When did she die?"

"A long time ago. When I was a kid."

Seven-year-old Tess had jumped on top of her mother's casket as they were lowering it. They'd had to fish her out of the mud. Her psychologist father had put her on kiddie antidepressants, because he already had a weird wife and he didn't want a weird daughter.

"After she died, I decided she was magic," Tess continued. "I made up this story and told it to myself for years. I was in high school before I really let it go."

Jake leaned against the doorframe again, and Ross could see his profile. He could also see Jake's hands balled into fists in his pockets. The fade *must* be feeling an urge to feed—why was he standing so close? He could ask her to go away. He could cross to the other side of the room. He could break through the glass and grab her. Why was he standing there, enduring discomfort?

You know why, asshole. He likes her.

"What was the story you made up?" Jake asked.

She gave him a sheepish smile. "Did you ever read *A Wrinkle in Time?*"

"Sure." He nodded. "I worked in a bookstore for ten years."

"Well, I must have read that book a dozen times, and it was a lot like that. She was off visiting another dimension, and someday, when I was older, she was going to come back and take me there too. I didn't fantasize she'd come back and we'd all be a family again, like in the book. I didn't want to share her with my dad. Isn't that awful?"

"Not if he's anything like *my* dad," Jake muttered, glancing away.

While Jake's gaze was off her, Tess dabbed at her eyes, and Ross dug his fingers into his thigh. *Emotionally impenetrable*, one evaluation had read. He remembered thinking that didn't sound like something a psychologist should say, especially about a little kid.

"Okay," said Jake. "You held up your end. You wanted to know what it felt like—what I did to you?"

"Yes," replied Tess. "Let's start with that."

"You may be sorry."

Jake shifted so he was standing in front of the door. He planted a hand on either side and leaned in, so Ross could no longer see Tess.

Ross drew his weapon and stepped toward the observation room door, still watching the window.

"I could feel you, the whole time we were talking. Your warmth. Your energy. Something emanated out of you, like a field of tangible light. Warm and amber. Thick like honey."

Ross reached for the door handle.

"When you touched me . . ." Jake shook his head. "It was like I plunged into molten light. It enveloped me, seeping into my pores. I tasted you on my tongue, in the back of my throat. Felt you pulsing through my veins. Along my nerve fibers. I didn't want to stop."

There was a long, electric pause. Ross couldn't see Tess. Was she afraid? She sure as hell *should* be.

She cleared her throat, replying in a voice that quavered, "But you did."

"I knew I was hurting you."

Tess drew a deep breath, letting it out slowly. "That's good, Jake. A good sign. It means you have some control over it. We can work with that."

Jake nodded his head, but he didn't reply.

"Your description . . . it was really beautiful. Like a poem."

Jake stared at her, and so did Ross. Could she possibly have missed the overt sensuality in Jake's description, or was she choosing to overlook it?

"There's something wrong with you," Jake said, giving voice to Ross's own thoughts. "I've just told you I wanted to eat you."

Tess smiled. "Is that what you said? It sounded much nicer than that. You're a writer, aren't you?"

"Songwriter. I'm a musician. I *was*."

Jake shuffled his feet through another pause, and Tess said, "Listen, I need to go upstairs for a while. But there's something I want to try, and it's safer to do it now, while you're still feeling strong."

The hairs stood up on the back of Ross's neck. He twisted the door handle.

"Will you put your hand against the window for me?"

Tess turned at the sound of rapidly approaching footsteps. Ross came out of nowhere, inserting an arm between her and the door.

"I can't let you do that, Dr. Caufield."

She scanned the hallway behind him. "Were you in the observation room all this time?"

"I'm sorry," he said. "I should have let you know I was back. I didn't want to interrupt."

It was difficult to ascertain how sincere he was because of his controlled exterior.

"Well, there are two of you now." She glanced at Agent Swain, standing a few yards from the door, and steeled herself for the battle to come. "I want to try an experiment with Jake."

Ross stared at her, his tone icy calm as he replied. "You almost died last night, Doctor." His eyes moved over her and she flushed, knowing her legs shook from the effort of supporting her weight.

He was right. But when it came to Ross, it somehow felt like they had the history of a failed relationship between them. All defensiveness and mistaken assumptions. She was no longer sure when she was asserting herself professionally or reacting to him personally.

"Jake is a gift, Ross," she said, matching his all-business tone. "And he's *my* subject. If you keep interfering, we'll learn nothing from him. This is not what you were sent here to do."

The agent's expression darkened. "I was sent here to protect you. And what you seem to most need at the moment is protection from yourself."

Resentment flared, burning through the dregs of her strength. Her breathing shallowed from the hard work of remaining upright.

But uncertainty gnawed away the edge on her anger. What if he was right about this too? Jake was important—her work with him was important—but what if she was risking herself just to spite Ross?

She needed time to think. Turning from Ross, she said, "We'll talk soon, Jake."

"Okay, Doc," he replied. When she reached the end of the hallway she heard him murmur, "You're in over your head, G-man."

OFFERINGS

The Higgs boson essentially holds the universe together. It gives particles mass, which allows them to bind together and form things, like stars and planets and Donald Trump's hair.
—Rex Huppke, "God Particles for Dummies,"
Chicago Tribune online

TESS NEEDED sleep to cope with Jake. She needed sleep to cope with Ross. But there was so much to do. She was halfway through an email to the task force when her body decided to take what it needed.

Two hours later she was awakened by a knock on the door.

"Who is it?" she croaked. It was Ross, of course. There was hardly anyone else left.

"I brought a peace offering," he replied through the door.

She couldn't help smiling at the conciliatory tone. "What makes you think I want to make peace?"

"Oh, I think you do. Don't you want to know what it is?"

How did he know she was childish about surprises?

She sat up in bed, shoving her laptop to one side and running a hand through her hair. "It's not locked."

The door opened and in he came, carrying a tall paper cup in front of him like a shield. The coffee was from the café down the street. The cup bore the silhouette of an angular man who looked like a century-old, film noir version of Ross—fedora, trench coat, and pointy shoes. Cigarette, complete with a little curl of smoke.

The smell reached her before he did, and she held out her hands.

"I apologize," he said, handing it over.

Their fingers brushed as hers closed around the cup. The chill had crept back over her while she slept, but the contact—with both the cup and the man—warmed her.

"And what are you apologizing for, Special Agent McGinnis?" She gave him a tired smile. "Just so I'm clear which element of your behavior struck you as inappropriate."

He fixed his eyes on her, dark gray and inscrutable. It occurred to Tess that he was the only person she'd ever known with sexy eyelids—heavy and slow-blinking, like he'd just woken up, no matter what time of day.

"The remark I made about protecting you—it was unprofessional."

Tess sipped her coffee. Double twelve-ounce latte, no syrup. Observant. But then he *was* an FBI agent. "I accept your apology. I apologize too."

He raised his eyebrows.

"Don't look so shocked."

"What are *you* apologizing for, Doctor Caufield?" He almost smiled. It touched his eyes but not his lips. "Just so I'm clear which element of your behavior struck you as inappropriate."

Tess studied him, gauging his mood. He was guarded, as usual, but his expression had lost the closed-off, professional coolness. It was as good a time as any to start again. To let go of that unfortunate first meeting and try to find a better footing for their working relationship.

"I know I can be naïve, Ross," she began. "But I do understand you're answerable to your superiors and not to me. I know the work we're doing here is too important not to be closely monitored by Washington. Especially now that we've got one of them *here.*"

The tight line of his shoulders relaxed. He waited for her to continue.

"I work with people on a very personal level. I'm guessing it's not what you're used to, but I don't know how else to be."

Ross turned, grabbing the armchair across from the couch and angling it toward the bed before sitting down. "You *are* a psychologist."

"And a researcher. I'm used to being completely open with my colleagues. Sharing information. I'm used to them trusting me. I'm used to being able to trust *them.*"

He leaned his elbows on his knees, causing those David-like muscles in his arms to bunch and flex, stretching the thin cotton of his T-shirt. The damned sexy eyelids lowered to half-mast, and he looked up through his eyelashes at her. Long, black eyelashes no man had a right to.

"You and I don't trust each other," he said.

"Right." Tess sighed. "It's driven me crazy since the day you arrived. At first I thought it was *you* driving me crazy." Ross chuckled against his folded hands. "But really, I think it's because I know I can't build the kind of working relationship with you I'm used to. It makes me uncomfortable."

Ross nodded. "I can understand that. I just don't know that there's anything I can do about it."

"No. It's one of the things I need to accept about you, so we can move on. I'm also trying to accept that you can't tell me everything about why they sent you. But, Ross—"

"There's something you want from me in return."

She ran her thumb over the image on the coffee cup. "I need to take the lead in managing Jake. You can report whatever you want—whatever you need to—to the people you work for. But you have to let me make the decisions about how to interact with him. About how to study him." She glanced up. "Do you think you can do that?"

Ross took a deep breath and leaned back in the chair. "I'm trying. I really am. You have to understand . . . it's not that I don't trust you to do your job, but it's my responsibility to keep you alive. Goff's only been dead a week. The French scientist was killed two weeks before that. We can't afford to keep losing Echo experts." He leveled his gaze at her. "And you take risks, Tess."

She nodded. "Yes. But we won't learn anything new if we don't take risks. The whole body of scientific discovery rests on that premise. Jake's important to my research. He and others like him are critical to resolving this crisis—something we *all* want. And the clock is running down for him."

Ross covered his face with his hands, rubbing his forehead with the tips of his fingers. He thought for a minute, and he said, "His life is not more important than yours. If we can agree on that, I will make more of an effort to take care of my responsibilities without interfering with yours."

He dropped his hands and looked at her, and she nodded. "Agreed." She drained the last of her coffee and set the cup on the nightstand. "Are you ready to go back downstairs?"

"Are you? You look exhausted."

Noting the half circles under his eyes, she smiled. "That makes two of us."

"I didn't almost die last night."

"Hmm, true."

As she slipped on her shoes he said, "Dr. Bakshi wants to check you before she goes. Why don't we do that first?"

She didn't want to spend another minute away from her fading subject, but she'd just agreed to compromise. "Okay, good idea."

Jake was still able to come to the window when she tapped on it, but he moved slowly, and he'd lost the catlike sense of alertness. Just over twelve hours had passed, but leaving Tess alive may have also left him with less than a full charge.

"Isn't there some law of physics that says mass can't be lost?" Jake said, glancing at his semitransparent arm. "I'm pretty sure I'm short about half a measure."

"You think you're joking," said Tess, "but there's a biophysicist on our team that believes your degeneration—and regeneration— has to do with the Higgs field."

"God knows I love it when you speak geek, Doc. But you'll have to explain that one."

"The Higgs field is a sort of cosmic goo that imparts mass to subatomic particles. Without mass, they'd flit away at the speed of light."

"Is that what's going to happen to me?"

"We don't know for sure, but . . ." Tess trailed off as something occurred to her. "It's interesting you used the phrase 'thick like honey' when describing the energy transfer."

"Yeah?"

"The Higgs field has been described as a pool of molasses." She tapped her fingers against her arm, thinking. "It's easy to pick up a foam packing peanut from the ground. But if you submerged it in molasses—or honey—you'd have to work a lot harder to pick it up. That's basically how the Higgs field works."

"So you think I might have been feeling this Higgs field. The Higgs field in *your* universe."

She shrugged. "A few months ago it would have sounded crazy. We don't discard anything anymore."

She fished around in her pocket for a notepad, but found she didn't have one.

"I'll text you," said Ross from behind her.

Jake shifted in the window, peering over her shoulder. "So, did you guys kiss and make up?"

Tess rolled her eyes as warmth spread over her cheeks. "There was a kid like you in my kindergarten class, Jake."

"Wow, I'm sorry to hear that."

"One time he called me 'Messy Tessy,' and I got so mad I threw my shoe at him. From that point on he said it every time he saw me."

Jake grinned. "You going to huck your shoe through the door, Messy Tessy?"

"It was a bid for attention. The best way to stop it is to ignore it."

"So I like making you blush, Doc. It's not like I have anything else fun to do."

"You do now. I want your cooperation with an experiment."

Jake looked uneasy. "Yeah?"

"I want to see if we can conduct an energy transfer through the window. Glass has low conductivity. I think it might help to slow the transfer."

Jake's expression hardened. "Fuck that."

She raised her eyebrows, startled by the change. "What's wrong?"

"I like you, Tess. You're sexy and smart and kind." His gaze slid to one side as his features softened. He chewed his lip, and his gaze pulled back. "Your life's worth more than mine. I won't do it."

Surprised by this uncharacteristically earnest pronouncement, she hesitated, studying him. "We're going to be careful," she argued softly. "We won't even touch each other. Ross and Agent Swain are right here. There's nothing to worry about."

"G-man, have you gone to sleep on the job again?"

Before Ross could reply, Tess said, "You'll die if we can't make this happen."

He gave her an anemic smile. "Everyone I love is dead, Doc. I don't *care*."

She moved closer to the window, holding his gaze. "If we *can* make this happen, we may be able to teach others to do it. Maybe no more of you have to die. Maybe no more of *us* have to die. This is bigger than you and me, Jake."

He sighed and slumped against the doorframe. "God, you're annoying."

Guilt warred with relief. She was using him, she knew. The poor man had lost *everything*. She couldn't begin to understand how that must feel.

"Thank you."

"What is it you want me to do?"

"Step away from the door, Doctor," said Ross, touching her arm.

She turned, prepared to remind him of their agreement, but he beat her to it.

"I'll do it," he said.

She blinked at him. "You?"

"You're not strong enough to do this again. Remember our agreement."

Her gaze moved between Ross and Jake. "I don't know that I'm comfortable risking your life on my experiment."

He frowned. "But you're comfortable risking your own?" Before she could reply he continued. "You said you were going to be careful? No touching?"

She nodded. "Yes. Hands close to the glass. I want to see if it will work without actual contact. I thought you could pull me away if I got in trouble. I don't think I can pull *you* away."

Ross called down the corridor to Agent Swain. The broad-chested, red-haired agent strode over and joined them.

"Stand here with Doctor Caufield and be ready to pull me away from this door, understand?"

Swain looked wary, but he nodded. "Yes, sir."

Ross took Tess's place in front of the glass, and he and Jake eyed each other coolly.

"Feeding time at the zoo," muttered Jake.

"Let's start with each of you a couple inches from the glass," said Tess. "Now just tell me what you feel."

Ross wiggled his fingers. "I don't feel anything. Wait . . . yes, I do. It's like—"

Jake groaned.

"What's wrong?" asked Tess.

Tess saw Ross's fingers move closer to the glass. "Ross, wait!"

Their hands sucked together like magnets, smacking against the window.

"Ross!" she cried again.

"I'm okay," he said through clenched teeth.

She panted, eyes moving between them. The transfer was happening. Jake squeezed his eyes shut, leaning away from the door, but his hand stuck fast.

"It *hurts*," said Ross.

"I'm sorry," Tess replied, trying not to panic. "I should have warned you. Are you in pain too, Jake?"

"No, but I gotta tell you—he doesn't taste as good as you do."

She could see Jake solidifying. Ross was uncomfortable—perspiration beaded across his forehead and above his lip—but he was lucid and upright. She was about to ask him if he wanted to stop when suddenly he slumped against the door and moaned.

"Let him go, Jake!" Tess shouted.

Tess and Agent Swain grabbed Ross, but the moment she touched him, currents of heat raced up her arms. She gave a yelp of surprise.

Swain dislodged Ross from the door, and Tess was sucked against it. Her face only an inch or two from Jake's, she felt the door shudder on its hinges. Jake's eyes went wide with horror.

"Get her away!" he cried, muscles in his neck straining.

Through the slashing pain of the energy transfer, Tess felt hands clamping down on her arms. But Jake stumbled away from the door, and Tess and the two agents spilled backward onto the floor.

"Shit," panted Agent Swain, "what just happened?"

"The fade expressed a preference," muttered Ross, crawling over to Tess.

A cold drop of sweat slipped from his forehead to hers as his fingers searched her throat for a pulse. She knew her heart was beating—fast, in fact—but she didn't realize she couldn't breathe until he bent his ear to her mouth.

Her hand flailed out and grabbed his wrist.

He lifted his head and looked at her. "You're not breathing."

She shook her head and dug her fingers into his arm.

His hand came to her cheek and he bent close, like he was about to kiss her. "Try to relax," he urged.

Relax? She was suffocating!

He tilted her head back and stuck his fingers in her mouth, probing carefully along her tongue to her throat. He withdrew his fingers and took hold of her chin.

"I need you to trust me."

He pinched her nose closed, and she panicked and struggled.

"*Relax*, Tess." His mouth closed over hers, and his breath forced its way into her throat. The panicky feeling eased as her lungs expanded with his air.

Ross waited, watching to see if she'd start up again on her own. But her diaphragm had seized, like someone had punched her, and it seemed in no hurry to get going again.

"You're going to be fine," he soothed. "I think it'll pass if you'll calm down. I'm not going to let you suffocate. I have more than enough air for both of us."

Finally some of his calm seeped into her, and she nodded. Realizing she'd knotted her hand in his shirt, she opened her fist.

"Good." He bent and breathed for her again. She closed her

eyes and let her thoughts drift to his lips . . . the soft, firm feel of them against hers.

Suddenly her chest heaved and filled on its own. She pushed him away, rolling onto her stomach, gasping and coughing. As the spasms subsided, she let her head fall against Ross's leg.

"Jesus *Christ*, Doctor."

COMPROMISED

> If you drink much from a bottle marked "poison," it is almost certain to disagree with you, sooner or later.
> — Lewis Carroll, *Alice's Adventures in Wonderland*

Y OU OKAY?" croaked Tess.

Ross stared down at the reddish waves of hair cascading over his thigh. "Yeah."

But the calm he'd willed himself to feel for Tess's sake had now evaporated. His breaths came quickly as he relived the last moments of the transfer. The way Jake had snatched at Tess *through* him. Jake had fed on Ross, but he *hungered* for Tess. Everything Jake had described that morning about how it felt to feed on her, Ross had experienced as the conduit between them. And it was much more complicated than hunger. Jake wanted her emotionally. Sexually. The impression had been so strong it had left *Ross* with a painful erection.

Tess lifted her head from his leg and sat up, propping herself against the wall. Ross did the same, raising his knees to conceal the evidence.

"Next time we have to do it before he's started to fade," said Tess. "He was too desperate."

Ross jerked his chin, motioning the other agent away. Swain holstered his weapon and moved off down the corridor.

"I'm not doing that again," said Ross. "And neither are you."

Tess met his gaze. He was pretty good at reading people— *unnaturally* good, a colleague had once said—but at the moment he was coming up empty.

She rose slowly to her feet and started toward Jake's door.

Ross swore and yanked the Glock from its holster. "*Don't*, Doctor."

"Take it easy. I'm just checking on him."

Ross pushed himself to his feet and followed.

"Go away, Doc," Jake growled through the speaker.

"It's okay, Jake," said Tess. "You're not feeling the same need now, are you?"

"I don't *need* to eat a whole carton of Espresso Chunk ice cream, but that never stops me from doing it."

"Not the same. That's not hurting anyone but you."

Jake laughed bleakly, but he didn't reply.

"Don't overreact to this. We talked for a long time this morning, and you never came at me."

"He wanted to," said Ross.

"Listen to your boyfriend, Tess. You taste good. Better than Espresso Chunk."

"Fine," she agreed, "you wanted to. But you didn't. You stopped quicker this time. You're learning to control it. This is a breakthrough, and we can't afford to walk away from it."

She glanced at Ross, not exactly in challenge, but not pleading either. Was it a sign of how far his judgment had been compromised that she was the only calm one in this situation?

No, it's a sign of her being the only one who hasn't been in Jake's head.

"I'm going upstairs to rest," she continued. "But I'll bring you back some lunch. When you're solid you need food. We'll get a bed in here for you too. It's going to be okay, Jake."

Jake's defiant expression had slowly morphed to one of shock. "You are one beautiful, fucked-up guardian angel, Doc."

Ross shoved the Glock in its holster. *That's just great.*

Tess headed down the corridor and Ross followed, close enough that when her knees buckled he was able to catch her around the waist—and crash with her to the floor. At least they'd made it to the lobby where there was carpet.

"Sorry, Doctor," he groaned. "I feel like I've been run over by a truck."

"I think it got us both. I hope you caught the license."

Oh, I've got its number all right.

They lay tangled on the floor, too tired to move. Ross knew he should withdraw his hand from her stomach. Curious how long it would take her to notice and wriggle away, he left it there, letting it rise and fall with her breathing.

Ross thought about the power wielded by the tiniest motion in a moment like this. Under the circumstances, it was easy enough to imagine they'd both forgotten where his hand was. But were he to allow the tip of a single finger to press or rub, she would understand it, even if she didn't acknowledge it. It would change everything between them.

He pulled his hand away.

As Tess started upstairs, she couldn't help thinking of Professor Goff—how excited and proud he would be about what she'd accomplished with Jake. His death had left a void no one else could fill. Tess's real father had called her the same day Goff died to tell her, yet again, that she was wasting her life. And the money he'd spent on her education.

"Doctor?"

"Huh?" Tess realized she'd stopped at the second-floor landing, fingers trembling on the handrail. Ross was eyeing her with concern.

"Come on, I'll walk you the rest of the way up. There's something I need to discuss with you."

The floor plan of Tess's apartment was the same as Ross's, but the similarity stopped there. Ross had only lived here a week, and Tess had spent the last two years making her space comfortable. She had a fat sofa and chair to soften the lines of the exposed-brick wall. An antique trunk, which had clearly been loved by many generations, to serve as a coffee table. Expensive plum-and-gold bedding to console her for the fact the bed was in the same room as her living space. Unfortunately at the moment the duvet, top sheet, and an assortment of clothing were locked in a still-life wrestling match on the floor.

Ross closed the door behind them, and Tess stopped at the kitchen table—another battered relic from a bygone era—to flip open her laptop.

"I'm ordering pizza," she said. "Anything you don't like?"

He pulled out a chair and sat down. "Anchovies."

"Coward. Anything else?"

"Mushrooms. Artichokes."

"I guess I should have asked what you *do* like."

"Everything else. Really."

Tess chuckled and filled out the form. She was usually a goat cheese and tomato sort of gal, but she desperately needed protein. She checked both pepperoni and sausage, and added a large spinach salad for good measure.

"Should I order enough for your people?"

"Yeah, go ahead. I'll text Swain and have them keep an eye out for the delivery guy."

Tess finished the order and hit Send. She sat down adjacent to Ross while he fiddled with his phone. Her eyelids began to droop, and she realized that after food she was going to have to rest. She was used to functioning on very little sleep—rarely did she go to bed before 1 or 2 A.M.—but the contact with Jake had taken its toll.

Tess spotted a sweater hanging on the back of Ross's chair, and he leaned out of the way as she reached for it. She slipped it on, gripping her fingers over the sleeve ends to cover her wrists and hands.

Ross set his phone aside and gave her an appraising look. "You need to take a break."

She smiled. "That's what I'm doing."

As Tess waited to hear whatever it was he had come up here to say, more than hunger fluttered in her stomach. She didn't want a lecture. She was too tired to argue. And she liked him much better when he wasn't telling her what to do.

"I wanted to let you know that I'm requesting reassignment."

Tess felt like she'd swallowed a stone. It sank into the pit of her stomach.

"You're going back to Washington?

Nodding, Ross rubbed a thumb over the palm of his hand. "If they approve my request. I think they will."

"Damn." She gave a hollow chuckle. "I'd just about got you broken in."

Ross grinned. "I thought I was breaking *you* in."

"That explains a lot, doesn't it?"

Their laughter was strained and short-lived. Tess folded her hands on the table. "I'd ask you why, but I think I know."

Ross raised his eyebrows. "Do you?"

"It's because I've been so hard to work with, isn't it? I was just starting to get past that. I *had* noticed you have a few good qualities—in addition to being controlling, overbearing, and arrogant." She softened this with a teasing smile.

"You've grown on me too, Doctor."

His gaze felt heavy, and Tess dropped hers. She dug a fingernail into a gouge in the tabletop, but the old wood was too hard to yield to such an attack.

"Despite the fact I'm moody, impulsive, and generally a pain in the ass?"

"Please let the record reflect that you said that, not me."

"Hmm." She cut her gaze at him. "If it's not because I'm a bitch, or because you're risking your life for me every five minutes, or because we're having the rainiest summer on record and it's two thousand miles to the nearest decent bagel, then what's not to love about this assignment?"

If she thought she'd make him laugh, she was mistaken. Granite was more jovial.

"I want to be the one to let you know I am leaving, but I can't talk to you about why. I'm sorry."

"You mean because you'd have to kill me, or because it makes you uncomfortable?"

A brittle smile was his only reply.

"You know they're just going to send someone else, Ross." She couldn't keep a note of resentment from her tone. "I'd rather not start all over with a stranger without knowing what went wrong here."

She wasn't being completely honest with him, but to do so would require being more honest with herself.

"That's not really my problem, Doctor."

Stung, Tess got up and walked to the windows on the other end of the apartment. She frowned at the street below, folding her hands to stop the trembling.

"No, of course it's not."

"Jesus," he muttered. His chair creaked as he got up. "I don't know why I said that. I'm sorry. This isn't easy for me."

Tess heard him crossing the room to stand behind her. She kept her eyes on the downtown skyline, a couple miles to the northwest, and the glittering water of Puget Sound just beyond.

"I've never had to leave an assignment before. To be honest, Doctor, I thought you'd be relieved."

"I guess we don't know each other as well as we think we do." She rubbed her hands over her shoulders. "I wish you'd tell me why."

Her heart thumped heavily through the long pause that followed.

"All right. But don't make me talk to your back."

Tess turned, and Ross ran a hand through his hair, sighing. His fingers made it stick up in a few places, and she liked that. Almost as much as she liked the uncharacteristic dark stubble sprouting over his chin and jaw. The man was dangerously sexy. She found herself thinking about how many times he'd had his hands on her over the course of the last day.

"I feel compromised," he said. "I'm not sure whether I'm following orders anymore. I've become indecisive, and uncertainty on my part is unacceptable in a situation like this. Our lives are at risk every minute. And mistakes have consequences beyond the two of us."

"What's making you indecisive?"

Ross's gaze shifted to the window, and his tongue ran over his bottom lip. "You."

Her heart startled off its lily pad. She dropped her arms by her sides and waited for him to continue.

"You're persuasive, and determined. You care about people, and you're passionate about your job. All of that's great, but . . ."

"It's making you second-guess the orders you've been given?"

His eyes met hers. He looked startled.

"I'm not sure that's a bad thing, Ross."

He closed his eyes and turned back to the window. "I'm not either. That's the problem."

She stared at his profile, surprised by what he'd revealed. Surprised that one of his walls had come down, if only a little.

He turned. "But my biggest concern right now is the risks you're taking. I agree there's risk inherent in what you're doing. I have to *accept* that you're going to take risks—within reason. But the line between reasonable and unreasonable risk has become so blurry I can't see it anymore. And I can't do my job that way."

"I think you're being hard on yourself. This is an unusual situation. One you couldn't have trained or prepared for. The line between reasonable and unreasonable risk would be blurry for *anyone*. It's blurry for *me*. I'm operating on instinct and hunches."

Ross shook his head. "I've been an agent for ten years. The specific circumstances may be unusual, but the situation . . . I've faced it many times. I should be able to handle it."

She studied his face, trying to grasp the subtext. Was he hinting at . . . at duty compromised by personal feelings? She shivered, flashing back to that moment in his bed when she'd woken to find her head on his chest.

Her heart drummed as she waited for him to continue.

But when he did, he said, "Get some rest, Tess. I'll bring up the food when it comes."

He was turning, but she reached for his arm. "I know this has to be your decision, but I hope you'll . . ." She swallowed. "I hope you'll think it over."

He gave her the smallest of smiles. "Do you?"

"You've saved my life twice. I trust you. I value your opinions, though I know I don't say so." She wiped her sweaty palms on her jeans. *Just say it, Tess.* "I wish you wouldn't go." The surprise that flickered in his eyes made her want to backtrack. "I really don't think there's anyone else who'd put up with my crap."

His smile deepened. "You're not as scary as you think you are, Doctor."

She laughed nervously, raising a hand to her temple. "Even with my new Bride of Frankenstein look?"

"Mysterious, maybe." The breath stuck in her throat as he took the end of the white strand between his fingers. "A woman with a secret. But scary? Sorry."

He tucked the lock of hair behind her ear and moved away.

Tess sank down on the bed, wondering who was going to get her heart started again now that he was gone.

Jake stood with his back against the one-way glass of the observation room.

"I'm coming in," Ross warned through the intercom. "Stay where you are."

Agent Perez stood nearby with her sidearm drawn as Ross entered the lab and set a plate of food on the floor. He was leaving again when Jake asked, "How is Tess?"

The fade looked relaxed, and solid. He still had the feverish look in his eyes, but nothing about his posture suggested he was tensed to pounce.

"She's sleeping."

Jake nodded.

Ross started again to leave, but Jake said, "You might be interested to know I learned a few things about the two of you during Tess's little experiment."

"I'm not." Ross stepped out and closed the door.

Jake walked to the door, and something about the way the fade looked at him caused Ross to hesitate. He sent Perez to the lobby.

"What is it you want to say, Jake?" he asked through the intercom.

Jake crossed his arms, staring at Ross. "A bunch of . . . *information* comes rushing in when I feed on her. It happened with you too.

Mostly it's just a lot of noise, and hard for me to really make any sense out of it. But a few things have come through pretty clear."

Ross's gut twisted with apprehension. He knew he should walk away before the fade told him something he had no business knowing. Something he didn't *want* to know.

"I'm not going to share any of her secrets with you, G-man. That's between me and her."

Ross bristled. "Then what is it you want?"

"I'm going to give you a piece of advice, and if you're not a complete asshole, you'll take it."

"Yes?"

"Don't leave her."

Ross's work as a field agent had made him an expert at controlling his reactions. But it was hard to imagine the jolt of regret that ran through him wasn't visible from the outside.

"What?"

"You heard me, Ross. Don't you leave her. I know you're thinking about it."

Walk. Away. Now.

"I'm not leaving her. I'm leaving the assignment. It's not personal."

"What a load of horseshit. They teach you to talk like that in special agent school, or is that just you?"

"Fuck you," growled Ross, turning.

"Listen, Ross, I've had a little peek inside your head. I know you want her, and it's completely fucked you up. But I'm interpreting these temper tantrums of yours as you actually giving a shit about what happens to her."

Ross's blood boiled. He stood rooted to the spot, waiting for the truck to run him down again.

"I'm going to give you the benefit of the doubt and tell you something you don't deserve to know. Tess is bruised and broken inside. She cares about this job more than anything else. Lots of people let her down when she was little, and she forgets about it by working hard, and by helping others."

Ross clutched the grip of his weapon in desperation. He didn't need the fade to tell him all this. He had the fucking *file*. "I don't know what this has to do with me."

"If you leave she's going to get herself killed. You might as well put a bullet in me right now."

Ross wiped the palm of his hand on his pants. He pushed damp hair back from his brow. "She'll be fine. They'll send someone else."

"That's another bullshit answer and you know it." The fade's eyes brimmed with fury, and a single tear drove down his cheek. "Fucking *coward*."

Ross gaped at him. How had Tess gotten so deeply under Jake's skin in only twenty-four hours? He realized the answer to that question was in the question itself. She *was* under his skin, literally. Circulating around in his body. She was the only reason the fade was still breathing.

Ross believed he had an inkling of an idea what that must feel like.

"It's done, Jake. I sent the request five minutes ago. She'll be safer with someone . . . more removed."

Ross turned off the intercom and stepped away from the door, only to whip around again as Jake's body slammed against it. He aimed the Glock at the window, and Jake's face moved into view. Jake gave the door a violent kick.

Ross pushed the barrel of the Glock against the window, and Jake closed his eyes.

Worried about oversleeping, Tess only managed to nap for about half an hour. She'd resolved not to let more than an hour pass before trying another energy transfer. It would all be on her this time; Ross wouldn't agree to do it again. And she couldn't blame him for that. No wonder he couldn't wait to get out of here.

She assumed she'd be bodyguard-free for a while, until they could send a replacement. Meantime she was going to have to work out a sustainable plan for Jake's care and feeding. She couldn't expect help or reinforcements from the Bureau, but Abby would be back Monday morning. Until then she'd just have to keep the transfers short and frequent.

Whatever Tess's regrets about Ross, she'd forget them soon enough. Besides Jake and the energy transfers, she had a mountain of task force email to catch up on. All of them were expecting an update on Echo 8.

When she reached the lab, Jake was lying on the cot they'd found in the basement storage. She tapped on the glass with her knuckle and he glanced up.

Glaring at her through the glass, he shook his head.

She frowned and turned on the intercom. "Come on, Jake. I want to try the transfer now, before you need it."

He rolled on the cot until his back was to her, folding his arms over his head.

DENIAL

TO: Ross McGinnis
FROM: Maxwell Garcia
SUBJECT: Re: Reassignment request
CLASSIFICATION: Classified

I respect your honesty, Ross, and I commend your professionalism. I do not, however, concur with your assessment of the risk posed by your continuing at Seattle Psi. Your actions in this current situation have, as far as I can determine from the information you've provided, in no way compromised our objectives.

Furthermore, the administration has asked us to submit new strategies for containing the Echo threat, and you are critical to a key proposal. More on this soon. In the meantime, I'm afraid I must deny your request for reassignment.

Sincerely,
Max Garcia
Director, Federal Bureau of Investigation

ROSS SAT staring at his laptop screen. Two paragraphs of polite, professional reply that could easily be summed up in three words: *Suck. It. Up.*

He wasn't as surprised as he should be. He didn't believe in fate, but the truth was, everything that had happened since he met

Tess had the feel of something that had happened before. He wouldn't go as far as to say it was *supposed* to happen, but it had a feel of inevitability.

Moreover, Jake had gotten to him. The fade had some kind of crazy, instinctive ability to get hold of Ross by the balls when it came to Tess. She was clearly bright and capable, but Jake was right about her vulnerability. Ross had been afraid of what might happen to her when he was gone, though he knew it was sheer arrogance to think he had any real power to keep her safe.

Sighing, Ross glanced up from the observation room desk—in time to watch Tess walk through the lab door. Agent Swain stepped into the doorway behind her, weapon trained on Jake.

"Get *out*." Jake's eyes were bright with anger, his hands balled into fists against his legs.

"The sooner we do this, the safer it will be."

"Tess!" Ross shouted from behind her.

She stayed focused on her subject. "I'm not leaving until you come back to the window."

"It's not gonna happen, Doc," replied Jake, pressing his back against the wall. "We're done."

"Why?"

"Because you're going to get hurt. *Worse*. Now get out."

"Come on, Doctor," said Ross, hand closing over her arm.

In struggling to hold her ground, she lost both her footing and her focus and stumbled toward the cot.

Jake sprang, and suddenly he was on top of her, caging her against the floor between his arms and knees, as close as he could be without touching her.

A gunshot whizzed over Jake's head, striking the mattress on the cot. "Hold your fire!" cried Ross.

"Back off, G-man!" growled Jake, moving his face close to hers. "You had your chance."

"That's enough drama, Jake," called Ross, his voice steady but tight. "You got what you wanted. I'm staying. Now let her go."

Jake didn't seem to hear Ross. He made a slow circuit with his head, moving his face over Tess's without touching. Her skin burned, and she felt the magnetic pull of the energy transfer.

"Don't . . . *move*," murmured Jake. "You feel *so* good."

She held completely still as Jake's face hovered over her neck. "Jake . . . ," she croaked.

"Stop fucking around!" yelled Ross. "You'll kill her!"

Jake lined up his lips with hers and closed his eyes. She shrank against the floor, giving a frantic little moan.

"Are you afraid of me *now*, Doctor?" purred Jake, still poised to kiss her.

"Yes," she panted.

Jake's head straightened. His eyes bored into hers. "You've tried to help me. You've been kind to me. I want to help you too. But you can't tame me. We can't be friends. I want to kiss you. I want to fuck you. I want to *absorb* you. One day I'm going to do one of these things, and you're going to die."

"You're *finished*, asshole." Ross's voice faded into the background.

Tess felt the energy transfer peeling away her layers. Gone was the woman, the parapsychologist, the grad student—the mantle of adulthood. She was a child again, alone and naked, and deep within her was a well that concealed a child's secret, from the world and from her grownup self. She pulled back from the shadows, afraid to look into the face of the thing that waited there. She could hear its hollow breathing. And she could feel how its tendrils had woven into her life.

"That's not who I am," she murmured, half conscious now as her energy drained.

Jake leaned close, his lips at her ear. "That's right, Doctor. It's not."

She closed her eyes as it sank in that he was witnessing these memories with her. A tear slipped from under her eyelid, and he bent and stopped it with the tip of his tongue, following its track up her cheek to the corner of her eye. Barely grazing her skin, but searing like a cattle brand.

Ross gave a cry of rage.

Jake jumped suddenly to his feet, holding out his arms. "Do it, G-man."

"Don't!" Tess choked out.

"Cover me," Ross ordered Swain.

Jake stood still, Swain's weapon trained on him, while Ross lifted Tess from the floor. Shaken and drained by the transfer, she curled her hands around his neck and pressed her head against his chest. She wasn't sure which of them was trembling harder.

He carried her out into the corridor, and she heard the lab door close behind them.

"Stay with me," she murmured.

He bent his head, stubbly chin catching at her hair. "I'm not going anywhere."

Tess was asleep by the time they reached her apartment. Her skin was cool, but her heartbeat was steady. He tucked her into bed before retrieving his laptop and the extra blankets from downstairs. When he'd dropped it all off, he went to the cafeteria to pilfer coffee beans.

He checked Tess once more before settling into the armchair next to the bed with his laptop and coffee cup.

There was a second email from Director Garcia.

As you're aware, you were selected for this assignment based on the results of your psi evaluation. I had not yet discussed with you my intention for you to work with the scientists at Seattle Psi to sharpen your abilities. Clearly the arrival of Echo 8 made that impractical.

However, this crisis has multiple fronts, and we are adjusting priorities.

I'll be traveling to Seattle to discuss details with you and Dr. Caufield. In the meantime, I'm giving you access to a portion of your confidential file—your test scores from the academy. Take some time to review your psi evaluation with Dr. Caufield. I'll be in touch soon.

Ross closed his eyes and let his head fall back on the chair. *Psi evaluation.* This particular souvenir from his weeks at Quantico kept coming back to haunt him. It had always been a sore spot—a piece of information he hated having as part of his official record—and the very reason he'd fallen out with Tess in their first meeting.

He logged onto the Bureau's secure site and found the new folder in his document library. He began opening and scrolling through files. As he scanned the psi evaluations, which were based on interviews and tests that probed for precognitive and psychokinetic abilities, a few comments jumped out at him:

> *Highly intuitive/perceptive*
> *Incorporates precog in routine decision-making*
> *Candidate suppresses*
> *Recommend blind test sequence*

Candidate suppresses. If that meant he didn't believe in it, whoever had written the note was right. Ross's work often involved quick decisions, which he sometimes made based on guesses and gut instincts. His guesses—and his gut—were almost always right. He believed this was due to his aptitude for noting and recalling details, and he rejected—even resented—the notion of a paranormal "gift."

But he'd been given an order, and the director himself was coming to reinforce it.

Ross read the evaluations more carefully, jotting down notes on a legal pad. When he finished, he got up to pour another cup of coffee. His hand strayed to a bottle of wine resting next to the coffee maker.

"Make mine a double," called Tess.

He grinned at her over his shoulder. "I made coffee. Do you want some?"

"Absolutely." Her voice creaked with fatigue. "I'm going for a record."

He walked back to the bed and set a steaming mug on the nightstand. "It's been sitting awhile. But I think it will still work."

"Thank you," she said, sitting up and kicking off some of the covers. She still had on her basketball sneakers, same style as his, only red.

"How do you feel?" he asked.

She sank against the headboard. "Probably about the same as I look." She wrapped both hands around the coffee mug. "I'm okay."

"What happened earlier, with Jake . . . that was my fault."

Tess frowned. "I don't see how that's possible."

"He knew I was planning to leave."

She gave an uneasy laugh. "And here I thought it was all about me. I thought he was trying to warn me. Prove to me he was dangerous."

"It *is* all about you." Ross chose his next words carefully. "He doesn't want me to leave because he doesn't want you to be without protection. He's in love with you, Doctor."

"He's *what*?" Ross watched the color steal over her pale cheeks. She shook her head. "He only thinks he is. Because I've helped him."

"Trust me. I've been in his head. Or he's been in mine, anyway. 'Love' is putting it mildly."

Tess swallowed and set down the mug. She fiddled with one of the blankets. "But you're not, are you?"

Ross's heart thudded. "I'm not . . . ?"

"Leaving. I heard you tell him so."

He let out his breath. "That's right. My request was denied."

"I see." She gave him a tight smile. "I'm sorry."

"I hope you understand—I was trying to do what was best for everyone. It was never about . . . it wasn't *you* I was . . ." *Shut up, asshole.*

"It's okay, Ross. There's no need to discuss it. I'm glad you're staying."

He smiled at her, and he changed the subject, because he didn't know what else to do. "There's actually something else I'd like to talk to you about, if you feel up to it."

"Of course." She glanced at her watch. "I think at five we should go down to Jake, but that gives us half an hour."

He retrieved the legal pad and sat down again in the armchair. "Can you read this and tell me what you make of it?"

She took the notepad and worked a blanket up around her shoulders. Her forehead creased, lips parting slightly, as she read the first page.

"What is this?" she asked, glancing at him.

"I copied it out of a Bureau personnel file. I'll explain when you finish."

He tried to relax while she read, propping his feet on the bed and resting his head against the back of the chair. Her sneaker grazed his as she crossed her ankles. He felt both soothed and unsettled by her presence, and that made no sense to him.

After a few minutes she said, "Who taught you longhand? A spider?"

He grinned. She grinned back, and some of the tension in his chest released.

"So, what this looks like to me is a researcher's notes on a subject with strongly demonstrated precognitive ability."

"Can you explain to me what that means? I mean, I know precognitive ability is the ability to predict things before they happen. I'm just wondering whether the person they're describing is really any different from anyone else."

"That's a more perceptive question than you realize." Tess sat up, folding her legs and angling toward him. "Psi phenomena aren't phenomena at all. Psi, including precognition, is a fact of life. It's part of the human experience and has been for centuries. We don't think in terms of individuals with 'special' abilities anymore. Everyone is capable to some degree—scientists in my field almost universally believe this. But some access these abilities more successfully, more consistently, than others. Some suppress them, either consciously or subconsciously."

"Why?"

"Why suppress them? There are a lot of reasons. Fear of the unknown. Cultural prejudices against the idea of psychic abilities. For some people, acceptance of psi wreaks havoc on their belief systems—dramatically alters the way they view the world, life and death, spirituality. It's understandable. For others, it creates a feeling of being out of control."

"I can see that." He studied his folded hands, but felt her eyes on him.

"Can you?"

"Sure. I personally would like to believe I make decisions based on logic and experience, not on vague intuitions."

"Ah, but you're revealing a prejudice. Why isn't precognition as valid a factor as logic, experience, intellect, or common sense in making a decision? Haven't you ever had a 'gut feeling'?"

"Of course. But again—based on experience and observation. It's not the same."

"Are you sure about that?" Her color rose as she grew more animated. "It's a paradox, Ross."

"What is?"

"The idea psi abilities cause a loss of control—it's actually the opposite. If you sense you're about to trip down the stairs and break your ankle, you can take the elevator instead, right?"

She had a point. But he replied, "Maybe I'd just trip on my shoelace and break my ankle anyway."

Tess laughed—a long, genuine laugh. He couldn't help feeling pleased that he'd caused it. "Okay," she said, "you're gonna have to buy me a drink if you want to talk about determinism."

Ross thought he'd like nothing better than to go out for a drink, like two normal people. This is how it should have gone between them from the beginning. This is the conversation they *should* have had at the summit. He could admit now that he'd felt threatened by what she represented. He suspected that sentiment ran both ways.

"Actually I think it's me who owes *you* a drink at this point," she continued. "What do you say we take care of Jake, microwave the leftover pizza, and open that bottle?"

Why not? He had to somehow work up the nerve to tell her Director Garcia was coming from Washington with an agenda of his own.

"You're on. But I'll take care of Jake. You take care of the rest."

Her expression registered surprise. "Are you sure?"

He wasn't. But he knew if he didn't do it, she would. "Yes."

"With the glass between you," she cautioned.

He nodded, rising from the chair. "I think he'll be more in control if you aren't there. I'll be back. Text me if you need me."

"I do," she said, then laughed and turned red as her shoes as she corrected, "I mean I will."

TRUTH AND CONSEQUENCE

TO: Echo Task Force
CC: Abigail Carmichael
FROM: Tess Caufield
SUBJECT: Urgent Update
CLASSIFICATION: Classified

Seattle Psi has succeeded in conducting a series of nonlethal transfers with Echo 8 (Jake Parker). Details are provided in the attached document. Be advised that transfers for depleted Echoes are still *extremely high risk.*

I'm working on a detailed report for the administration, which I will submit for your feedback and recommendations. Please contact me with any questions.

Tess Caufield
Precognitive Specialist
Seattle Psi Training Institute

WHEN ROSS left, Tess composed and sent her update to the task force. What she needed now was time to organize her thoughts for her report, but she didn't know when she was going to get it. Jake was turning into a full-time job. More than full-time. What would she do when it came time for bed—set an alarm to wake her every few hours?

But the truth was she never slept more than a few hours at a stretch anyway. Last night with Ross was the first time she'd slept a whole night through in as long as she could remember—though it hadn't exactly been a natural sleep.

By the time Ross returned she had reheated the pizza and poured the wine. He helped her carry the plates and glasses to the sofa.

"How'd it go?" she asked.

"Fine. He's stopped being such a prick. I think the last encounter wore him out."

She nodded. "Honestly I suspect he's bipolar. I wish I could do more to help him."

"You're doing a lot. He's alive because of you."

"I'm not sure he's grateful for that."

She lifted her glass for him to clink. "Thank you. For everything."

"You're welcome, Doctor."

They ate their dinner in silence and slid the plates back onto the coffee table. She sank against the sofa with her glass. "Can I ask you a question?"

"Sure, go ahead."

"The stuff you gave me to read earlier . . . that was about you, wasn't it?"

He gave her a wry smile. "What makes you think so?"

"Just a hunch." A good one, apparently. "Who sent you the file?"

"Director Garcia."

"Have you always known? Or was the Bureau the first to talk to you about your abilities?"

Ross shrugged and settled back against the sofa. "My father always said I had good instincts. Those are an advantage in my line of work. You really can't make field agent without them."

"They're an advantage in any line of work," she said. "But from what I read of your file, your instincts are better than most people's. Why do you think they're sharing this with you now?"

He met her gaze. "They intend for me to train while I'm here. Garcia notified me today."

She frowned. "Did he say why?"

"Not yet. I think it has something to do with the Echoes. He's coming here to discuss it with us."

"When?"

"I should know soon."

Tess eyed him, uneasy. She didn't like the idea of his agency getting more involved in their work. She knew full well she didn't have any right to expect they wouldn't. But the FBI viewed the Echoes as a threat to public safety. Ross's superiors didn't care that Jake and the others had once been human. What she and Jake had discovered could resolve all this—*if* she could make the administration listen to her. She was counting on Ross's help for that.

"It's interesting to me that you've used your ability without even being aware of it," Tess said. "When I spoke earlier about suppression, I was talking about individuals who block or sabotage their abilities. Can you tell me about a hunch you've had since you've been here? Something that's ended up happening?"

Ross stared at his glass, turning it in his hands. "I knew Jake would attack you when we went in there last night."

"That's right, you told me."

"Anyone could have guessed that. It's what they do."

"True enough. But tell me more about your hunch. Was it *just* your sense of the danger of me going into a room with an Echo?"

He considered this, lifting his eyebrows after a moment. "I'd forgotten this until now, but I had a dream the night before."

"About the attack?"

"Not really. It made no sense, like most dreams. You and I were arguing about something—I can't remember what."

"I'm sorry to inform you that was no dream. It really happened."

The corners of his lips turned up. He had a boyish, charming smile that she hadn't gotten to see often enough.

"We were sitting at a table in the cafeteria," he continued, "and there was a plate between us. There was a donut on it—one of those powdered-sugar ones. I was trying to give it to you, and you wouldn't take it."

"That doesn't sound very much like me." She laughed. "What makes you think the dream was related to the attack?"

"You never touched the donut, but at one point you showed me your hands and there was powdered sugar all over them. Then you just disappeared."

"Powdered sugar . . ." It tugged at her memory, but a couple moments passed before she figured out why. "You're thinking of that white residue I touched on the floor, before Jake reappeared."

Ross nodded. "After you disappeared I woke up in a panic. The dream made no sense to me, but the first thing I did was ask Abby whether she'd seen you. It could just be a coincidence, though, couldn't it?"

"Absolutely. That's why we conduct studies rather than relying on anecdotal evidence. But if you've had a lot of hunches play out in a similar way, I'd call that psi. Would you say you have?"

She lifted the wine bottle from the coffee table and refilled their glasses. Ross let out a sigh.

"Yeah, I would."

"But you don't always trust them. You didn't forbid me from going into the lab."

His jaw dropped as he turned to stare at her. "I absolutely did. You just told me why I was wrong and did it anyway. I'm pretty sure *your* special ability is always getting your way."

She laughed so hard she had to set down her glass. He handed her his napkin so she could wipe wine from her chin.

"I've second-guessed myself a lot here," he continued in a more sober tone. "It's part of the reason I thought I should leave."

"Calmer, nonemotional states are more conducive to success with psi. We've been under a lot of strain."

She studied his profile. He was clearly uneasy about all this.

"Listen," she said, "it doesn't matter what you call it—precognition, good instincts, intuition—it's part of you, and it's a good thing. You're lucky to have it. We can definitely help you enhance it. If you learn to use it more consistently, more confidently, it will help you in your job."

"Well, it sounds like I'm not going to have any choice about that. We'll see what the director says when he comes." He set his glass down and angled toward her. "You told Jake this morning that your mother had psi ability."

It didn't occur to him that he was more buzzed than he should be off two glasses of wine until he watched Tess's face fall and remembered this was something she didn't like to discuss.

"Yes," she said quietly, shifting her gaze to the coffee table. "Not as strong as yours I don't think."

"You were close to her?"

She gave a slow nod.

"Jake told me . . ." *Bad idea, McGinnis.*

"Jake told you what?"

Ross believed this discussion needed to happen. But he was keenly aware of the risk of mangling it.

"We had a strange conversation right before you came down the last time," he began carefully. "He told me he'd learned some things about you—about both of us, actually—during the energy transfer. He was worried about something that had happened in your past. He was worried the risks you were taking had to do with whatever it was."

She sank back against the couch, crossing her arms over her chest. "Are you sure this is your business, Ross?"

"I'm sure it's *not*. But as the person assigned to keep you alive, it would help me to know whether . . ." He trailed off, feeling less and less sure of himself. "I know you carry a lot of pain, and not because I have psychic abilities. I doubt it will come as a shock to you that the Bureau has a file on you, and that I've read it. I know about your mother's death. I know about the meds. I know you were hospitalized for depression when you were a teenager."

Her voice trembled as she replied, "You may have been in my file, but that doesn't make it okay for you to go fishing around in my head."

Mission mangled. He rose from the sofa and took a step away, trying to compose his thoughts over the effects of both the wine and the energy transfers.

"You're right," he said. "It's not my business, and I'm sorry. Really all I need to say is this: If you push me to a choice between you and Jake again, Jake's going to lose. What happened with him after lunch may have been a show, but he could have killed you. I won't let it happen again. If you want to keep him alive, you need to place more value on your own life."

As suddenly as the heat came it went, leaving her cold. She folded her hands over her shoulders and sank her face into her arms, shivering. She felt like the little girl with the dead mother. The girl whose father had just told her she was young and she'd forget.

She felt the sofa depress beside her as Ross sat down again, draping a blanket over her shoulders. "I'm sorry," he repeated, more softly this time. "Do you want me to leave?"

He reminded her of her father in many ways—self-assured and overbearing. Quick to judge others. But over the last twenty-four hours she'd come to believe that Ross had a heart.

And how was he to know about the thing in the well? He couldn't, because no one did. Not the shrinks, not anyone. She had to find a way to quiet it, because this was one thing she knew she could not face. Not now, when she needed every particle of concentration to do her job and stay alive. Maybe not ever.

Breathing deeply, she let herself sink against his shoulder. Slowly his arm came around her. She felt his breath in her hair, and she listened to his heart.

There was something else about Ross. She felt safe when she was with him.

Tess fell asleep in Ross's arms. He dozed for a while too but woke with a start as he remembered Jake. Glancing at his watch he saw it had been four hours since the last transfer.

She didn't stir as he eased away from her, lowering her to the couch and covering her with blankets. He'd have been worried about her if he hadn't just felt the slow, steady beat of her heart against his abdomen.

As he left the apartment the lights in the hallway came up automatically. He headed down and made his way to the lab. Jake met him at the window, scanning behind him for Tess.

"I know I'm not your favorite flavor, but you'll just have to deal."

Jake smirked. "Twice in a row now. To what do I owe this sacrifice?"

"She's exhausted." So was he, but he was reluctant to enlist the other agents to help with the transfers until they'd worked out the bugs. They couldn't keep going like this, though.

Jake must have been hungry, because he dropped the heckling and held his hand to the window. The fade closed his eyes, and his breaths came long and deep. Ross felt the tug of the current, and again he was surprised Tess hadn't complained of the pain. It was nothing like the first time, but it wasn't pleasant.

After a moment Jake's mouth curved down in a frown, and he said, "You really are an asshole. Could you think about something else?"

"What?"

Then he realized his thoughts had drifted to Tess—the sound of her laugh, the feel of her breath against his skin, the shape of her body where she'd pressed into his side. . . .

"Christ, come *on*," moaned Jake.

"So you're reading our minds now?"

"I told you I could see things." Jake glared at Ross. "Especially *loud* things."

Jake's hand dropped away from the window, and he walked back to the bed.

"You're welcome," Ross muttered, leaving him alone.

He went back to Tess's apartment to check on her, and so he'd be there when she woke in a panic about Jake. He'd spent maybe fifteen minutes scanning distractedly through email when she sat up, muttering, "Damn."

She swung her legs down, and he called, "Relax, Doctor."

She glanced up, startled.

"Sorry." He rose and crossed from the kitchen table to the couch. "I knew you'd be worried about Jake. He's fine."

She ran her fingers through her mussed hair and stood up. "He needs a transfer." Her voice was still hoarse from sleep. Creaky and sexy.

"I took care of it."

Her gaze shifted back to his face. "Thank you. Again. You should get some sleep. I can take the next one."

"Let's both get some sleep. Then we'll go down together and train one of the other agents."

She smiled. "Yes. Good idea."

Her hands came together in front of her, fingers fidgeting. She was uncharacteristically nervous and unsure.

"Are you okay, Doctor?"

Her gaze moved around the room. "I guess I'm just finding it hard to say good night." As soon as she'd said it she looked mortified.

"Today has been pretty intense," he replied, attempting to ease her discomfort. "I can stay if you want company."

Her hands relaxed at her sides. "How about some tea?"

"Thanks," he said, moving to the couch, "but I should probably dial back the caffeine."

"I have chamomile." She walked to the kitchen and flipped on the kettle. "And peppermint."

"Peppermint sounds good."

She came back with the mugs and sat next to him on the couch. Their sneakers lined up on the edge of the antique trunk.

"Are those standard issue, Agent McGinnis?"

"Only the black ones."

"Ah, of course."

She blew steam from the top of her mug. "Were you surprised that Director Garcia denied your request for reassignment?"

He picked up the teabag string, swirling it around in the water. "I was, yes."

"I'm less surprised after seeing your psi evaluation. Though I'm still not clear on what it was you thought you'd done wrong."

He cast her a sidelong glance, remembering what she'd accused him of earlier—"fishing around" in her head. He supposed it was fair enough.

"It wasn't so much what I'd done. I let something happen I shouldn't have."

"You're talking about Jake? The attack?"

"Not only that."

She waited for him to continue. There were plenty of reasons not to be straight with her, but he'd tried that before. She was damn tough to evade.

"Do you remember anything from the night of the attack?"

"Not much besides the attack itself."

"Nothing from after, in my apartment?"

Color rose to her cheeks, and her eyelashes fluttered. "No. Just the next morning."

"You woke once in the night, or seemed to. You . . ."

The words froze in his throat. *No turning back now.*

"You kissed me."

"I *what?*" She let out a nervous laugh. "Ross, I'm so sorry. I don't remember that at all."

"No, I know. It's not a problem, Doctor. I didn't believe you were conscious at the time."

"I really . . . right on the mouth?"

Now he laughed. "Yes."

"Jesus. What did you do?"

"I didn't do anything. I'm sorry. I should have told you. I should have . . ."

She rubbed her lips together, and she set down her tea. Folding her hands in her lap, she said, "Well, I'm sure it violated all kinds of stuffy, men-in-black regulations, but I think you're being a little hard on yourself. Requesting reassignment because your *assignment* kissed you."

"Not because of the kiss."

"Then why?"

He met her gaze. "Because I wasn't sure what I would do if it happened again."

Despite suspecting there was something like this behind Ross's request, she was completely unprepared for his confession. She'd dropped her eyes, and the blood rushed to her face as she realized she was staring at his lips. It was colossally unfair she had no memory of what they felt like.

"It's a dangerous complication," he continued, "and I—"

She reached out, laying her palm against his chest. He jumped, but his hand moved to cover hers.

"And you . . . ?"

"And I don't know which end is up anymore."

"I can help with that," she said softly, moving her face close to his. Dark eyelashes fluttered as his gaze dropped to her lips, and she felt a sympathetic fluttering in her abdomen. "This one."

His hands moved quickly, fingers in her hair, palms cradling her head, as he pulled her mouth to his.

"God, Tess," he murmured against her lips. He'd rarely spoken her name, and the sound of it left her tingling all over.

She slid a hand up his arm and gripped his shoulder. His hands reached around her waist, and though she'd only meant to angle toward him, she found her bent knee slipping over his thigh until she sat across his lap, belly pressing into his ribs. His arms scooped around her, pulling her against him so he could taste her deeper.

They struggled for breath, aching and arcing. She squeezed his hips between her knees, and her fingers sought the hem of his shirt. As she ran the palms of her hands over the hot skin of his back he moaned, breaking their kiss so he could nuzzle and nip her neck.

His flesh quivered, alive under her stroking fingers, as he slid his hands over her hips and squeezed her thighs. He found some pressure point she didn't even know she had, and her hips gave a spasm, causing her body to jerk against him.

Groaning, Ross lifted and spun until somehow she lay beneath him. He inserted a hand between them, fingers struggling with the tiny buttons of the summery blouse she wore. She reached up and finished the job for him, letting the blouse fall open, before tugging his shirt over his head.

He touched the lilac lace of her bra, pushing down the edge of one cup so he could thumb her nipple. Moaning, she arched against him, and he dipped his head to tease her with his tongue.

"Should we be doing this?" she hissed, because someone had to.

"No," he said, working at the button of her jeans now.

Her hands slid over his chest—rounded, firm, and statuesque.

He tugged her jeans down to the point they hung up on her backside, and he slipped down and planted soft kisses on the sensitive flesh just inside her hip.

"Oh Jesus, Ross."

"There's something wrong with me," he muttered.

"Not from where I'm standing."

"You're not standing." He laughed, nibbling her hipbone.

"You're right. How did that happen?"

"I can't believe how much I want you," he breathed. "The worst part is I feel like I've been given permission. I tried to—"

"Let's not bring anyone else into this room, Ross," she said, raising his head and holding his face between her hands. "Just you and me. Okay?" There was a desperate edge to her voice, and she knew the admonishment was as much for herself as for him.

"Okay," he whispered, sitting up and pulling her into his arms. "Just you and me."

She untangled herself from the embrace and slipped the blouse off her shoulders. Ross unhooked her bra and let it fall. He rose from the couch, lifting her in his arms. The heat of his body warmed her chilled skin.

He laid her on the bed and tugged her jeans free.

"Hang on," she said. She rolled onto one hip and gave the nightstand drawer handle a yank. Four foil packets jumped in the bottom of the drawer. *Thank God.* She grabbed one and examined it before tossing it aside and grabbing another one.

"Expired," she groaned. "How pathetic is that?"

He took the packet from her hand, examining it. "These things take years to expire."

"Um, yeah," she mumbled, embarrassed. "I don't suppose you have any?"

"I wasn't exactly expecting—"

"No, I know." She gave a nervous chuckle. "I'm not sure how I would have felt about you having one in your pocket."

Ross nudged her back down onto the bed. He ducked his head and gently kissed her. "Wait here. I'll go downstairs and check my bag. But first . . ."

He bent over the nightstand and plucked out the two remaining foil squares. He glanced at the first and tossed it back in, but as he examined the last one a smile crept over his face. Her heart stuttered and she sat up.

"Four more weeks," he said, waggling the condom at her. "What do you say?"

"I say get over here."

He crawled toward her and she pushed him onto his back, unbuttoning his jeans and tugging them off. She gulped as her gaze flowed over his abdomen to the triangle of musculature below, and the equipment at its base. She ran one finger down the length of taut, flushed skin, and he groaned and ripped open the condom. She helped him unroll it, fingers trembling.

He flipped her onto her back, settling between her legs. She gasped at the sudden hardness against her mound of sensitive flesh.

"How are you feeling about this, Doctor?"

She threaded her fingers into his hair. "Impatient."

He smiled, eyelids lowering, and let his thumb brush over her nipple. She felt a responding flicker of heat between her legs and eased them farther apart. His hand slipped down, cupping her, middle finger dipping and exploring as she let out a soft moan.

"Jesus, Tess," he hissed.

Heat flashed over her skin and she gave a self-conscious laugh. "I told you."

"I intended to tease you a little, but I don't think I can take it."

"Thank God for that."

She wrapped her legs around his waist and he pushed inside her with a single, convulsive thrust.

"Ah!" she cried, clutching his shoulders.

"Sorry." He laughed. "Are we okay?"

She smiled and pulled his mouth down to hers. "We're okay."

Ross took a long, shuddering breath as he drew out slowly, then sank back into her as he exhaled. His lips trailed across her cheek and he murmured, "You're so warm, Tess . . . so *sweet*. . . ." She contracted her muscles around him, and he gave a low whimper.

She kissed his throat. "I feel safe with you."

She'd been thinking it all day, but it wasn't something she'd expected to share with him. He drew back, his gaze locking with hers. He cradled her cheek and jaw in his hand, tilting her head back, kissing her so deeply he left no hollow, aching place unfilled.

She began to rock—gently at first, then faster and harder as their rhythms merged. With each thrust Tess felt pierced by a million particles of light. The particles coalesced into waves, washing over her with surges of warm, tingling sensation.

Finally a starburst of pleasure detonated low in her abdomen, and she felt him tense and vibrate above her. The white-hot flash of light filled her, consumed her, erased her. . . .

Tess clenched her legs and softer tissues around him as he exploded in every direction. Ross couldn't remember the last time he'd gone off first, but he'd never felt so out of control with a woman. He was already planning how he'd make it up to her, but then came her answering cry of release, and his heart pulsed with relief.

He opened his eyes, seeking her soft, swollen lips with his own. . . .

And she vanished.

FALLING

TORN FROM the warmth and shelter of Ross's arms, Tess's
naked body rocketed down a muddy hillside.

She scrambled for a handhold—anything to slow her descent—
but the scrubby bits of vegetation she caught hold of broke off or
slipped through her fingers. Both the air and the mud were frigid,
and the sticks and stones that littered the hillside raked at her bare
skin.

At the bottom of the hill she slammed to a halt, headfirst,

against a half-submerged tree trunk. Crying out in pain and panic, choking on acrid air, she sat up and cleared the hair that had plastered over her eyes.

Frantically she surveyed her surroundings, but everything more than a few yards away was cloaked in a gray haze. She saw a couple of large, pulsing orange smudges off in the distance—fires? It would help explain the low visibility and stinking air.

"Ross?" she called, voice raw with fear.

She strained to muffle her coughing so she could listen for an answering cry. But there was nothing beyond the sound of her own short, frosty breaths. She called again, but still nothing.

Was it possible this was a dream? No dream had ever been so real, or so painful. She touched her hand to her forehead and examined the blood that smeared her already numb fingers.

Quaking with cold, she drew her knees to her chest. Her eyes fell on the tree trunk in front of her, and she noticed it was coated with a layer of frost. She would die of exposure—soon—if she didn't get someplace warm.

Get to the fire! Survival instinct asserted itself over the discomfort in her body.

Again she scanned the murk, fixing on the largest of the pulsing lights. She hooked an arm around the tree trunk and levered herself out of the muck, ignoring the bite of the bark against her naked flesh. She took a couple of unsteady steps—and then squealed as something wriggled out from under her foot. As she leapt away from the wriggling thing, her back foot slipped and she pitched facefirst into the soft mud.

"Fuck!" she cried, choking on a sob. "Where am I? Jake?"

This had something to do with him—with the transfers. It had to. But was it *real?*

Please don't let it be real.

She clambered along on her hands and knees and found she made better progress. But with her face inches from the ground she could see—and *smell*—all the things embedded in the muck. *Dead* things. Putrefied frogs, mice, even a squirrel. Her arms and legs were so cold they were like clubs, and she couldn't help brushing against the little carcasses as she crawled.

Another sob heaved out of her, and again she called Ross's name.

She felt the brush of a sleek, fur-covered body as it scampered along a bit of wood between her arms. She reared up on her knees with a shout. A chorus of squeaks broke through the silence, and her head whipped around.

The flotsam around her was populated with little bodies—rats, living ones—sniffing at the air and watching her.

She thrashed sideways and struck something hard. Sensation in her fingers was long gone, but she crab-crawled backward over the solid surface. *A rock*, she thought at first—*no, a slab of concrete*. As she craned her neck to look behind her, her hands struck open air and she pitched backward, tumbling off an abrupt edge.

She plunged, weightless, through the choking atmosphere.

Ross gave a cry of shock and confusion.

He ran his hand over the sheet, still warm, still bearing the impression of her body. *"Tess!"*

His mind flailed. He sat up, scrubbing his hands over his face. He looked around. *Her* apartment. He'd touched and tasted her. He could still smell her on his skin. He hadn't fallen asleep and dreamed the whole thing.

He jumped to his feet, discarded the condom, and pulled on his jeans. His shoulder holster hung over the back of a chair, and he snatched up the Glock.

What the hell are you going to shoot?

He stood with the length of the barrel pressed against his forehead, rubbing his thumbs over the grip. *Think think THINK.*

It must have something to do with Jake—something to do with

last night's attack, or with the transfers. The fade had done something to her. Changed her somehow. Was it possible she was downstairs with him now?

She fucking vanished.

A desperate moan clawed its way out of his throat. He sank to his knees, her voice echoing in his head. *I feel safe with you.*

Ross's phone rang from the kitchen table and he scooped it up—Director Garcia. *No time for that.* He sent the director to voicemail and texted Agent Swain. He gripped the phone, counting the seconds. . . .

Negative. Haven't seen her.

"Fuck fuck *fuck!*"

He sprang to his feet and headed for the door. He didn't want to go—what if she came back? But he had to talk to Jake. He had to do *something.*

Halfway to the door he heard a shriek and spun around. Something dropped through the ceiling and crashed onto the bed.

"*Tess?*"

He ran to her side, dragging her violently shaking body closer. Holy Christ, she was filthy. And bleeding. Her eyes were wide with terror.

"C-cold," she chattered, curling her icy, mud-slicked arms around his neck.

He lifted her from the bed and carried her to the bathroom. He turned the shower on and got into the tub with her. Warm water jetted down on them and she curled into his chest, one arm hooking tightly around his neck. He needed to check her—see where the blood was coming from. But it could wait. He locked his arms around her.

"Hold on to me, Ross."

"I've got you."

Even as he said the words he knew how impotent they were. He'd been inside her, and she'd just slipped away.

SACRIFICE

We are human. *They* are human. In this century of technologically facilitated connection, how have we not grown beyond valuing the well-being of our own tribe above that of all others?
—Professor Alexi Goff, University of Edinburgh, *Echo Dossier*

TESS HAD stopped shivering, and her weight sank fully onto him as her body shut down in the aftermath of shock. He didn't want to wake her, but far worse than disturbing her rest would be to have her disappear again before they had a chance to talk about what happened.

"Tess." He pushed wet hair back from her face, eyeing the nasty cut and bruise in the center of her forehead. "Doctor, wake up."

She woke with a cry and a start, arm clenching around his neck.

"It's okay." His placid tone was an astonishing feat of mind over matter. "You're okay. Let's get you dry and dressed."

They crawled out of the tub, and Tess dried herself while he peeled off his wet jeans, replacing them with his T-shirt and boxer briefs—the only dry clothing he had in her apartment.

He opened her closet, not bothering to ask permission, and

pulled out a pair of purple corduroy pants, a long-sleeved top, and a hooded fleece jacket. As he was closing the door he stopped and grabbed a scarf as well.

"Put these on," he said, handing her the clothing.

She gave the pile a bemused look. "It's August, Ross."

"Just do it, okay?"

Their gazes met and understanding crystalized between them, no psi ability needed. *In case you go somewhere cold.*

He watched her fiddle with the clothing with trembling hands and then moved in to help. When they'd gotten her dressed he led her to the bed. Her gaze fell on the mud-splattered sheets.

"Where's your phone?" he asked.

She blinked and glanced around. "On the kitchen counter." He retrieved it and handed it to her.

"Dr. Carmichael."

"Right," she agreed. Her thumb worked over the keypad, and he heard the text whoosh away.

"How long before she can be here?"

"The meeting is on Whidbey Island. There's no ferry at this time of night, so a couple hours to drive up to the bridge and back down. That's *if* she's still awake."

He considered for a moment and replied, "There's no point in that. We'll videoconference her when she texts back. Now tell me what happened."

Her gaze moved around the room like she hadn't heard him. "*Tess.*"

She fixed wide eyes on his face.

"Stay with me, okay?" Some of his panic leaked into his voice this time, and she sat up straighter.

He walked over to the fridge and opened it, hoping for orange juice. There was nothing but a bottle of fancy grapefruit soda. He twisted the top off and carried it to the bed.

She took the bottle and gulped half of it down. "Thank you."

"Talk to me."

"I feel like I've gone crazy. I don't know if it was real, Ross."

His gaze grazed her forehead. "I think we can safely assume it was."

She hugged her arms around her chest. "I went someplace cold and muddy. There were dead things. Fires in the distance. Really bad air. Smoke and decay."

His heart picked up speed along with her words. "Where do you think you were?"

"The site of some natural disaster. I think . . ." She fixed her eyes on his face. "I think it was Jake's Earth."

He didn't want to believe it. But he did.

"It could have something to do with the transfers," she said.

No "could" about it. And that meant it might happen to him too.

"Do you think it was Seattle?"

"I don't know. It was basically a mudslide. Though there was some concrete. Is it important?"

"It could be. If it happens to both of us."

Her eyes moved over his body. "You're right. You should get dressed."

"Agreed. Come on."

She rose from the bed without question, and they walked together to his apartment, heedless of his state of undress. He wasn't sending her anywhere without him, not even upstairs for dry clothes.

"Did you feel anything unusual before it happened?" he asked, pulling on a pair of jeans.

She raised an eyebrow, and he thought about that shared moment of release, right before she'd vanished.

"I meant was there any kind of warning," he said.

She shook her head. "Not that I remember. But I can't help wondering whether we . . . whether we *triggered* it somehow."

She could be right. The timing seemed like it could be significant. "I hope you're right."

By her expression she was surprised and also a little wounded.

"It would mean we can prevent it from happening again," he explained.

"True." *But at a cost* was the part he knew she was holding back. That couldn't be helped.

After a few moments of silence she said, "We need to talk to Jake. And he needs a transfer."

Ross stared at her, incredulous. "Are you serious?"

She took a deep breath. "I know what you're thinking. But can we afford to let him fade out before we get to the bottom of this?"

"What if more transfers make it *worse*? Do you want to go through that again? Because I know I don't. You *vanished*, Tess. You're lucky to be alive."

She raised her hands to her face and rubbed her temples. Drained from the transfers and wrung out by adrenaline, it was a wonder her brain was functioning at all. But she couldn't let herself power down until they had some answers.

Adrenaline.

She looked at Ross. "You asked me if I felt anything unusual before it happened—the dislocation. I did feel something. Right before I left, and right before I came back."

"Tell me."

She dropped her gaze, hugging her arms around her chest. "I felt afraid." She let a breath out slowly, trying to stop the wrenching in her stomach. "I mean I was afraid the whole time I was gone. But right before I came back I fell off something—a concrete ledge."

"What about before you vanished?" he asked quietly. When she didn't answer right away, he continued. "You mean me. You were afraid of me."

Another slow exhalation. Her gaze moved to the window. "It's difficult for me, Ross. I don't . . . *trust* easily." She shook her head, knowing she'd told him all she could. "I think maybe the dislocation was triggered by a fight-or-flight response."

"Sounds like just the flight part to me."

His expression had flattened, but the words came out like an accusation. She was about to remind him that he was the one who'd requested reassignment, when his phone rang.

Grabbing it off the table, he answered, "McGinnis."

The color drained from his face. "In the morning?"

His eyes moved to hers, and she lifted her eyebrows.

"I understand." He slipped the phone into his pocket. "Director Garcia is on a red-eye to Seattle."

"Now?"

"There's a layover, but he'll be here by 7 A.M. He wants to meet with us right away."

She glanced at her watch and saw it was nearly 1 a.m. Realizing her heart was outpacing the second hand, she focused again on her breath. Another quick inhalation followed by long exhalation to activate the parasympathetic nervous system. *No more flight tonight.*

"What's this about, Ross?" she asked. "Garcia isn't coming all this way to talk to us about your psi training."

He shook his head. "That's a piece of a larger puzzle. But I don't know more than that."

"Do you think it has to do with Jake?"

"I can guarantee you it has to do with Jake."

She rose from the bed. "I'm going down to talk to him." He deserved to know what was happening, and if they didn't do a transfer soon he'd become dangerous. That was not the Jake she wanted the director to see.

"Doctor—"

She jumped as her phone vibrated against her hip.

"Hi, Abby."

Ross breathed a sigh of relief. He needed Abby for backup on what he was about to say.

Tess's jaw hinged open, and her eyes locked onto his. "Can you say that again?"

After a moment she shook her head, and she flushed an angry red. She walked to the window and looked down at the street. "They can't do that. This is a private facility."

Ross closed his eyes. *It's all coming down on us at once.* In his mind's eye he could see Abby, standing out front with her weekend bag, arguing with two men blocking the entrance. He had these kinds of visions all the time. He'd never thought twice about the fact they most always turned out to be accurate—never before now.

"Director Garcia's arriving in the morning. I'll stop this, Abby. I promise you."

Tess turned from the window, frowning. "No, I'm okay," she continued. "I don't want you to worry."

She sank onto the edge of his bed, listening. "Abby, are you still there?" She glanced at the touchscreen and her frown deepened. "I lost her."

"The building's been sealed off," he said.

She stared at him. "You knew about this."

He shook his head. "I saw it, just now."

"How did you see it?"

He raised his hand to the back of his neck, sighing. "In my head."

Tess gave a slow nod. "Abby had left the island before I texted her. She's outside right now. They can't do this," she repeated.

He didn't bother to correct her.

She rose from the bed. As she was crossing the room he reached out and blocked her way.

"No, Doctor."

"Let me go, Ross."

"I can't let you go down."

"What if they stop the transfers? This might be my last chance to talk to him."

"I'm going to recommend the transfers stop."

She glared at him. "It's good to know where you stand."

"That's not fair. You know it's not. I told you I wouldn't choose between your safety and Jake's again."

She folded her arms and turned away from him. "So we just wait for orders, is that it?"

"Yeah, that's it." He pulled out his phone and texted the agents downstairs that Jake was off-limits. "You take the bed," he told her. "I'll take the couch. Sleep in your clothes."

If he'd expected to see anything in her expression but anger, he was disappointed. "So I'm under arrest."

"You're under protection, Doctor. Let's get some sleep."

Gremlins rioted in Tess's mental clockwork, wrenching the cogs of logical thought. She lay sleepless, alternately fuming at Ross and craving his arms around her. Working herself into a jittery state of exhaustion.

Their interests were diverging, as she had known they inevitably would, and it was up to her now to choose her course. She refused to accept the Bureau would choose it for her. But she grieved for the loss of Ross's companionship. For his clear head, and his plainspoken ways. For his body lying close, and the refuge of his embrace.

It was doomed from the outset.

With that fatal thought she closed her eyes. The moment the

voices inside her stilled, she dropped off to sleep. Her eyes didn't open again until Ross rose at sunrise.

They parted long enough to change into more professional attire—this time with doors closed between them. Afterward they met on the landing and walked down together.

And apart.

Director Garcia waited for them in the abandoned cafeteria. Tall and lean, with a suit that looked like it came from the same store as Ross's, there was a clean-cut, no-bullshit air about him. He stepped forward to shake Tess's hand.

"Dr. Caufield. It's good to meet in person." Penetrating, intelligent eyes flickered from her to Ross, and she suddenly felt naked. What had Ross said to him when he requested reassignment?

Garcia's brow creased as his gaze lifted to her forehead. "What happened to your head, Doctor?"

"Director Garcia," she began, ignoring his question, "are you able to explain why this institute's director—who lives on the premises—was forbidden entry last night?"

Garcia exchanged a glance with Ross. "If you'll join me, I'll answer your questions and also explain my reason for coming here."

Another agent entered the room carrying a bulky paper bag and a tray of coffee in to-go cups. As she set the load on a table, Garcia ordered, "We're not to be disturbed."

"Yes, sir," replied the agent, leaving again.

"Please." Garcia gestured to the table, and as much as it irked her to fall into line, she knew that food and coffee were necessary fortifications for what was to come.

She accepted a cup and spread cream cheese on a bagel, listening to the casual exchange between Ross and his superior—questions about the flight, about the weather in D.C. and Seattle. Apparently commandeering buildings and relieving people of their constitutional rights was all in a day's work for them.

That's not fair. No, she could feel Ross's discomfort. No doubt the director could too. For the moment she and Ross were in the same boat, paddling toward an unknown shore.

Finally Garcia brushed crumbs from his sleeves and folded his hands on the table, shifting his attention to include them both. "Please consider everything said in this room to be classified. It shouldn't even be discussed with the agents outside."

Tess stared at him, sensing she was approaching a point of no return. But if she remained in the dark she could help no one, least of all herself.

"I came to Seattle to assess the potential for a covert operation," said Garcia. "Specifically to assess the potential of yourself, Agent McGinnis, and Echo 8 as our first participants."

This was exactly what Tess and Goff had feared would come of the Bureau's involvement—and the reason she had resented Ross almost on sight.

"Covert operation," she replied evenly. "That's more than classified? Something the rest of the government doesn't know about."

"That's right," said Ross. He was seated next to her, and she felt his foot slowly slide against hers. Was it meant to be reassurance, or warning?

"The Bureau is interested in working more closely with Echoes," continued Garcia.

"*With* Echoes? I thought your agency was more concerned with containment. With eradication."

Garcia didn't flinch. "Our interest is public safety, first and foremost."

"I see." She didn't bother to filter the skepticism from her tone.

Garcia continued like he hadn't noticed. "I'm here because I'm very interested in the work you've been doing with Echo 8. In the method you discovered for keeping him alive."

She felt Ross stiffen beside her. "There was no need to exile Dr. Carmichael for that," she said. "I'm eager to tell you about my work."

"Ross may have told you that I'd also like you to work with him on sharpening his ability. We're specifically interested in remote location."

"He did mention your interest in his psi ability. I'm happy to work with him. But I'm not sure that should take precedence over our current crisis."

"The two are related, Doctor. First of all, there are a number of targets we'd like to track using Ross's ability."

Her gut tightened. "Targets?"

"We'd like to see if he can learn to locate Echoes, which I'm sure you'll agree is in the interest of public safety."

"I believe it is in the interest of *our* safety. I'm not so sure about *them*. It depends on what you plan to do once you find them."

"We plan to recruit them."

She blinked at him, confused.

"We have something they need, and you've discovered a safe way to give it to them. We offer to sustain them, and they agree to work with us."

"Work with us to . . . ?"

She risked a glance at Ross, wondering how long before he told the director about the dislocation. Impassive as his expression appeared, she could see the tension in his jaw muscles.

"To help us address a problem," continued Garcia. "Or a series of problems. We have a list of individuals who pose a threat to national security. We believe Echoes could be very effective in helping us neutralize them."

National security. It was a sort of magic password these days. But she still couldn't get her brain around this. She wasn't sure if it was fatigue or the words the director was using. She glanced again at Ross, and by his expression—the relaxing of his jaw muscles, the narrowing of his gaze—she knew that he was ahead of her.

"Black ops," he said quietly. "Echoes kill without weapons."

Tess's gaze jerked back to Garcia, the frozen gears in her brain finally spinning free.

"We can send them anywhere," said the director. "They can look just like us, or they can be almost invisible, as the situation requires. They are lethal, and we can train them to be precise."

"No collateral damage," continued Ross.

"Exactly. And what they do doesn't look like a hit."

Ross straightened in his chair. "It's not really our purview, is it? State-sponsored assassination."

"Historically, no," replied Garcia. "It's not precisely within our jurisdiction. The operation will be a cross-agency collaboration. But as the agency with the most experience dealing with Echoes, we're taking the lead."

Her gaze moved between them, jaw frozen stupidly open. It was far beyond what she'd originally feared.

"Why is it necessary to go around constitutional process?" she asked weakly, knowing it was pointless.

Garcia folded his arms over his chest. "Some of them have proved too elusive for capture. With others, we've given up hope of ever procuring enough evidence for the desired outcome at trial."

"Doctor," continued Garcia, "what we're offering you is an opportunity to serve your country while doing the work you want to do. We're giving you a chance to save Echoes."

She swallowed her rising panic. *You're the expert here. That's why they're consulting you.*

"What makes you think they'll do it?" she asked. "They're not killers. They're no different from us."

Garcia raised an eyebrow. "They *are* killers, Doctor. And I'm not worried about their compliance."

Understanding clamped its jaws over her heart. "You don't intend to give them a choice."

"Live or die. That's a choice."

She took a measured breath and steadied herself. It was Garcia's job to be forceful and confident. To bowl her over with his presence and authority. But a mouse chewing a corner of a flour sack could work a world of mischief.

"There are holes in this scheme, Director. Deadly ones."

He gave her a thin smile that raised chill bumps on her arms. "Like how do we manage them in the field? What's to stop them from running? From killing other people? It's all I think about. And now it's your job to think about it too."

Before the protest made it out of her mouth, Ross inserted, "Director, we've discovered the transfers have a dangerous side effect."

It squeezed her heart to think about how this revelation was going to affect Jake, but as much as she had grown to care for him, the situation had always been much bigger than a single Echo. For the moment she and Ross were on the same side again.

"Oh?" replied Garcia, finally looking less like the man with all the answers.

"Yes, sir." Ross glanced at Tess.

"Last night I dislocated to Jake's Earth."

Garcia's mouth opened, but he shook his head. "Explain."

Ross elaborated on the dislocation, omitting what had immediately preceded it.

Garcia sat staring at the table for a full minute before replying. "That must have been terrifying, Doctor."

"It was." *Almost as terrifying as what's going on in this room.*

"It's a shocking development. One that bears further investigation."

She could feel the energy of Ross's tension, stronger than when they'd first sat down.

"We wouldn't want to subject you to that again personally, Doctor. But . . ."

She practically hovered in her seat, waiting for his next words, but when he continued he said, "Why don't you look in on your subject, Doctor. I have a few things to discuss with Agent McGinnis. We'll reconvene for lunch."

Surprised by the sudden dismissal, she studied him as she rose to her feet. Like Ross he was a master of blunted affect, but she didn't think she was imagining the change to the light in his eyes.

He's already thinking about how he can use this.

"Thank you, Doctor," Garcia said.

Unequal to the task of returning a courteous reply, she simply turned to go. She felt Ross's gaze on her back until the door closed between them.

The brain gremlins returned as she walked toward the lab. She needed someone to talk to—someone she could trust. She needed Abby! She couldn't help feeling her whole life had just changed over bagels and coffee. The director had been polite and professional—had expended energy to persuade her—but were they really giving her a choice? Or had choice exited the building at the use of words like "covert operation" and "national security"?

And what about Jake and *his* choice? Her heart beat out ahead of her body as she neared the lab. He would be suffering by now, and dangerous to feed. But if she didn't, they'd lose him. Despite what Garcia had said about sparing her, she didn't want anyone else conducting energy transfers until she could learn more about the dislocations.

She was relieved to see fresh faces in the corridor—agents who probably hadn't had any orders from Ross to keep her away. Pulling her shoulders back and hardening her expression, she strode purposefully toward the lab door.

As soon as one of the agents glanced up she said, "I'm Dr. Caufield. I'll need you to stay alert while I interact with the subject."

Both agents straightened, but neither tried to stop her. She noticed the door had been crudely reinforced with bars fitted into hooks and brackets at the top and bottom.

She pushed the intercom button. "I'm sorry, Jake."

He rose slowly from the cot, crossing the floor like it pained him.

"I'm the one who should apologize," he said, joining her at the glass. "I'm sorry about last time. I was trying to be a hero, but since then I've remembered that 'selfish bastard' is what I do best. I'm glad you're back."

"Let's take care of you. Then we'll talk."

"Where's your Fed?"

"There are two agents with me in the hallway." She held up her hand to the glass. "I know you were trying to scare me yesterday, but what you did took amazing control. You can do this."

Jake heaved a tired sigh, but he raised his hand.

After a moment she frowned. "I don't feel anything."

"That's because I'm pinching the hose."

"That's great, Jake. Now just let go a little. You need this transfer."

"You don't have to tell me, Doc."

She moved her hand closer to the glass, letting the pads of her fingers touch. Slowly his hand flattened against the other side. Now she could feel it, like pinpricks all over her body.

"You've made huge progress over the last twenty-four hours."

"I finally realized when it comes to pigheaded you're in a whole different league."

She smiled.

Don't look so damn pleased with yourself.

It took a moment to sink in that his mouth hadn't moved.

"Jake, did you just—?"

Maybe we should keep it our little secret.

Her gaze cut to the agent a couple feet away, but he was staring at the opposite wall.

What's going on, Doc? Feels like you've got about a hundred Super Balls bouncing around in your head.

Her thoughts had quieted when the transfer began, but now

she'd spun back up to full speed. She recognized the value of this moment. Ross and Garcia closeted together. New agents who didn't answer to Ross. This might be her only chance. It might be Jake's only chance.

It was risky, to herself and potentially to others. But no more so than the Bureau's back-alley agenda.

We have to get out of here, she told him.

His brow furrowed. "*We*" as in . . . ?

You and me. Things are changing. The FBI director is here. They want to turn you into an assassin, and they're going to force me to help them.

Whoa, Doc. Are you sure about this?

Yes. And we don't have time to argue.

Much as I'd love to go all Bonnie and Clyde with you, they're not going to let us walk out of here. You know that.

They will. All we have to do is get you out of this room. We have to stop the transfer now. We need you faded.

What? Why?

Theoretically you should be able to walk through this door. The second point of no return she'd crossed. Or third. She'd lost count.

The drip of the energy transfer slowed. *Come again?*

Bullets go through you. That suggests walls can too. You must be manipulating energy to interact with your surroundings. You're doing it involuntarily. I'm betting you can voluntarily stop doing it.

Doctor, I don't know. But he gave the window a shove with the palm of his hand.

Don't think about pushing against it. Think about it not being there. For you, that door is nothing more than a habit.

He closed his eyes, and she watched the rise and fall of his breathing. She pulled her hand away from the glass—and gasped as his hand followed it through.

It had puzzled everyone on the task force that none of the confined Echoes had ever done this. She suspected it came down to being stuck in a certain way of thinking. They believed they needed to interact with a knob to open a door, so they did. She'd agreed with the others it would be irresponsible to ever raise the topic with one of their subjects. Until now.

The rest of Jake followed his hand, and there was a shout and a gunshot. The bullet passed through Jake's chest and punched through the door.

"Come on!" she cried.

She took off at a run, the heels of her shoes slapping against the hardwood, and assumed Jake was behind her. The shouts of the other agents would soon draw Ross and Garcia, so there was no more time for talk.

She headed for the back exit, where they pushed past another startled agent. But the woman caught Tess's arm and jerked her backward.

"Jake!"

He reached for the agent, just grazing her shoulder with his hand, but it was enough to stun her and shake loose her grip.

Tess scrambled to her feet, and they sprinted down the side-walk. She had no purse, no money . . . nothing but the clothes on her back. Luckily she lost her keys at least once a week, so there was a spare hidden under the fender.

JAKE

"In THAT direction," the Cat said, waving its right paw round, "lives a Hatter: and in THAT direction," waving the other paw, "lives a March Hare. Visit either you like: they're both mad."

—Lewis Carroll, *Alice's Adventures in Wonderland*

JAKE FOLDED himself into the passenger seat and closed the door, and Tess whipped out of the parking spot, tires wailing like a banshee.

"I shouldn't be driving," she muttered.

"I'll second that," he replied, grabbing the Oh Shit handle. "Just out of curiosity, why do you say so?"

"I'll explain later. Just be ready to catch the wheel."

"Right. Terrific."

Jake closed his eyes and pressed against the car door.

"Are you okay?" she asked.

"This isn't as easy as it looks." He desperately needed to feed, and he was sitting less than a foot away from her in her ridiculous little hybrid. He shivered as her warm honey washed over him in waves.

"Hang in there, Jake. We're going to ditch the car soon."

He opened his eyes and focused his attention outside the window. "Well, fuck me."

"What's wrong?"

"This is my neighborhood." He craned his neck to glance back the way they'd come, and he let out a bark of laughter. "We were in my building the whole time."

"Your building?"

"I live here. I mean on my Earth, I *lived* here. The building was a museum on the bottom, and affordable housing above."

She shot him a questioning look before accelerating onto the ramp for I-90. "You're sure about that?"

"Looks exactly the same, except for the grounds."

"It's hardly the first overlap we've found with your world, but wow. We thought . . . *Ross* thought you showed up here because I'm on the task force. Something seems to be drawing you to us."

"I don't know about all that, but 'drawn to you' is an understatement."

Jake leaned against the headrest and sighed. Hard as it was to be in the car with her, he couldn't deny he felt happier—and more alive—than he remembered feeling in a very long time. And there was no small amount of satisfaction in the fact Tess had chosen him over Ross.

I really am a selfish bastard.

The Fed was a protector by nature. He was good for Tess—even Jake could see it. Her childhood had been sadly devoid of protectors. But Ross didn't really understand her. Jake *did.* They'd both lost something so dear to them they walked around half-empty. And when Jake was with Tess—despite the insanity into which he'd materialized—he forgot about the emptiness.

"So we're running away together," he said. "Very romantic. Where are we going?"

She cast him an anxious look. "I don't know. I have no money, no ID, a quarter charge left on the car, and we need someplace to stay where an occasionally psychic FBI agent won't find us."

Jake grinned. "You're an epicenter for chaos, aren't you?"

A laugh burst from her lips, and she flashed him a smile—a smile made infinitely more interesting by the fact he could see tears in her eyes.

"Don't tell anyone, okay? I've got them all fooled into thinking I'm very studious and professional."

"No, no, you should put it on your business cards. 'Tess Caufield—Specialist in Dimensional Travelers, Epicenter for Chaos.'"

She laughed again, and a tear spilled onto her cheek. She flicked it away with her thumb.

Jake's smile faded. His mouth went dry. He felt a tug at his heart, and another at his groin. "I want to swallow you whole."

"Maybe later. Now be quiet. I need to think."

She thinks I'm joking.

Tess had been flying down I-90, and now she veered right onto I-5 north, toward downtown Seattle. Another wave of warm honey blasted over him, and he dug his fingers into his leg. Jake knew his body would already be curled around hers, heedless of the car careening into the concrete divider, but for his subconscious compulsively chanting: *You'll kill her.*

"This is a bad idea," he groaned. "I can't be this close to you."

"I'm sorry, Jake. I'm going to find someplace to park and then we'll take care of you."

"Until then you better talk to me or something bad is going to happen."

"Why don't you tell me something about your life? All I know about you is your profession—smartass moonlighting as a musician."

"That's really essentially it."

"Oh come on."

He sat glaring through the windshield. The little silver car zipped alongside the downtown corridor. There was something strange about the buildings—they were all crowned with some kind of dark, lumpy matter, like they were wearing wigs. Jake took a closer look at one mass hovering close to the elevated highway and discovered the lumpiness was organic—a rooftop garden.

As they passed the Mercer Street exit Jake scanned for the city's most recognizable landmark. The morning was bright and clear, sunlight glinting across Lake Union, yet he couldn't find the six-hundred-foot structure.

"Where's the Space Needle?"

Tess's eyes darted to his face and then back to the road. "It was damaged in the Millennium explosion at Seattle Center, at the end of the New Year's Eve fireworks show. The city had to take it down. They salvaged the saucer section, though. You can see it there at the south end of the lake." She nodded to the window. "They turned it into a museum and memorial, for the people who died. What about your Space Needle?"

"I guess it made it eighteen years longer than yours did."

Jake closed his eyes, thinking. Trying not to think. He wondered about the "overlap" she'd referred to earlier.

"Doctor, how alike *are* our Earths? I mean, is there another Jake Parker around here somewhere?"

She shook her head. "We don't really know. From Echo interviews we do know our Earths were very similar. The geography, the political and social structures, the level of technological advancement— none of these were different enough that Echoes have found any difficulty blending in here. Both Earths had a United States, for example, and a European Union. But we have a different president. That's a significant difference, and we have to assume even small differences would have huge ripple effects. But as improbable as a high percentage of matchup may seem, several multiverse theories allow for a whole range of other Earths, from identical to unrecognizable."

"Your city looks almost like mine. You live in the same building I do."

She acknowledged this with a sideways nod. "Exactly. But like I said, there's a lot we don't know. One multiverse theory suggests a distinct universe exists for every possible outcome in a given situation. With an infinite number of variations, anything is possible. It could very well be that the close similarity between our worlds is allowing the dislocations from your Earth. And it's a safe bet this isn't the only other Earth where Echoes are popping up."

The skin on the back of Jake's neck pricked, and a feather of hope tickled his stomach.

"Jake," said Tess, hesitation in her voice. "Can I ask something about your death?"

He fidgeted in his seat, repositioning his long legs in the short space. "Maybe."

"We know that at least three of the other Echoes died just prior to impact. Two killed themselves over fear of the impending catastrophe, and one was likely killed in an unrelated accident. I think there may be some connection between you ending your life and ending up here. Possibly the asteroid impact temporarily interfered with a process for reintegrating your energy into your own universe."

"The irony is cloying, isn't it?" He turned to stare out the passenger window at the University of Washington campus as it flew by, too fast to compare to the image in his memory.

"You killed yourself for some other reason, though, didn't you?" she asked quietly. "You didn't actually know about the asteroid."

Jake pressed his forehead against the cool glass and closed his eyes. The window bounced the moist warmth of his breath back into his face. "Do you have Ballard here, Tess?"

A few beats of silence passed, and she said, "Sure, we have Ballard."

The Ballard neighborhood that Jake knew had been a very

desirable area. The original, unincorporated town was built by immigrant Scandinavians right on Puget Sound. But over the last several years, rising sea levels and intensifying weather had resulted in frequent flooding. Abandoned by the wealthy and overrun by rats, it had devolved into slum housing.

"I want to go to Ballard. Is that possible?"

She didn't answer, and he took it for a no. He suspected she intended to drive straight out of Seattle. But she guided her car off the highway at the next exit.

"Okay, Jake. Your question about the Space Needle gave me an idea, and Ballard is not much out of the way. Plus there are newer cash machines there than in my neighborhood, with finger-scan access. It'll point them right to us, but we'll do our best to disappear after that."

A cash machine in Ballard? He doubted it. But he didn't want her to change her mind so he kept his mouth shut.

Tess parked the car on Market Street, and Jake gaped at a neon cupcake sign in the window of a café—a café identical to one he remembered from the pre-flood Ballard. There was no sign of flooding here. No rats or stray dogs. No condemned buildings. No ragged children digging through the garbage.

Coming here had been a waste of time. Even if Emily existed on this Earth, she wouldn't live here. She couldn't afford an area like this. He settled back against the seat, muttering, "I'm such an idiot."

"What's wrong?" asked Tess.

"Long story."

She studied him a moment and then held her hand out to him. "Let's do the transfer and get out of here."

He flinched against the car door. "Watch yourself, Espresso Chunk."

"Come on, Jake. We have to do it."

He picked up his hand and looked through it. He balled it into a fist and pressed it under his leg. He looked at Tess and swallowed. Her proximity was a fire in his throat. A fever in his head. A hunger, petulant from denial, gnawing its way out of his belly. His whole body quaked from the effort of maintaining the seven or eight inches of space between them.

He wiped his sweating palms on his jeans and let out the breath he'd been holding.

"One thing before we start," said Tess.

He raised an eyebrow.

"I'm not so keen on the word 'chunk.' Maybe I could be Strawberry Swirl."

He laughed and rolled his head on the seat. "You can be *dead* if you don't start doing a better job picking your friends."

"Lean back and relax. Rest your hand on the console between us, and try to think about something else."

He gave another bark of laughter but did as she asked. "I really don't get why you're doing this. I've already killed myself once, and even if my Earth hadn't been destroyed, there'd be no one to care—I'm pretty much a waste of oxygen. Why wreck your life for this?"

Warm honey seeped in through his hand. He sensed how close she was—no more than a couple inches away—and gripped the console.

"*I* care," she replied. "I don't believe you're a waste of oxygen. I don't believe you deserve to die. None of you deserve to die."

"You can't save us all. You can't even save me." He looked at her, noting the little upside-down "v" of irritation over the bridge of her nose. "Sweetheart, I know I talk a lot of shit, but I'm not screwing around now. Let me out here, and go back to Tall-Dark-and-Angsty. Go back to your job and your life. You deserve to be happy."

"It's more complicated than that, Jake."

"Is it?" But he knew what she meant, or thought he did. Better than anybody. Maybe even better than Tess. "All of this is really about your mother, isn't it?" The pain in her face should have been enough to stop him. "Because you couldn't save her."

"You've been talking to Ross. The pair of you think you've got me figured out."

He scowled. "I have not." Then he closed his eyes. "Okay, yeah. I have. But that's not the point. I get it, Doc. Trust me, I get it."

He felt her hand inch closer, and his breath stopped. Every nerve ending strained toward the source of the energy that trickled into him, maddeningly slowly, like the last dregs in a bottle of syrup. He fought the urge to reach for her. To take more, faster. It was torture and ecstasy together.

Blood surged in Jake's ears, and he couldn't take it anymore. He opened his eyes and turned in the seat, holding out his other hand. Understanding what he wanted, Tess reached out slowly with her other hand, and the current doubled in strength.

Jake groaned and dug his shoulder into the seat.

"Do we need to stop?" she asked.

"Uh . . ." Energy surged to a crest, expanding in his chest. The bones of his fingers itched, and he wiggled them toward hers. He opened his eyes and looked at her—relaxed and focused, lips parted, oblivious to the threat swelling an inch away from her.

Then she saw it in his eyes and dropped her hands, flattening her body against the car door. "Snap out of it, Jake."

Even as he leaned closer, his hand reached for the door handle. He shoved it open and flung himself out onto the sidewalk.

"Holy shit," he muttered, panting against the curb. But staring down at his knuckles he noted he was solid again, and with a few feet of distance between him and Tess, the spike of need began to flatten.

"Jake?" A woman's voice, but not Tess. Someone outside the car. He rolled over, blinking up at a feminine silhouette. The sun was directly behind her.

"Are you okay? What are you doing here?"

Sweet Jesus. "Emily?"

The woman laughed. "You're high, right? It's too early to be drunk, even for you. You better not have had a gig in my neighborhood last night and not even told me."

"Emily!" Jake jumped up. He almost pulled her into his arms, and then he remembered that was the last thing he could do.

"Jake?" Tess had gotten out of the car and come round to his side. Her gaze flitted warily between him and the newcomer.

"Hello," said Emily, smiling. "I'm Emily, Jake's sister."

Jake drank her in with his eyes—she was so beautiful. More beautiful than he remembered.

"Sister?" Tess's voice rose with surprise.

Emily offered her hand, and Tess shook it. "I'm Tess."

"Nice to meet you."

"Emily," said Jake, "where's Lucas?"

She gave him a puzzled look. "Who?"

"My nephew—your *son*?"

She frowned, her big brown eyes narrowing with worry. "You're worse than high."

No Lucas. His heart flinched at the familiar pain. But *Emily* was alive here. "No, I'm sorry, Em. Forget it. I'm feeling a little confused. How are you? You look amazing."

She came a few steps closer, and he backed against the car. Tess stepped closer to Jake, almost between them.

"*You* aren't looking so good," said Emily. "Are you sick?"

"Yeah, I think I am—don't touch me or anything." He glanced again at the cupcake sign. "Do you want to get coffee?"

"Jake!" Tess glared at him.

Right. Stupid. BAD idea. He took a quick look around, noticing a mosaic-tile orca fountain at the convergence of Market Street and the old brick-paved Ballard Avenue.

"Maybe we could sit down for a minute, over by the fountain?"

"Are you sure you don't want to go back to my place? I can make you some breakfast. You could lie down. I have to work, but you could stay there as long as you want. You really look awful."

Jake shook his head, sick with regret. "Thanks, Em, but I have to be somewhere. I'd just like to talk to you for a few minutes, if that's okay."

Emily nodded. "Let me grab a cup of coffee. I'll meet you over there. Can I get either of you anything?"

Tess gave her a strained smile. "No, thank you."

When she was gone, Tess said, "Seriously, Jake?"

He closed his eyes nodding. "I know. *Shit*." But he was so happy it was hard to be appropriately repentant. "I can't believe this."

"How many reasons do you want for why this is a bad idea?" she asked.

He fixed his eyes on her face. "She *died* on my Earth. It was *my* fault. I have to make sure she's okay."

"Oh, Jake." She sighed. He knew she understood. She wouldn't deny him. "What if she hugs you or something?"

"I won't let her. *Please*, Tess."

"It's not like I can stop you." She rested her hands on her hips, studying him. "You look fully charged. But just a couple minutes, no longer. Then we're heading for the light-rail station."

He nodded and they started for the fountain.

"Another thing—obviously there's another *you* here. If you're not careful you could really confuse and upset her."

Tess was right; this was nuts. But he couldn't help it. "I promise I'll be careful."

She waited near the street while Jake sank down on the edge of the pool at the fountain's base. A couple minutes later Emily crossed the street to join him.

"Your friend's pretty," she said, sitting down beside him. "She seems nice. A little possessive, maybe."

"She's okay. She knows I . . . don't feel well. She's worried."

Emily grinned. "She doesn't seem afraid of getting it."

Jake let a dark chuckle escape. "She's already had it. Listen, Em, I don't have long."

He couldn't help contrasting this Emily with his Emily. Married and divorced too young from a worthless, abusive punk, his sister was always losing jobs as she struggled to raise their asthmatic son on her own. Life had stamped the light out of her eyes, but she'd been too proud to accept any help from Jake, who, admittedly, had been only marginally better off than she was.

This Emily was like a different person. Yet his gut—and his heart—told him she was the same in all the ways that mattered.

"Tell me what you've been doing."

"What, since I saw you last week?"

Jake cleared his throat. "Yeah."

She sighed, drumming her fingers on her coffee cup. "Working my ass off as always. We hired a new designer, and he's turned out to be a real diva. But our marketing budget is microscopic, so we can't be choosy. I think Alex wants to get married. Beyond that, SOS."

"Alex wants to get married?" Relief washed over him. The worthless punk's name was Tyler.

Emily gave him a sheepish smile. "Yeah, I know. Twenty-six is too young. But he really *is* a good guy, Jacob." Her mouth curved down. "I think he may be too old-fashioned for me, though. I don't think I could marry someone without living with them for a while. What do you think?"

"I think you should do whatever makes you happy, Em."

She shook her head, bemused. "Have you just found out you're terminal or something? Last time we talked about Alex you said he was an arrogant ass. No, wait—that wasn't it. You said he was a 'neo-conservative, pseudo-intellectual, retro-riche, arrogant asshole with no soul.'"

Jake raised his eyebrows. "I said that? I'm sure I was drunk. I'm the asshole, Em. You should know that by now."

"No, you're not. You're just passionate, and borderline bipolar. Now are you going to tell me what's going on with you? Why you look like forty-days-and-nights-at-sea, and why that woman is lurking over there watching us?"

The reference to Tess reminded him what he was messing around with. "I can't, I'm sorry. I have to go."

"You've been here two minutes!"

"I know. I just wanted to be sure you're okay. That you don't need anything."

She watched him, baffled, as he stood up.

"Do something for me, baby sister."

"Yeah?"

"Don't come to any of my gigs on the east side, even if I forget and ask you to. It's too late to be driving home that far. People drink and get in their cars." Jake swallowed, folding his arms over his chest. "It's just a bad idea."

"You know I never go anywhere I can't get to on the Slinky. Besides, when did you start doing gigs on the east side? I thought you hated those people."

"Uh, yeah, I guess you're right. Good for me?"

Emily stared at him, possibly beginning to be alarmed. "Don't I get a hug or kiss or *anything*?"

"Not today. I'm sick, remember?"

"Right. Can you come for dinner next week? Just you and me, no PUs, I promise. I'll make puttanesca."

He smiled. His favorite on both worlds, apparently. "Sure. Give me a call in a couple days and remind me? I'm feeling a little fuzzy."

"Oh, I will. Don't even try to wiggle out of this, Jacob."

He fixed his eyes on her face. "Make me stick to it. There's no one more important to me than you."

Emily rolled her eyes. "Go home and sleep it off, Jake. Say good-bye to your friend for me. She seems nicer than the last one. And not so top-heavy she defies the laws of physics just by walking around. Why don't you bring her next week?"

Could he possibly be this much of a hypocritical asshole in this dimension? Offended by pseudo-intellectuals and suburbanites while sleeping with girls with titanic breast implants?

He swallowed, casting a glance toward the street. He was tempted to pretend, just for a moment, that Tess was his. But he'd already created enough problems for the other Jake.

"I can't, Em. She has a boyfriend."

Emily gave a trademark snorty laugh. "Like that's ever stopped you."

"Don't forget to call me, and I'll see you next week. Take care of yourself, okay, sweetheart?"

"Bye, Jacob."

Jake joined Tess and they hurried down the street, Emily waving after them. A warming peace stole through him, easing the cold ache of loss.

"Are you okay?"

He couldn't look at her. "Yep. Let's catch a train. Where are we going, anyway?"

"I've had a brilliant idea. I'll tell you on the way. But it could be dangerous."

"Great. I was counting on it."

DERELICT

The *Kalakala* began life as the *Peralta*, a 1927 San Francisco Bay steam ferry that was towed north in ruins after a fire destroyed its wooden superstructure. At the old Lake Washington Ship-yards in Kirkland, workers grafted a daring new aluminum top on the salvaged iron hull, and the *Kalakala* debuted on Seattle's waterfront on July 3, 1935. It soon became a world-famous, state-of-the-art attraction, synonymous with Seattle long before the Space Needle became a landmark. Billed as the world's first streamlined ferry, it excited imaginations about the future with its Buck Rogers rocket-ship lines and art deco style.
—"*Kalakala*'s Table Set for Unseen Guest,"
Seattle Post-Intelligencer, February 13, 2002

ROSS SAT frozen and helpless as Tess walked away. With Director Garcia watching him from the other side of the table, Ross could do nothing but try to mask his rising panic.

He told himself Tess wouldn't be foolish enough to go through with a transfer. Especially not now. She'd know as well as Ross that Jake would be hungry and dangerous. And then there was the dislocation.

But this was *Tess*. She was never afraid when she should be. And the director had painted her into a corner. *She's more afraid of Garcia than Jake.*

"Ross?"

He snapped back to attention. "Sir?"

"I said I'm counting on you to control Dr. Caufield. I want

the two of you focused on your assignment, and I want regular updates on your progress."

"Yes, sir," he replied vaguely, refraining from pointing out it would take more than Ross and Garcia to control Dr. Caufield.

"Can I be frank with you, sir?" he asked, trying to stay in the conversation while worst-case scenarios played in his head.

"Please."

"Dr. Caufield took the position on the task force because she wants to help these people. I'm not sure involving her with something like this is going to produce the results you're hoping for."

"You seem to have established a rapport with her. I'm leaving it to you to bring her around. We can achieve our goals for this operation with three to six individuals. After that she is free to pursue her own research." Garcia slid his cup out of the way and leaned toward Ross. "But she needs to understand if she doesn't cooperate her career will be over."

Ross knew this was no idle threat. It didn't matter that she worked for a private institution.

"Now I need you to tell me more about the dislocation," continued Garcia. "This could affect our plans."

"Yes, sir. It raises the stakes considerably."

"We're in agreement about that."

"Dr. Caufield and I have both conducted transfers. The dislocation came with no warning. We need to take measures to ensure—"

A gunshot sounded in the building, and Ross jumped from his chair. A moment later he and the director were running through the lobby.

As they reached the lab he saw the door was secure, but he knew it was too late. His "worst case" had involved Tess running, but his brain had refused to believe it was possible. How many times did he have to learn that bad things happened when he ignored his gut?

"The fade went right through the door!" an agent shouted at them from the lobby. "Just like a damn ghost!"

"Caufield?" called Ross as he ran to meet him.

"Both of them—out the back exit!"

Ross knew what her car looked like, but why in hell had he not made a point of knowing where it was parked? There was a lot on the south side, but there was also street parking closer to the entrance.

Street parking, prompted his gut. So now he had a choice: Follow her to the street, possibly not catch her, and have no vehicle to follow her in. Or go for his car and miss seeing which direction she'd gone.

Either way he was fucked.

An agent burst into the lobby. "Heading west on Massachusetts."

As Ross ran for his car he snatched his phone out of his pocket and started typing a message to the Seattle Field Office.

"Ross, *wait,*" ordered the director.

Ross froze and glanced back.

"The fade's got Dr. Caufield?"

More likely the other way around. "They left in her car. I'm asking the field office to issue an APB—"

"Put your phone away, Agent McGinnis."

He stared at the director. "Sir?"

"Calm down and think. We can't involve the local police if the fade is with her."

What *had* he been thinking? He'd been thinking about the woman he'd just made love to, and her lifeless body discarded beside the road.

Or ravaged by rats on some post-apocalyptic Earth.

"No, sir," agreed Ross. "I'll go after them."

Garcia nodded. "I'll debrief the others and contact you with any additional information. Bring back Echo 8 alive if you can. Promise him anything you need to."

"Yes, sir," said Ross, hardly hearing his superior at this point. Thinking better of heading straight for the car, he turned and bounded up the stairs to his apartment.

As he changed into civilian clothes, he tried to focus on where she might go. The Bureau believed he had a gift for this. Tess seemed to believe it too. Time to put it to the test.

But he soon found that focusing on Tess only further addled his brain—thoughts of her were steeped in strong emotions he couldn't afford to let sidetrack him right now. His current state of mind was the opposite of what Tess had told him was most conducive to psi.

He switched his focus to Jake. *Where are you?*

Ross jumped as his phone gave an alert. He glanced down at the text . . . the field office confirming the APB—which he had sent *despite* the director's reminder about the classified nature of all this. "No engagement," he'd warned them. But it was better for everyone if *he* found them first.

Now to get to the car without Garcia seeing him leave without backup.

As Ross stuffed extra ammo into the pockets of his jacket, an image formed in his mind, too abstract to identify—a cigar shape with rows of tiny round windows. The more he tried to concentrate on the image, the more it fragmented and blurred.

He started for the stairs, and the image flashed again. He froze and closed his eyes. What was it? A bus? Ditching the car would be a smart move, something Tess was sure to think of, but Jake on a *bus?* It didn't really look like a bus—more like one of those bus-shaped trailers. An Airstream—a *huge* one.

That made no sense.

———

"We're going *where?*"

Jake stared at Tess as the Slinky—Seattle's light-rail commuter train—whisked them along the track toward Seattle Center. She'd known this was going to be a hard sell.

"They'll assume we'll head out of town. No one will think to look for us there."

Jake glanced around at the other passengers. The nearest one was half a car away.

"Because it's *crazy*," he hissed.

"Do you have a better idea?"

The Slinky slowed, and Tess stood up. "This is us. South Lake Union. Come on."

Jake growled his dissatisfaction, but he rose and followed her off the train.

In the course of their journey, the summer-blue sky had swollen and distended into a bruised-looking belly of rain cloud. Now it was spitting a chilly rain, and only a few other passengers hurried with them off the platform and down to the sidewalk below. Tess headed for the Space Needle saucer, which rested atop a single-story building at the south end of Lake Union. When they reached the huge disk, she veered left and passed along the west side of the building.

Out back they crossed a waterfront park—a postage stamp of well-manicured grass dotted with abstract metal sculptures. Off to the left was their destination—a rusted-out hulk from another era, the decaying *Kalakala*. Three hundred feet of riveted sheet metal hole-punched with tiny windows, the century-old ferry looked more like an abandoned spaceship.

As the nonprofit that had hoped to restore her went bankrupt over the last couple months, the *Kalakala* had evolved into an unofficial shelter for the homeless. They kept inside the ferry and out of the public areas, which meant they weren't panhandling around shops and restaurants, so the police had left them alone so far.

One of the downtown shelters had donated portable toilets to keep them from fouling the waterfront.

They stopped a few yards from the dock. Jake eyed the huge art deco artifact with alarm. "It's a fucking ghost ship. What if it's full of junkies, or worse? "

"I know it's creepy," she said, stuffing down her own misgivings. "But no one in there is going to mess with us, Jake. At least not more than once."

She gave Jake a significant look, and he frowned his disapproval.

"Listen, it's temporary. We just need a place to hide until I can figure out what to do next."

"Hide from Ross, you mean. That's really what this is about, isn't it?"

She pushed her fingers through her damp hair, shoving it back from her face. She stared at the hulk of the *Kalakala*.

"This is bigger than me and Ross, and even you. But if we'd stayed, I'm pretty sure they would have stopped me doing the transfers at least for a while. And you didn't have a while."

She looked at Jake. His brown eyes rested softly on her face.

"God knows I'm no fan of Agent Ross—he's way too alpha for you, Doctor. But I can't say I blame him. If you were my girl there's no way in hell—"

"Jake, don't." Tess cleared her throat, swallowing the possibilities she'd left behind her.

A police siren sounded in the distance, reminding her of the danger of lingering in public places.

"I don't want to get picked up right now," she said. "I don't want any decisions made for me. Something happened last night that I need time to process before it happens again. Please get on the ferry with me. I promise I'll tell you everything."

Jake gave an exaggerated sigh. "You know damn well I'll do anything you want. But if I wasn't first cousin to the Grim Reaper, I'd sure as hell make you at least kiss me for this. I'm getting all the aggravation, and your bodyguard is getting all the rewards."

"He might argue with you about that," Tess muttered as they headed for the boat.

Jake answered with a loud bark of laughter.

The *Kalakala* had two sets of wide, double doors, fore and aft, to allow cars to drive on and off the main deck. One of the aft doors had been propped open, leaving a ten-foot-high, cavelike entryway.

"Let me go first," said Jake, stepping around her onto the dock. "Let me do the talking."

"Absolutely. I can't wait to hear this."

They ascended the short ramp and passed through the open door. Blackness swallowed them.

Small, round windows spaced about three yards apart down the length of the main deck did little to dispel the gloom on such an overcast day. But gradually Tess's eyes adjusted enough to make out a few shadowy shapes.

"That's far enough." A woman joined them in the square of light that barely penetrated the cavernous main deck. She was tall, with red dreadlocks that hung to her waist. She stood eyeing them, arms crossed. "What do you want?"

"We're looking for a place to stay for a few days. Do you have room for two more?"

The woman's eyebrow hitched up with surprise. She scanned them both from head to toe.

"This ain't a hotel," she grunted. "Police looking for you?"

"We're not in trouble with the police, no." True enough. Just barely.

"Social workers? Reporters? Jesus freaks?" She bent closer. "Don't lie to me, honey."

Tess had acquired an excellent poker face from her work with research subjects, but the wiry redhead unnerved her. She froze, pinned down by the unrelenting gaze.

"Her boyfriend's stalking her," Jake said. "Police won't issue a restraining order. Guy's gone completely apeshit. I'm afraid he's going to kill her."

Tess winced as the woman's gaze jerked, hawklike, to Jake. "Now see, that's just the kind of trouble we don't want here." She smirked. "But I have a nose for bullshit. Wanna try again?"

"Listen," Tess cut in, "how about we pay you, and you let us keep our secrets. It's just for a few days."

The woman raised long, bony fingers to her black-denim-clad hips and continued to study them. She was tall enough to look Jake in the eye.

"How much you got?"

They'd stopped by a finger-scan cash machine before getting on the Slinky, and Tess had given five hundred dollars to Jake for safekeeping. He reached into his jeans pocket and came out with a twenty. He held it up between two fingers, and the woman snatched at it.

Jake jerked the bill away before she could take it. "What's your name?"

The woman scowled. "Maggie."

"Twenty for each day we stay, Maggie. We want our own space, right here by the door. I have posttraumatic shock, and I don't like strangers close to me. Tell the others."

"Tell them yourself, Slim."

"Do you want the money or not?"

Maggie frowned, but she held out her hand and Jake gave her the twenty. "If you plan to share our food, you need to hand over another one of those."

Jake eyed Tess, and she nodded. He handed Maggie another bill.

"There's food and blankets belowdecks." Maggie sniffed. "No

cooking inside—use the stoves on the deck outside the front doors. Piss in the Sani-Cans, not in the boat and not in the lake. Crash where you want"—she pointed the folded bill at them—"but the captain's bridge is off-limits."

Maggie moved away, and Jake withdrew into a dark corner by the doors.

"I don't like this," he muttered as Tess joined him.

They pressed their backs against adjacent walls, watching the movement of the others in the car compartment. There were three small groups within about ten yards. Tess could hear murmurs of their conversation, but beyond a curious glance or two, no one seemed to be taking much interest in the newcomers.

"I don't like it either. Three days at most, I promise."

"Tess, that woman . . . she feels *wrong*."

"What do you mean?"

He thought for a moment. "I don't know what I mean. She feels cold, I guess." He shook his head. "That's not it. She feels *wrong*."

Tess rested her head against the cold metal hull, considering. Her brain was foggy from the transfer in the car, and at the moment she was just grateful to be sitting down.

"We'll keep an eye on her, and on the others. In the meantime, I think we need to start doing shorter, more frequent transfers. I'm going to be the only one doing them for a while, and they're much less draining when we do them before you're faded."

"You know that's not sustainable, Doc."

"Yeah. I'm trying to think of something else. You're doing so well with control, I thought maybe you could try stealing a little here and there from other people. When there's some distance, or something in between, the sensation is really very subtle. Much as I hate the idea, I think it's possible you could do it without people noticing. But . . ." *I don't want to expose anyone else to the side effects.*

She held out her hands to him. "We'll figure it out. In the meantime, let's do a few minutes while we're sitting here. Then we'll find something to eat, and maybe you can watch while I nap. Sleep and calories help with the recharging."

Jake raised his hands, and soon he was relaxing into the transfer, his breaths coming slow and even.

"I feel more in control this time," he said.

"Good. That's what we want."

Jake closed his eyes, and Tess tried to ignore the burning/buzzing sensation in her palms. Her thoughts drifted to Ross and one of the last things he'd said to her.

Sounds like just the flight part to me.

Was Jake right? Had this been more about running away from Ross than anything else? She believed she'd done it for Jake, and to protect herself from getting locked into the Bureau's agenda, but would it have hurt to stay awhile and hope for a chance to talk to Ross? She'd just assumed that with Garcia there he'd go happily back into the fold.

And why shouldn't he? His job was just as important to him as hers was to her.

Tess turned, scanning down the length of the ferry, easily half the length of the Seahawks' stadium, maybe more. She could still hear the low conversation of the others, and now loud laughter ringing at the far end of the deck. She noticed a partially enclosed stairway about five yards away, and wondered if it led belowdecks.

Tess felt the connection break and returned her attention to Jake. "Enough?"

"Never enough," he murmured, his eyes soft.

They sat cross-legged, facing each other.

Warmth stole into her cheeks as she remembered Ross's declaration about Jake: *He's in love with you.*

Jake raised his hand toward her face, and her breath caught.

"I don't feel . . . *dangerous* right now," he said in a languid tone, hand still hanging in the air. "I almost feel like . . ."

Like you could touch me. She knew what he was thinking, and she wasn't afraid.

"Why don't we try it?"

He blinked at her, and his fingers moved closer. But he dropped his hand before touching her.

"We need to go back," he said.

"Jake—"

"I mean it, Tess. You need to give Ross a chance to help you fix this. You and me off on our own—there's no way it's gonna end well. It's like the three of us are a fucking hydrogen atom."

Tess frowned in confusion. "A what?"

"Come on, try to keep up, Doctor. One arrogant proton cozying up inside one sexy, certifiably insane nucleus, while poor, lonely, negative-charge boy is doomed to circle in the distance."

"That's one hell of a metaphor." Tess laughed.

"Tell me why I suddenly became more of a threat to Proton Man."

She'd been both dreading and craving this moment. She knew how he was going to react, but she desperately needed to talk it over with someone. Because there was no reason to think it wouldn't happen again.

"Something happened last night that scared us both. Before we really had a chance to talk about it, the Bureau director showed up with all this talk about covert operations and training Echoes to be killers."

"Forget about that for now. Tell me what happened."

She folded her hands together, squeezing. Feeling her own solid flesh. "I dislocated."

Worry creased his forehead. "Why do I get the feeling you don't mean you threw out your knee?"

"For ten, maybe fifteen minutes, I went somewhere else. Just like you did when you came here. I think I was on your Earth."

Tess described her harrowing descent down the muddy hillside. The fires and the rats. The final plunge into light that closed round her like a tunnel and spat her out the other end.

"It was real, Jake. I didn't dream it. Ross said I was there, and then I wasn't."

When I came back, he held me until I stopped shaking. Until I almost felt safe again.

"I don't doubt it was real," growled Jake. "This is because of your contact with me. We're running because Ross knew that, and he didn't want you doing the transfers anymore, and he was fucking right, Tess."

She nodded. "I agree. It's the transfers. And it could happen to him too." Fear sucked at her stomach as she thought about him dislocating and not being able to get back.

Jake stared at her, angry and incredulous. This was going about as well as she'd expected. "So let's hear some geek-speak, Doctor. Explain to me how this is happening and what you're going to do if it happens again."

"I can't explain it, but I assume our exchanges have created some kind of link to your world. And there was a trigger too. . . . I think it had to do with Ross." *With running away from Ross.* "It's like you said about the hydrogen atom—you and me and Ross are hopelessly tangled up. I *feel* that, Jake."

"You could have died. We have to stop."

"You're right; I could have. And I won't lie to you; it scared the hell out of me. But I think it's possible I may be able to control it. I think it may be related to fight-or-flight response, and if that's true, if I get into trouble I should be able to come back." It was the only thought that had kept her from losing it in the twelve hours since the dislocation.

"Not only that, Jake. If it happens again, maybe I can learn more about your Earth. If rats survived, other mammals may have. *People* may have. Many omnivores survived the K-Pg event—the one we believe killed off the dinosaurs. What if you could go home, Jake?"

Jake leaned close, eyes bright with anger. His voice burned low as he said, "Back on my Earth, I lost the only people I loved. They died because of me. I didn't want to go on living without them, so I blew my brains all over the wall of my apartment. I haven't changed my mind about that decision. I've never regretted it, not even for a moment. On this Earth, *you're* my reason for living. I go along with your crazy ideas to make you happy. I like talking to you. I like feeling your energy running through me. But I won't let you die because of me."

He stood up. "Come on."

Tess sat gaping at him, still taking in the stream of revelations.

"I said *come on*."

She ground her teeth together and folded her arms over her knees. "Do you have any idea how tired I am of the two of you telling me what to do?"

"You need handlers, Tess," he snapped. "Deal with it."

"Unless you plan to throw me over your shoulder, I'm not going anywhere. If you want to go, go."

"Christ, do *you* have any idea how aggravating you are?" He gave a loud groan and sank down beside her. His hands clenched in his lap, and he sighed. "I can't leave my orbit, remember?"

She raised her hand toward his face, and he flinched away. Her hand followed, index finger touching a dark-blond curl, light as a feather.

"Tess . . . God . . ." He turned his head slowly, until his lips brushed the tip of her finger. "I think I'm falling in love with you."

Tess dropped her hand, guilt collapsing her chest.

Jake didn't break eye contact. "I'm not sorry I said it, but I don't expect you to answer."

There was a part of her that thrilled to his confession, and that confused her. Yet why should it be hard to understand? Beneath a thick protective coating of anger and sarcasm, Jake was *lovable*. Scruffy good looks, a quick wit, and a sexy smile. He had a bizarre ability to make her feel his regard even while baiting her. And they had shared a bond neither of them really understood.

But it was a ridiculous thing for him to say. For more reasons than she could count.

"You don't mean that, Jake. You hardly know me."

Anger flashed again in his eyes. "I'm not confused about the fact that the last thing we can be is lovers. And I know you love someone else. But don't try to make yourself feel better by talking me out of how *I* feel."

"That's not what I'm doing." Was she? "I'm only suggesting the possibility you've mistaken gratitude for love. I've been taking care of you. Keeping you alive. You've lost your home, and it's not surprising that—"

"Jesus, Tess! Is it so hard to believe that I love *you*? Not your bedside manner. Not your energy. Not your suicidal superpowers. *You*." He shook his head. "Let's just drop it."

She sighed, frustrated with her lack of tact. "I'm sorry. I care about you, and I don't want you to be hurt. I guess that's why I'm trying to talk you out of your feelings."

Jake's shoulders drooped as his anger ebbed. "Can I ask you something?"

"Sure."

"Promise to tell me the truth?"

"Hmm. Let's hear it first."

"Would I have a chance? I mean if I wasn't toxic, and if you'd never met Tall-Dark-and-Angsty?"

"Ah, Jake." She wished with all her heart he hadn't asked. Lying to herself was easy. She wasn't so good at it when it came to other people. "I can't see any good coming of answering that."

He frowned. "Coward."

She studied his downcast face. "All right. You are exactly the kind of guy I'd go for if circumstances were different. Now do you feel better or worse?"

Jake grinned. "I knew it. How could you resist?"

She rolled her eyes and stood up, brushing grit from her skirt.

"Where are we going?"

"We skipped lunch. My judgment has clearly been affected. Let's go downstairs and see what they've got."

Stubby candles placed on alternating steps lit the way belowdecks. Dribbles of wax collected in pools around them, and in some cases had run off the stair edges to form colorful stalactites. Fire on board a ship seemed like a bad idea, but there was probably no power source. And the thing *was* basically a giant tin can—not much to burn.

Next to the candle on the bottom step was a shoebox full of flashlights and batteries. Tess bent and picked one up, shining it around the small room at the foot of the stairs. Lockers lined the walls, some open and partly filled with garbage. At the other end of the room was a jagged, rounded opening hand-cut into the wall—obviously not a part of the ship's original architecture.

"Normally I'm in favor of dining by candlelight," muttered Jake, "but this is creepy."

"I don't see anything that looks like food. Do you?"

Jake flicked on another flashlight, and the second beam bounced over the walls. "No. Let's go back up."

She grinned at him. "Afraid of ghosts?" It didn't seem the right time to tell him she knew of at least one documented death down here—a suicide. There'd also been some amateur documentation of paranormal activity.

"I'm more afraid of the living," he said.

"You keep forgetting you're a walking weapon."

Jake scowled. "*You're* the one who keeps forgetting that. And I'd rather not go looking for trouble."

"We'll make it quick. Find the food and get out."

"I could slip Myrtle another twenty. Make her do it for us."

"I'd like to limit our interaction with *Maggie*—and everyone else—as much as possible."

"Right." Jake sighed. "Okay. I'll go first."

He stepped into the room and opened one of the lockers, jumping back as something tumbled out—a stack of paper coffee cups. He opened the locker below it more carefully, shining his light in.

"Rat poison. That's encouraging."

The next six lockers contained toiletries and stacks of folded clothing, but nothing edible.

"Come on," she said with a shiver. "There's nothing in here."

They ducked through the hole in the wall into the next room. Though larger than the room with the lockers, the clutter of furniture and the absence of any light source made this space feel close and heavy. An ornate bar carved of dark wood lined one wall, and half a dozen small tables had been shoved against the adjacent wall. Velvet-covered stools still formed an orderly row along the bar.

A thick layer of dust coated everything, and cobwebs hung like dark lace curtains in each of the corners.

"What was this thing, anyway?" asked Jake, directing his beam along the bar until it came to rest on a large work of stained glass.

"A ferry."

"Why is there a bar in the basement?"

"It has a couple bars, and a restaurant, I think. It used to be really fancy." She dragged a finger through the blanket of dust on the bar.

"When? A hundred years ago?"

"Yeah, something like that."

He cast her a look of disbelief. "I was joking."

Tess shrugged and started toward the other side of the room. "Doesn't look like anyone's disturbed anything here in a long time. Let's keep going."

She stepped over a prostrate barstool and landed on something squishy—it squealed and so did she. She hopped to one side, and Jake shone his light on a retreating rat. It gave her a sick feeling, reminding her of last night's dislocation and the perils that seemed to be multiplying around them.

"I *hate* rats," she muttered. "Give me a huge, hairy spider any day."

"I'm sure they've got some of those down here too."

She swallowed. "I take it back."

She moved closer to Jake. He didn't flinch away from her this time, but he said, "How is it I'm not on the list of things that make you scream and run away?"

"You're not hairy or creepy. Well, maybe a *little* hairy."

"Do you like the beard? I could shave it."

"You wouldn't be Jake without the beard."

"Emily always hated it." He ducked and stepped through another roughly cut opening.

"I'm not your sis—"

Suddenly Jake yelled and slipped out of view. She heard a series of scuffling and thumping noises, accompanied by *"Fuuuuuuck!"*

"Jake!?"

She ran to the hole and popped her head through, pointing her light down. The opening hung over a steep stairway, and Jake lay at the bottom.

"Oh my God, are you okay?"

"I found the engine room," he groaned. "In case you were looking for that."

Tess crawled through the hole, careful about where she put her feet. She grasped the metal rail and made her way down.

"Did you break anything?"

"*Can* I break anything? I don't know. Feels like I might have twisted my ankle."

She reached for his pant leg and then drew back, remembering. "Can you walk?"

Jake hauled himself to his feet and tested his weight on the ankle. "It's not bad."

He bent and picked up his flashlight, and she shone hers over a huge iron cylinder that ran the length of the wall.

"Wow, look at the size of that engine," said Jake. "When did you say this was built?"

"1920. -Ish. Or maybe that's just when they changed the name; I can't remember."

"That's bad luck, isn't it?"

"What is?"

"Changing the name of a ship."

"You know . . . I read a story in the paper a couple years ago, and now that you mention it they said it was a bad-luck ship. It burned once. The original was made of wood. It also crashed a few times."

Jake rolled his eyes. "Well how about that. The two of you were made for each other."

She scowled and opened her mouth to accuse him of engine envy. Before she could, he asked, "Do you hear anything funny?"

Pausing to listen, she heard nothing but silence made heavy by the water that pressed against the sides of the ship, and the occasional loud creak. Then she noticed a faint *drip, drip, drip.*

"Maybe there's a leak."

"You don't get to pick any more hideouts, Doctor."

"Come on, it's perfect. Who's ever going to look for us here?"

"Uh, *no one.* Don't know that I'd call that a selling point."

She groaned. "Okay, it's stupid to be down here. I admit it. We wouldn't be if I weren't starving."

Jake eyed her guiltily. "Sorry—I know I'm being an asshole. I hate boats. And if something happens to you because of me . . ."

"Let's check one more room. If there's no food, we'll go back up and find Myrtle."

"Deal."

They waded through a layer of trash to more stairs at the far end of the engine. Ten steps up they found another hole in the wall. Jake shone his light in, and her stomach growled, the sound amplifying in the mostly empty double-deck room.

"Well, no food in here either. Just a pile of . . . rolled-up carpets?" He stepped through the opening and she followed.

Dust coated the floor in this room, so thick it rose in a choking cloud as they walked.

"What the hell?" grumbled Jake, pulling the collar of his shirt up to the bridge of his nose.

He stopped, but Tess took a few steps forward. They did look like carpets, piled higgledy-piggledy at the back of the room. And this was apparently the end of the line. No more holes cut through the wall.

"Let's go," muttered Jake. "No telling what kind of nasty shit we're breathing."

"Hang on a minute." Tess followed his example, covering her nose and mouth with her shirt, and took one more step into the room. There was something strange about those bundles. The shapes were too irregular—too lumpy—to be rugs.

She tapped her foot against the closest one, gasping as a bit of it broke away. Kneeling, she ran her beam along its length. Something reflected light back at her, and she bent closer.

An oval locket. Under the locket was a patch of moth-eaten fabric, and the long fibers lying on either side of the locket were—*hair.*

"Oh Jesus," Tess whispered. Her heart had already scuttled up to the main deck and out to the dock.

"What is it?"

"Come on, Jake!"

She bolted past him and crawled through the opening, careful of the stairs on the other side, and Jake came through right behind her.

"We have to get off this ship. Those are *bodies*—the kind that are left after Echo attacks!"

"Christ, Tess! Are you sure?"

She tripped near the bottom of the stairs and tumbled to the deck below, banging her knee so hard tears sprang to her eyes. Jake watched helplessly as she scrambled to her feet.

"Why the hell didn't I listen to you?" she moaned.

"Calm down," muttered Jake, his face setting in a grim mask. "Watch where you put your feet. Keep quiet and stay behind me."

Halfway across the engine deck, a light appeared on the stairs at the other end. Jake and Tess froze as someone started down.

"Who's there?" Jake barked.

"Welcoming committee," replied a woman's voice. Maggie. "Stay where you are. Your host wants to meet you."

"Change in plans. We're checking out. Keep out of our way."

Maggie chuckled as three other figures ducked through the hole and started down behind her. The light from the lanterns they carried illuminated the room and threw long shadows on the walls.

A dark-haired man at the back of the group made his way forward and a wave of recognition cooled Tess's rising panic.

"Ross!" she cried.

"What the . . . ?" began Jake.

Ross's gaze fixed on her with surprise. What she saw in his eyes—rather what she *didn't* see—started a cold trickle of terror.

ALPHA

> With a finite amount of matter in a cosmos that is infinitely expanding, we would expect to find not only twin Earths, but twin individuals. Somewhere out there *your* twins are thinking, "What a preposterous notion."
>
> —Physicist Brandon Black, Echo Task Force,
> UC Berkeley

R OSS GESTURED to his companions, and one of the men strode forward and stuck a gun in Jake's face.

"Hey!" Jake cried, grabbing his arm. The man didn't react at all to his touch—except to jam the muzzle against Jake's forehead.

"You're solid enough for a bullet, brother," warned Ross.

"Take it *easy,* G-man!"

"It's not Ross," Tess croaked, numb with terror.

Again the leader's eyes anchored on Tess. He stepped closer. "No one's called me that in a very long time. But how interesting to know I have a double on your world. Most people call me Mac. Beautiful women call me anything they want."

"Oh shit," said Jake. "Oh *shit.*"

Tess faltered back, and the Ross look-alike stepped forward, inclining his head her direction. "Come here," he murmured, taking another step. "You smell good."

"Don't you touch her!" warned Jake.

"We all share here, brother." Mac glanced at his man with the gun, who had balled the front of Jake's shirt in his fist. "Shoot him if he moves."

Tess backed away, but Mac's hand shot out. She screamed as red-hot iron tongs closed over her wrist.

"I'll kill you, asshole!" Jake sounded like he was shouting under water. Boiling water. It seeped into every opening in Tess's body.

Her legs folded and she moaned.

Mac pulled her into his chest, murmuring in her ear like he was gentling a horse. "*Easy* now, easy. . . . Fear makes it flow faster. It'd be a sad waste to add you to our mummy museum."

Jake and the others faded away as the pain took over. Firebrands scalded everywhere he touched, radiating out a searing poison to the rest of her body. She had never experienced anything like this with Jake. This Echo's control was amazing—somewhere between Jake's desperate gorging and the slow throb of the energy transfers.

As he drained her, Mac continued whispering in her ear. "It doesn't have to hurt if you'll just *relax*. Mmm, you taste as good as you smell." Even through the pain she felt her body relaxing to the sound of his voice, going limp in his arms.

Then it struck her that his voice wasn't in her ear—it was in her head, just like Jake's had been.

Now, Tess, let's see what you have for me. . . .

He combed through her mind, sifting through thoughts and memories, searching for something . . . searching for *Ross*.

Tess felt the jolt of recognition as he found what he was looking for. Felt him locking on and replaying the last week of her life. She fought the pain, clenching against him, working desperately to wall off those last scenes with Ross—the intimacy they had shared.

Let me in.

Fuck you.

Dark laughter rippled through her. *Let me in, or I'm going to kill bachelor number two.*

The breath she was holding came out in a sob.

I'll do it, Tess.

She released her death grip on her memories, and probing tentacles wrenched open the last twenty-four hours of her life. His low moan rolled like thunder through her mind.

What have we here?

Please . . . don't . . .

Suddenly he released her.

She landed in a pile of trash, and Jake crouched beside her. The Echo with the gun now had his hands in the air. Before she could make sense of what had happened, a loud voice sounded in the room, reversing the slowing throb of her heart.

"Kick the gun over here. *Now.*" Ross. *Her* Ross.

She turned in time to see his shock as he stared into the face of his twin. In the moment of confusion, one of the men lunged at him, and Ross went down with a shout.

"Help him!" cried Tess.

Jake lurched toward the dropped weapon, but Maggie rushed at him with a section of pipe. Before Tess could shout a warning, the pipe connected with a solid whack, and he collapsed to the deck.

Tess rolled onto her hands and knees, her body protesting every movement.

As Maggie snatched up the gun, Mac strode over and kicked at the man feeding on Ross. "Get off!"

Ross groaned as his attacker peeled off, and Mac bent over him, closing a hand over his throat.

"Don't!" pleaded Tess.

She stared, paralyzed, as Ross's body lifted a few inches off the deck. With a crackle of static, a bluish glow enveloped them. Ross's form suctioned against Mac's. Their bodies overlapped and merged, convulsing . . . edges blurring.

She scrambled toward them. "Ross!"

Their bodies contorted and finally collapsed into one solid form. His eyes fixed on her, face drawn in an expression of profound shock.

"Ross? Can you say something?"

He rolled to a crouch, his gaze sweeping over the others.

"Keep them here," he said to Maggie. Then he rose and ran up the stairs.

Maggie and the others followed Mac, and Tess could hear the low muttering of voices as they conferred in the room above.

One of the lanterns lay on its side on the floor, and by its light Tess could see Jake's slumped form. She crawled through the rubbish—a mix of food wrappers, cups, crumpled newspaper, and paper bags.

She felt the pull she always felt when they were close, but in her drained condition she had no resistance, and her body tipped toward him. Scooting to a safer distance, she called his name.

Jake stirred and groaned, hand moving to the back of his neck. Her heart pulsed with relief.

"Are you okay?"

"Christ," he rasped, sitting up and looking around. "No. Are *you?*"

"I'm okay," she replied feebly, her throat closing over the words.

"Where is that asshole?" growled Jake. "Where's Ross?"

She did her best to explain what had happened. Jake stared at her like she was talking nonsense. Maybe she was. Her head buzzed and throbbed, and her stomach had begun to gnaw at itself. She wasn't sure anymore what she'd seen.

"Do you think he's gone for good?"

She hugged her arms around her chest, trying to hold herself together. "I don't know."

"Jesus, sweetheart." He reached a hand toward her face, drawing back as her head pulled toward it. "You're completely wasted."

"The other Ross—Mac—he *did* something to me. I could feel him in my head."

His jaw clenched. "What do you mean?"

"He was feeding on me and, God, it hurt, but it was slow and controlled. While he was doing it he talked to me. Telepathically, like you did. Then he started going through my thoughts, trying to learn about Ross. I couldn't stop him. It felt like he was . . ."

Violating me from the inside.

Tess shuddered, and Jake squeezed his eyes shut. "That fucker is dead. The next time I see him."

"Not until we figure out what happened to Ross."

Jake studied her, and whatever he saw made him pull himself together.

"Could he have gone to my Earth? Dislocated, like you did?"

Was that possible? Was it *preferable*? Finally she shook her head. "I don't think so. He didn't disappear. I watched them fuse together."

All my fault, she thought wretchedly. If she hadn't run . . . if she hadn't come *here* of all places. She tried warming herself with her hands, and Jake watched in silence.

"Keep talking, okay?" she said. "We have to figure a way out of this. We have to help Ross."

Jake thought Ross was finished; she could see it in his face. But he kept it to himself. "Did you say those are bodies in the other room?"

She nodded. "Just husks, really. That's what usually happens with Echo feedings. These people have learned how to do it without killing, even better than you and me."

"Sometimes."

"Sometimes. Mac told me fear makes it flow faster. It helps explain our success with the transfers."

"Because you don't have the sense to be afraid of me, you mean?"

She managed a weak smile. "Honestly I think Ross has always scared me more than you. I'm not sure what that says about me."

"You're more scared of yourself than either of *us*, Doctor."

She reabsorbed the smile. "I know you've been in my head too, but don't you start analyzing me. I've got a pretty thin grip on sanity right now as it is."

Jake's long fingers fiddled with a rubber band he'd picked up off the floor. He glanced at the doorway the others had exited through. "Can you explain why this keeps happening? First we run into my sister, now a Ross twin."

Tess raised her hands to her face, rubbing her temples. "God knows I didn't see it coming, but remember what I told you about quantum theory and links between nonlocal entities?"

"I remember you saying a bunch of stuff that confirmed my suspicion you're much smarter than I am."

"Well, the point is I agree with you it's more than coincidence. I'd guess it has to do with the psychic and emotional bonds between us—between you and Emily, between Ross and me. We're connected in ways we can't see or feel. I ran from Ross, but my subconscious pulled on a thread with him at the end."

Jake frowned. "This guy isn't Ross. I've seen inside your bodyguard's head, and I can tell you the last thing he would do is hurt you. It's the only reason I put up with him being such a dick."

"Mac is a version of Ross," she said, her throat constricting the words. "Something made him turn out different. There is a huge number of variables."

"You mean this Ross had a crappy childhood?"

"Possibly. But they're essentially the same person, and that's about the strongest connection you can get. I can't help but wonder if they merged because the existence of both of them in the same space-time created some kind of disruption that tried to normalize itself. The question is, can it be undone?"

It's probably not going to undo itself.

"I have to see Mac," she said.

Jake stared at her. "The hell you do."

"I have to try to help Ross."

He shook his head. "You're too weak."

Tess rose on quaking legs, calling, "Maggie!"

"Jesus, shut *up!*"

But Maggie was already headed down the stairs. "Come on, honey. Mac wants to see you on the bridge."

Jake rose beside her, and Maggie barked, "Just her."

"No fucking way." He clenched his fists.

Maggie pointed her gun at him.

"Jake," Tess pleaded, "this won't help."

"You won't survive another feeding." His voice came out rough with emotion.

"He won't kill me. He could have done that already."

"Let's go," said Maggie.

Tess started for the stairs.

"Go slow," snapped Jake. "She can hardly walk."

Every movement cramped the muscles in her legs, and she gripped the railing, lungs heaving after only a couple steps. She cast a glance back at Jake before ducking through the cut opening.

The agony of helplessness and dread stamped lines all over his handsome face. "Don't you do anything stupid, Doc."

"Same to you. I'll see you soon."

HIDE-AND-SEEK

Gentle reader, may you never feel what I then felt! May your eyes never shed such stormy, scalding, heart-wrung tears as poured from mine. May you never appeal to Heaven in prayers so hopeless and so agonised as in that hour left my lips; for never may you, like me, dread to be the instrument of evil to what you wholly love.

—Charlotte Brontë, *Jane Eyre*

CURIOUS EYES followed them as they made their way down the car deck.

Tess returned their interest as she passed, surprised to find they in no way resembled any street people she'd seen. Their clothes were clean and in good condition. None of them looked sick or underfed. There was no smell of stale spaces or unwashed bodies, and unlike the deck below, this part of the boat was clean and free of clutter.

She kept alert for a sympathetic face, but their gazes quickly dropped away. The whole thing was eerily reminiscent of something from *Watership Down*, a book she'd had to read in college. Were the Echoes keeping these people healthy and happy so they could feed on them? It was inspired, she had to admit. No one kept tabs on the homeless. If some of them disappeared into the bowels of the ship, who would notice? Only the others who risked the same fate for a dry bed and full belly.

At the opposite end of the car deck they climbed another set of stairs—wider and less steep this time, embellished with art deco flourishes. They led to a spacious seating area on the next level, with larger windows and rows of benches running the length of the boat. More people gathered here, playing cards or chess and talking quietly. Though many of the benches were soiled or ripped open, this level too was free of clutter and dust.

As Maggie led her to a third flight of stairs, Tess stumbled and fell to the deck. She hauled herself up by the railing, wheezing and coughing. Maggie stood a silent sentry while Tess rested and recovered. Was there a scrap of pity in the woman? Tess glared at her.

"Not there yet, honey, keep going."

Tess stared down at her foot, willing it to move to the next stair.

"I'll take it from here, Maggie."

Tess glanced up to find Mac standing at the top of the stairs. She thought about how she'd walked and talked with Ross on the stairs at Seattle Psi. Mac was even dressed like Ross—like *civilian* Ross. Faded jeans and T-shirt, but instead of the basketball sneakers he wore motorcycle boots. Mac was the same height, roughly the same weight, though the muscles in Mac's arms had more of a bulge, like he spent more time at the gym. His hair was a bit longer, and stubble darkened his chin.

Maggie hesitated, eyeing her boss. Tess realized that Maggie was probably as concerned about what had happened belowdecks as she was. Who was this man?

"Are we going to have a problem?" Mac asked sharply.

Maggie frowned. "Nah."

"That's good, because I need you to go down and make sure the others understand that nothing has changed. Make sure they're keeping an eye on our new friend, and make sure lunch crew is covered. Business as usual, got it?"

Maggie's shoulders hunched, and she turned and started down the stairs. "Okay, boss."

Mac descended quickly, and Tess braced herself as he reached for her. But when he lifted her in his arms, there was no pain. Only an uncomfortable tingling sensation, like a sleeping foot.

"Ross?" she breathed. Her hand curled around his neck as she looked into his eyes.

His lips curved into a smirk. "Interesting."

Her heart dropped all the way back down to the engine room. She let her head fall to his shoulder so she could master her tears unobserved.

Don't give up. He may still be in there.

They emerged into a more upscale seating area, with individual chairs arranged in a half circle around the front windows. The damn thing was like a floating hotel. She noted that *here* was where the food was kept. Maggie had apparently set a trap for them.

Mac wound around to a final set of stairs that took them up to the bridge. This space had been converted to sleeping quarters. She noticed a series of doors open to the deck outside, which pointed out the fact that there had once also been a series of walls dividing the space. At the end of the room was a gleaming copper wheel. A stick of incense burned on the instrument panel, filling the space with the aroma of sandalwood.

The room's only furnishings were a bed—just a mattress on the floor—and a leather chair and ottoman with a small side table. Mac set her down in the chair and crossed to the bed, where he lifted a cutting board laden with cheese, bread, and fruit. He placed the board on the table. Then he closed and bolted the door at the top of the stairs and sat down on the ottoman.

"No one will bother us now."

She shivered.

"I know you're hungry." He gestured to the cutting board.

"Is this how you fatten up the lambs?" Exhaustion had scrubbed the wry edge from her voice.

"You don't want it?" He reached for the board, but she grasped the edge of it with her fingers.

"Smart girl."

She'd moved past hungry to nauseous, but she knew she had to eat to keep her brain working. She nibbled a few bites of bread and cheese, and soon her appetite returned. Mac lifted a carafe from under the table and poured two glasses of water.

"Why did you want to see me?" she asked.

"I want to know what you make of what happened down there."

"How about you let me talk to Ross, and I'll tell you my theory."

Mac moved suddenly closer, caging her in the chair by gripping the armrests. Emergency sirens whined in her head.

"Answer my question, or I'll go looking for answers myself."

Tess rubbed her lips together and said carefully, "You sure you can still do that?"

He smiled. "I have no problem with putting my hands on you again to find out."

She swallowed and set down her water glass with trembling fingers. "It would help me if you'd answer a few questions first."

She held her breath while his eyes moved over her face. Finally he said, "Go ahead."

"Can you tell me what it felt like?"

Mac sat up, releasing the chair and crossing his arms. "I felt invaded."

She arched an eyebrow at the irony. "How do you mean?"

"He's nothing like me. He's rigid and obedient. A prisoner to his job."

Keep him talking. She needed to gather information without making him suspicious, but her heart pounded so loudly it threatened to give her away. "So you've seen all of him? His thoughts and feelings. His memories."

Mac grunted. "He shut me out fast, like you tried to do. Limped off wounded and hid himself in some hole I haven't been able to uncover. *Yet.* I actually learned more about him from your mind than his."

Not gone! The thought thrilled through her, and she struggled to keep her expression from betraying the surge of hope.

"Do you feel him inside you? Does he communicate with you?"

"Oh, he's there. I can feel him . . . *watching.*"

She almost sobbed with relief. Could she help him fight Mac?

She needed time to think, and for that she needed to keep him talking. Glancing down, she saw the fingers of one hand rubbing at his biceps. There was a tattoo there—a dragon, with a long tail that coiled around his arm.

"What were you on your Earth? Not FBI, I take it?"

Mac snorted and swallowed the rest of his water. "I was a meth dealer, Doctor. High-end. I lived in a penthouse with a view of the Sound. I had a collection of vintage bikes, a rockstar girlfriend with a million-dollar habit, and enough guns to arm a militia. *No one* fucked with me. How's that for irony?" He laughed. "Speaking of irony, you know your boyfriend's little brother is a meth addict? It's good to be an only child. Poor Ross . . . I'm his worst fucking nightmare."

Anger surged, and her mouth skipped out ahead of her brain. "You've certainly come up in the world. Captain of a rusty, floating graveyard."

A smile twisted his lips. "All of the people I knew are dead. I'm not. That makes me a survivor."

"That makes you a parasite. Just like you were on your Earth."

Mac lifted an eyebrow. "And your faithful companion down below is different *how?*"

"Jake? He hates what he has to do to survive here. You've made it your new career."

Mac laughed. "I get you, Doctor. You like the men in your life to have a healthy measure of self-loathing. No one could keep up with *you* in that department."

"I like myself fine," she replied, holding his gaze.

"I've been in your head."

"Funny how the people who really *should* loathe themselves never do."

"Careful," growled Mac, leaning close again. "I put up with a lot from a sexy woman, but you can cross a line with me. Now, I've answered your questions. It's time for you to answer mine."

Pressing back against the chair, she told him what she'd told Jake—that she thought he and Ross were so closely entangled they couldn't exist separately in the same space.

"So you think this is permanent," he said.

"I think once you grabbed him it was inevitable. But you existed separately before he came here. I think it's possible you could again. I might be able to help you."

She shuddered as a slow smile spread over his face. "Why would I want to do that? I'm not tied to this shipwreck anymore. I can start my life over." He reached up and dragged a fingertip from her cheek to her chin. "I feel human again in all the most important ways."

Tess sat up slowly, holding his gaze as she reached a hand behind his neck and pulled him closer. His lips curled again into a grin, and she closed her eyes and thought about Ross.

The kiss was hard and hot, and when it finished she murmured against his lips, "Let me talk to him."

He gave a bark of laughter. "Not a chance, sweetheart."

"Let me talk to him," she repeated, threading her fingers into his hair, "and I'll do anything you want." Until the last word she managed to keep her voice steady.

His arm curled around her waist as he murmured, "Have you fooled yourself into thinking you have a choice?"

Her heart pounded, her breaths coming in little gasps. How closely fear mimicked passion in the body.

She felt the same tingling she had on the stairs—she was still transferring energy, but the stream was very weak.

His lips came down on hers, but this time she pulled away. "Do what I asked, or I'll fight you."

His hand came to the back of her neck, closing like a vise. "You really *have* got yourself fooled. But I tell you what, Doctor. You go on and look for Special Agent McGinnis. I won't stop you."

She let Mac take her lips, and he immediately opened his mouth, devouring her, groaning into her throat. She dug her fingers into his hair, letting him take over as her mind went searching.

Ross, where are you?

Yes, come out, Ross. Come and see what I've got.

She shuddered at the sound of Mac's voice in her head, and it struck her that he was using her too, trying to force Ross into the open. What would happen if Ross surfaced? Would Mac absorb him completely? Or could Ross break away?

Ross was strong enough to fight. She just had to give him a reason.

Levering herself up from the chair, she broke the kiss. She walked to the bed and Mac followed, pushing her back and covering her body with his.

Jake listened to his guards argue about what would happen if they fired one of the pistols they were waving around like idiots. Would the bullet punch a hole in the boat? Would it ricochet? How many times?

Jake shut them out and focused on his hand.

He always cut the energy transfers off before he was sated. He hated seeing how they drained her. Hated the dark depressions under her eyes, and watching her stumble as she walked. Besides that it hurt his heart—and parts farther south—being so close to her and not being able to touch her.

He still hadn't recovered from the long, hungry stretch the night before. The transfers since then had been brief. Was he starting to be able to see through his hand? How much was enough? he wondered, eyeing the idiots with the guns.

Listening now to their ridiculous argument, he realized it might be enough for them to *believe* the bullet would pass through him.

"Hey, dumbass!" he called, rising to his feet.

Mac made a hungry sound as his lips pressed against her throat. His hand slid down and began fumbling with her skirt.

Tess, stop this! Now!

Ross!

His voice came urgently, an angry echo across her consciousness.

Hurt him, Tess. Make him STOP.

I need you, Ross.

As Mac spread her legs with his knees, she sank back into the memory of Ross in her bed. Mac reached down between their bodies, pulling at his own clothing.

"Ross," she murmured, blocking out the sound of silky laughter in her ear.

He pushed into her with a groan that slowly built in his throat to a shout. His eyes snapped open and bored into hers. Two tears slid down his face in quick succession.

His head sank against her neck. "I don't know how long I can fight him," he rasped. "You have to get out of here."

"Ross!" cried Tess, relief cresting like a tidal wave. He tried pulling out of her, but she held his face in her hands. "I'm not leaving without you. We'll fight him together."

He drew in a breath, shuddering like it hurt. "He's strong, Tess."

"He had the advantage of surprise before. But we know him now. *I* know him, and I know you're stronger."

Ross pushed his hands against hers, threading their fingers together as their gazes locked. "I won't let him touch you again."

Her mother once said the same thing. Mac's voice sliced between them and ricocheted around in her brain. *Then she died and left her with him.*

Ross froze and made a choking sound in his throat. "Oh Jesus."

Something primal and wounded keened from Tess's deepest hiding place. She closed her ears against the sounds of it stirring, clawing its way out. She clutched Ross against her.

Jake lifted the gun, angling it down, and blew a hole next to the doorjamb before kicking it open.

He burst into the room and saw them there—saw Ross's twin draped over Tess's body—and bile rose in his throat.

He snarled, blind with rage, and launched himself at the bed. Tess gave a cry of surprise as his hands closed around Mac's throat. She unwound one hand from Mac and clutched Jake's wrist.

A blinding light flashed, and Jake's stomach lurched as he felt himself suddenly falling.

DISLOCATED

> In another moment down went Alice after it, never once considering how in the world she was to get out again.
> —Lewis Carroll, *Alice's Adventures in Wonderland*

Tess plunged through empty space, light enfolding her, knowing any moment she'd be spit out onto some inhospitable patch of ground. When the landing came, it knocked the breath out of her, and her head cracked against something solid—something that groaned.

As she fought to right herself she discovered she was part of a multiheaded beast clawing and scrambling over slick ground. She came nose to nose with Jake, and his arms snaked around her as he pulled her free from the tangle of bodies.

Tess sucked in a breath as she felt—not pain, but a warm rush of pleasurable sensation. She closed her hands over Jake's arms, focusing on the massaging flow of energy.

"Oh *shit*," muttered Jake as she pressed him to the ground underneath her.

Random images fired through her brain—images of her, of Ross, of the woman they'd met in Ballard, a little boy with Jake's eyes.

Jake's memories! Tess jolted awake. She was draining *his* energy.

She shoved him away—or she thought she did. Her body refused to comply with the order that would break the flow of warm, liquid sensation.

She dug her heels into the mucky ground, groaning as she levered away, focusing all her strength on retracting her fingers.

"Relax, Jake," she choked out.

He replied through clenched teeth, "*You* relax while your skin is boiling off."

But he took a shuddering breath, and the muscles in his arms softened. Tess's fingers released, and she tore away from him, chest heaving from the effort.

She spun around in the mud, following the scuffling sounds to Ross and Mac.

Like a monster out of classical mythology, the two men inhabited one body from the waist down, but from the waist up they had separated. As they pummeled and clawed each other, Tess's gaze followed the two sets of arms until she locked onto the dragon tattoo. When Ross got his fingers around Mac's throat, she darted in and grabbed Mac's shoulder.

He gave a yelp of pain, and a shock ran through Tess, breaking her grip. Mac scrambled backward, and the fused forms peeled apart. He clambered away from them and up the hillside on all fours.

"The asshole's running," called Jake, struggling to rise.

"Good," muttered Tess, sinking beside Ross.

His lip was bleeding, but he was alive and whole. He spat on the ground and surveyed their surroundings. "Where are we?"

"Mordor," grumbled Jake, warming his arms with his hands.

Mud and charred sticks covered the rolling, open ground. Blackened skeletons of trees dotted a group of hills to the east, and to the south Tess could see some sort of structure, a dark scar against the hillside. It looked like castle ruins. The faintest smell of smoke tinged the air, and the sun was a dull white disk behind a hazy sky.

"Jake's Earth," said Tess.

"Are we sure?" asked Ross.

He hadn't looked at her yet, and now his tone left her cold. Not angry, exactly. *Businesslike*. Was he judging her for what had happened on the *Kalakala*? For what happened *before* the *Kalakala*? She crossed her arms over her chest.

"Well I'm sure," said Jake. "She gave me a little taste of my own medicine as soon as we touched down."

Ross's eyes flickered between them. "Are you saying we're Echoes here?"

"As if she wasn't scary enough." But Jake's expression was soft, and the question implicit in his gaze was, *Are you okay?*

She pressed her trembling lips together.

Ross's gaze swept again over the blighted landscape. "This doesn't look like Seattle. Or even what might be left of Seattle."

"No," she agreed, wiping her muddy hands down her skirt. "When it happened I was consciously thinking 'not Seattle.' I couldn't go through that again."

Ross's gaze swung around to rest on her face. "Do you mean you controlled the dislocation?"

"I didn't start it, but I knew it was about to happen." She thought back to the moment Jake had burst in. "I had the same pulling feeling in my stomach."

"Why do you think we all dislocated together?"

She had been touching them both, but she and Ross had been in very much the same position the first time she dislocated.

"If I'm right about the fight-or-flight response," she said, "I'd say it's because I was running from something different this time. Because I was afraid for *all* of us."

Ross glanced away, nodding, and she knew he'd filled in the blanks. Her heart sank a little, craving the tiniest gesture of warmth from him. But his shields had been activated, and it occurred to her this could be the reason he had yet to dislocate on his own; his defense mechanisms were different from hers. He powered down instead of up when he felt threatened.

"Maybe this place is connected with you," said Ross. "Someplace else you've lived, or visited."

Her eyes moved to the ruin at the base of the hill. If it *was* a place she knew, she'd never recognize it now. She hugged her knees to her chest. The frigid air had leeched all the heat from her body, making it progressively harder to think.

"Do you think there could be survivors?" asked Jake.

"It's possible." Her words passed through chattering teeth this time, and Ross took off his jacket and moved closer, draping it over her shoulders.

Her heart warmed at the gesture, and the almost-touch. "Thank you." She cleared her throat and continued. "Anyone close enough to see the asteroid would have been incinerated. And worldwide there would have been lethally high temperatures and raging fires. But the impact was predicted, so people would have taken shelter. Survivors would have faced an impact winter caused by debris in the air. Plunging temperatures, and a severe shortage of food and water."

"Holy shit," muttered Jake. "I missed all the fun."

"Do you think you can you get us back?" asked Ross.

She considered a moment, watching her breath vaporize in the air. "The fact I'm controlling it at all, plus the fact that I made it back before, suggest that I can. But so far it's happened more like a reflex." She threaded her fingers together, breathing into her hands to warm them. "I don't know. I'm so cold."

Ross stood up. "We need to find shelter. Let's take a closer look at that ruin."

He reached for Tess's hand and pulled her to her feet.

"Did you see where Mac went?" Tess asked Jake.

"He disappeared over the hill. One of us should have ended that fucker."

"Maybe we'll get another chance," muttered Ross.

Tess followed him down the hillside, with Jake bringing up the rear. The ground was the consistency of wet clay, and she kept skidding into Ross. At one point Jake lost his footing and slid the rest of the way down.

When a burst of oaths rising from the bottom of the hill assured Tess he wasn't critically injured, she laid a hand on Ross's arm and spoke in a low voice.

"I was wrong to leave like that. I know I put us all in danger. Garcia's scheme scared the hell out of me, and I couldn't see another way out."

He took a couple of careful steps down the hillside. Without glancing back he said, "I know, Doctor."

She'd thought she hadn't wanted anything in return for the apology. Now she realized she was wrong.

Together they caught up to Jake. "Sorry, Jake," she said, kneeling beside him. "The transfer's made you weak."

He smiled at her. "You're welcome to anything of mine that you need, Doc. What I told you back on that death ship, I meant."

"We should keep going," said Ross.

They made progress over the more level ground, and were almost to the ruin when something crunched under Tess's foot. She bent down and poked at an orange-and-white crab shell.

"So we're close to the ocean," said Jake, sniffing at the air.

"Not necessarily." She rolled a broken pincer between her fingers. "The asteroid impact would have generated massive tsunamis."

She dropped the pincer and picked up a bit of charred wood. "That would also explain why these weren't burned all the way—they were underwater when the fires started. What are these, anyway? See how they're all crooked and close to the same size?"

"Vines?" suggested Ross. "Maybe this was a vineyard."

"Ah, maybe so." Tess remembered what he'd said earlier, about her possibly having a connection to this place. She looked at him. "My mother was born in the Willamette Valley—Oregon wine country."

Tess's grandparents had owned a drafty century-old house on a hill overlooking a vineyard. She scanned the tree graveyard to the east, and her eyes followed the slope of the hill down to the ruin below. She felt a sudden chill that had nothing to do with the cold. The modern chateau had not been very authentic—seemed more so now that it was reduced to a ruin—but it had inspired many childhood fantasies.

"How close are we to the coast?" asked Ross.

"Maybe fifty miles. *Before* the flooding. It may be closer now."

Ross stared at the ground, hands squeezing his biceps, and Tess realized both she and Jake were waiting for him to tell them what to do. He was probably the only one with any survival training.

"We should gather up a bunch of these sticks," he said finally. "We need to build a fire."

"Do you think they're dry enough?"

"Let's hope so. It feels like about forty degrees out here. It'll be even colder when the sun goes down."

"I'll do it," said Jake. "You two go on to the shelter. I sure hope one of you was a Boy Scout, or we're gonna have to make coats out of these sticks for them to do us any good."

Ross and Tess continued across the valley to the ruin. Like the chateau from Tess's memory, it was constructed of smooth river stone and mortar. One wing of the sprawling structure had been flattened like it was made out of Legos. The roof was completely gone, as were the windows and doors. Rain-streaked soot coated everything.

Except for about an eight-by-twelve section, the interior was naked and open to the elements. Wet ash and piles of rubble littered the floor.

"It'll keep the rain off, anyway." Tess sighed.

Her foot struck the edge of something hard, and she reached down and brushed ash from a slab of square steel with a handle—an oven door.

She carried it to the small sheltered area and used one edge to plow away ash and debris, clearing a space for their fire.

"Come here for a second," called Ross.

Tess dropped the door and followed the sound of his voice through an arched opening. He stood in the middle of another empty room, adjacent to the flattened wing, staring at a hole in the foundation.

"Cellar?"

She joined him, gazing down at a staircase that descended into blackness. "Must be."

He probed the first step with his foot. "Seems stable enough."

"You're not thinking of going down there?"

"There could be food and water down there. Maybe matches."

Tess squatted and dug around in the wet ash until she found a shard of broken tile. She tossed it down and forward, and they heard a quiet splash.

"Sounds like your tidal wave theory was right, Doctor."

"I wonder how deep the water is."

"One way to find out."

He moved to step down, and Tess grabbed his pant leg. "Ross, don't!"

He'd made an excellent point about what might be down there, but the idea of him lowering into that wet, black hole made her want to crawl right out of her skin. And what if he got hurt?

"Let's see if we can get the fire started first, okay? Then at least we can get some light down there."

Ross looked at her, and for the first time since the dislocation, his expression softened.

"Okay," he agreed. "We need to look for tinder."

Realizing she was still gripping his jeans, she uncurled her fingers and slipped her hands into the pockets of his jacket. One hand closed over something cold and oblong. She pulled the object out and looked at it—a clip for his weapon, heavy with bullets.

"I was never a Boy Scout, but I'm thinking this doesn't hurt."

Ross reached for the clip, his fingers brushing hers.

"Now all we need is kindling," he said, glancing around. "Everything is so wet."

As he moved away, she felt something in the other pocket. She drew it out.

A delicate white gold and emerald bracelet—her *mother's* bracelet. Tess never took it off.

As she stared at it, long-dormant memories wormed bony fingers around her heart.

A tug at her arm. A whiskey-moistened murmur.

Drunken fingers fumbling to fasten the bracelet around her wrist.

A kiss, so wrenching and wrong she was almost sick.

Tess folded her arms over her knotting stomach. She squeezed her eyes shut.

No time for this now.

As she reached to return the bracelet to Ross's pocket, her trembling fingers let it slip to the ground. She gave a gasp that was out of proportion to the small accident, and Ross came to see what was wrong.

He stooped and picked it up. "I found this on the sidewalk outside Seattle Psi. Must have come off when you left."

"Thank you," she murmured, taking it from him.

She dropped it back into his pocket, and her hands fluttered to her sides. She let her gaze fall away as he continued to study her.

Please don't ask me.

"Jesus, it's cold." Jake was back.

She turned and walked through the archway to the other room and found him dumping an armload of sticks on the floor.

"Did you figure out how we're going to turn this into heat?"

"We need something dry to get it started," said Tess. "Do you have anything in your pockets?"

Jake stuffed his hands into his jeans pockets, shaking his head. He froze for a second, digging deeper. "Wait—how about this?"

He drew out the fistful of twenties Tess had given him, and she couldn't help laughing.

"Perfect," said Ross, joining them.

"So much for ordering beer and pizza later."

Ross reached for the money, but drew back quickly. "Hang on to it for a minute."

Tess scrutinized his form as he gathered a load of sticks. He looked solid enough, but in the heavily filtered light it was hard to be sure.

"How do you feel, Ross?"

"I feel cold."

She frowned. There were two of them and only one of Jake. They couldn't expect him to sustain them both, even if he was willing.

Ross carried the wood to the space Tess had cleared and started working on their fire. As if he'd been reading her mind, he said, "Jake, I think you should try a transfer with her."

"The doc had her way with me already," said Jake. "That means it's your turn."

"He's right, Ross."

"I'm fine," Ross replied, not looking up from the sticks he was arranging. "I want you to take care of her."

"Fucking heroes," muttered Jake. "Spoil it for the rest of us."

Jake tossed the wad of bills at Ross and turned to Tess. "Okay, sweetheart."

"I don't need it yet. Rest up for Ross."

Jake rolled his eyes. "Vampires for roommates, and I can't *give* it away."

Ross removed one of the bullets from the clip and tried wrenching it back and forth between his fingers.

"That looks dangerous," said Tess.

"No. This probably is." He gripped the bullet between his teeth, clamping down and yanking on it.

"Ross!" The dark-scary-hole option was increasing in appeal.

But there was no explosion, and after a few seconds he managed to work the bullet apart. He used the casing and a small stone to spark the powder, and a thin curl of smoke rose from the crumpled bills. He blew on the nascent flames until they licked up the sides of his teepee of sticks.

Jake scooted closer to the fire, for once keeping his smart-ass commentary to himself.

Ross stood up. "I'm going for more wood. Keep feeding it."

"I think we should try to stay together," said Tess. "What if I suddenly transport back?"

He eyed her, hesitating.

"What is it?"

"Nothing. Just . . . I don't know that it matters whether I'm five feet or fifty away from you."

"You mean you think we need to be touching?"

"Yes. But I also think when you want to go back, you'll go back. And if you want me to go back with you, I will."

Her cheeks warmed, and Ross turned to go. She slipped out of his jacket.

"Wait, take this with you."

Ross nodded toward Jake. "Give it to him. He doesn't look so good."

Jake sat close to the fire, hugging his arms around his chest and shivering.

She walked over and dropped the jacket across his shoulders. Then she sank down a few feet away. As she stared into the flames, an urge kindled inside her. A gnawing feeling, like hunger . . . or more like an itch. She scooted closer to the woodpile, feeding a couple sticks into the fire.

"Doctor?"

Jake had put on the jacket, and he was staring at her bracelet in the palm of his hand.

"Yeah?"

"Back on the boat, when I found you upstairs . . . which of them was with you?"

Tess poked at the fire.

"I know it's not my business," he continued, "but it's killing me thinking I was too late. That he had time to hurt you."

"It wasn't like that. I made a choice to try and help Ross."

Jake's expression darkened.

"Ross came back, and I'm okay."

"Why don't I believe you?"

Tess tossed her stick into the fire. "I don't know."

"Come and sit next to me. I promise not to ask you any more questions."

She shook her head. "Not a good idea right now."

"Never stopped you before."

"As you and Ross like to point out, sometimes I exhibit questionable judgment."

Jake watched her as she watched the fire. It wasn't going to last long. They needed denser wood.

"Is he pissed at you for leaving? Seems like he's gone surly. *More* surly."

"I thought you weren't going to ask me any more questions."

Jake patted the floor. "Only if you come sit next to me."

She stayed put, and Jake sighed. "He'll get over it, Doc."

"I don't know, Jake. There can be too much mess between two people, you know? People can have too many flying monkeys in their own heads to let in someone else's."

Jake shook his head, muttering in exasperation, "For the love of God."

Tess raised her eyebrows at his tone.

"Both of you are making problems out of nothing. I couldn't be with you back on your Earth because I'd kill you. I can't be with you here because you'd kill me. *Those* are problems. There's nothing standing between the two of you but his ridiculous pride and your fucked-up childhood. How long are you going to let him poison your life?"

She stared at him, confused. "Ross?"

"Your father."

Tess gritted her teeth and looked away. She felt the faint buzz in her limbs that always warned her the tremors were coming. They'd started when she was seven, while her mother was in the hospital. Got worse when she was a teenager, when the psychologists asked questions about her father. Had the bastard ever worried she'd tell them about him? Probably not. He knew she was terrified of him.

She closed her eyes. *Don't dislocate. Not now.*

"He was a prick," said Jake, softening. "Nothing can change that. But you're all grown up now. He can only hurt you if you let him."

Her father would go out late and come home drunk. She'd hear the creak of his foot on the bottom stair, and she'd pretend to be asleep. She'd been in college a year before she could fall asleep without shaking. Mostly because she stayed up studying until her eyes closed themselves.

"You don't know anything about it," she whispered.

But he did. He'd been in her head too.

"I'm sorry." Jake's voice was tight with emotion. "But you want to know what I think? The Fed is just trying to hold it together so he can take care of you. It's what he's been doing since the day I met you."

She raised her chin and looked him in the eye. "Why should he do that? I don't want him sacrificing for me."

Jake blew out an exasperated breath. "You are in serious denial, Doc. What you're really afraid of is that you'll let him bring you back to life, and then he'll reject you. That's life, sweetheart. That's *love*."

FLAILING

> There is no happiness in love, except at the end of an English novel.
>
> —Anthony Trollope

Ross was barely holding it together and he knew it.

How was he going to get them out of this? Little of his training or experience was of use to them. He had no weapon to fight the threats they faced. Nothing but his instincts, and Tess's, to guide him. His instincts were better than most people's—he'd come to accept that after discovering Tess's hiding place based on what he could only call a vision. But he was in way over his head.

And that was only the surface layer of problems. Even if Tess did manage to take them all home, Garcia was waiting. How could he turn her over to the Bureau after what she'd done for him? How could he *not*?

What she'd done for him. He clenched his teeth against the memory. It was his job to protect *her*. What would have become of him if she hadn't done what she'd done? Even if every other obstacle between them magically smoothed, this one would remain. How could he ever forgive himself for what had happened to her on that boat?

It shouldn't have gone down the way it did. If she'd only given him more time to regain his strength, so he could fight his own battle. Hell, if she'd only given him a chance back at the institute instead of taking off like that, so his hand was forced. He was furious with her.

He was furious with himself.

He walked back to the ruin with his bundle of sticks. Gathering them was a waste of time—they'd burn through them in no time. He'd taken the time away from Tess and Jake in hope of clearing his head. But his thoughts were more tangled now than when he'd left.

Tess and Jake sat warming themselves by the fire. The air was charged with tension, like they'd been arguing.

Good, he thought. *Let Jake be the bad guy for a while.*

Tess lifted her head as he walked in, smiling thinly before looking away.

As Ross drew closer to the fire, he smacked up against his need to feed. How could Tess stand to be so close to Jake? How had *Jake* stood it—both needing to feed on Tess and wanting her? He caught himself wondering whether Tess wanted Jake that way before deleting the question like a corrupted file.

He dumped his bundle and fished out three sticks, propping them in the fire. When the ends caught enough to stay lit, he grabbed them and headed for the cellar.

Tess got up to follow, but he called, "Stay in here where it's warm. I'll be back."

"Keep the fire going," she told Jake, ignoring Ross.

"Where are you going?"

"There's a cellar. Ross is going to check it out."

"Doc?"

"Yeah?"

"Sorry I was a jerk. It's none of my business."

"You're right, it's not. But I can't seem to stay mad at you."

Ross could hear the grin in Jake's voice as he replied, "Probably shouldn't have told me that."

"I regret it already."

Easy as that, Jake and Tess were friends again. *Sorry I was a jerk.* Jake didn't have a copyright on the words; he just had balls enough to say them.

Tess followed Ross into the adjacent room. "Do we really have to do this?"

"Me, not *we*," he corrected. He met her anxious gaze. "I just want to see what's down there. Food and blankets will make it worth getting a little wet."

She nodded and stared bleakly into the hole. "Please be careful."

He started down with his makeshift torch. He tested each step before resting his weight on it, balancing caution with the need to have at least a quick look around before his light went out.

"Tess," he called, eyes straining in the spider blackness.

"Yeah?"

"Can you light some more wood, in case these go out?"

"Sure."

His eyes adjusted, and he could see where the steps dipped below the waterline. His skin prickled in anticipation, and he reminded himself it couldn't be more than a few feet deep. He took the next step, scanning a wall of shelves to his right, and the wood beneath his feet buckled. His legs went out from under him.

He shouted a curse as he splashed into the cold water. He scrambled to right himself, but his head dunked all the way under before his feet struck the floor. He swallowed a mouthful of gritty saltwater.

"Ross!" cried Tess.

"I'm okay," he called, spitting the foulness out of his mouth.

His torch was gone. He couldn't see anything but the stairs behind him. He swept out his arms, feeling for a wall or anything to help orient him.

Ross heard a loud creak and turned. Tess was making her way down the stairs holding more burning wood. He could see her face clearly—she was terrified.

He opened his mouth to stop her, but he needed the light. And he was man enough to admit he didn't want to be down here alone.

"Wait there," he warned before she took the step above the one he'd broken. "The bottom ones are rotted."

Ross sloshed through thigh-deep water around the side of the staircase and reached for the bundle of sticks. Then he turned and took a good look around.

"Here, Doc." Jake joined them. He handed another torch down to Tess.

Shelves lined the wall that ran alongside the staircase. Ross moved closer, holding out his light. Cases of bottled water. Four whole shelves of canned food.

"Jackpot," he said. "Food and water, all sealed."

"Thank God." Tess sighed.

Ross gripped the edge of a large plastic tub and pulled it toward him, rattling the contents. He peeled up the lid, and it popped open with a whoosh of air. Peering inside he saw flashlights, cooking utensils, and a first aid kit—all of it dry. He grabbed one of the flashlights and discovered it had a hand-crank for charging. He cranked a couple dozen times and flicked the switch. It sent out a weak stream of light, and Tess gave a murmur of relief. Ross dropped his burning sticks in the water, where they extinguished with a hiss.

He sloshed back and handed the crate up to Tess.

"Empty everything out of this and send Jake back down with the box."

Ross inventoried a second set of shelves, which contained an assortment of camping gear—most critical, sleeping bags and a tent. One container had leaked, ruining the two bags inside. But there were other containers with two dry bags and a stack of blankets.

He crossed to the opposite wall, moving slowly to avoid stumbling over the debris that littered the bottom, and found a rack holding hundreds of wine bottles. He waded farther into the room, freezing when he saw movement.

As the surface of the water stilled, the movement did too. Ross swallowed drily and took a cautious step forward—the movement started again.

He pressed on, sweeping his light as he walked. Finally he let out a chuckle of relief. Wooden wine barrels. Oak, most likely—hardwood. It would burn slower. He grabbed one and pushed it back toward the stairs. Jake was waiting with the empty box, and he traded him for the barrel. He hauled out the rest of the empty barrels—fifteen in all—and then headed back down for a more thorough look at the far end of the room. While retrieving the barrels he'd bumped against something else floating that was more level with the surface.

There were four of these partially submerged objects, all about five feet in length. This was something Ross had seen before, but the hair stood up on the back of his neck anyway. There was no smell of decay—the water was cold and salty. He wondered whether they'd been unaware of the flood danger, or if the smoke had gotten them. He wondered how many other basements had been turned into tombs by fire, flood, or starvation.

Hallways branched off to the right and left at the back of the room. Ross waded a few yards into each, far enough to ascertain both were lined with more barrels. Some empty, some heavy with wine.

His inspection complete, Ross worked with Jake and Tess to

transport up food, water, and supplies. He hoped they'd be gone before they went through it all—he didn't want to have to come down here again. He especially didn't want anyone *else* to have to come down here.

When Ross emerged, he searched through the rubble for a stone heavy enough to break up the wine barrels. He found one roughly the size of a soccer ball, mortar still clinging to one side, and bent to lift it.

He couldn't shift it an inch. He tried again, and this time his fingers slipped *into* the stone.

"What the hell?" he cried, yanking his hand back. The surface of the stone caught weirdly at the tips of his fingers, and Ross looked at them, expecting to see blood.

"Looks like you haven't got enough juice for something that heavy, G-man," said Jake.

Jake came over and lifted the stone. He hefted it shoulder height and brought it down on the wet side of one of the barrels. The rotted wood crumbled under the rock, and he had an easy enough time breaking it up from there.

The guy was stronger than he looked. Tess stood watching him work, and Ross couldn't help speculating about what she was see-ing. To Ross he looked scruffy and underfed, even with muscles bulging under the weight of the rock. But maybe that passed for sexy in Seattle.

Ross glanced again at Tess, but now her eyes were on *him*.

Jake stood up, panting, and leveled his gaze at Ross. "It's time, tough guy. I've been where you are, and I promise you're going to go downhill fast."

"He's right," said Tess. "Come over to the fire. You must be freezing."

Tess picked up a tarp from the pile of supplies and spread it close to the fire.

"Go on," said Jake, moving close.

Ross staggered back a few steps. His body fought him, straining toward what it needed.

Jake glowered at him. "I can't figure out if you want to be a hero, or if you're trying to punish her, but either way it's starting to piss me off. Sit your ass down and let's get this over with."

Ross moved away from him, horrified by the violence of his own need. Hard as it was for him to be close to Tess right now, being close to Jake was harder.

He moved to the tarp and sank down. Tess knelt beside him, tossing more charred vines onto the fire, and he reached for her wrist.

She flinched and tugged at her arm, and he thought of the other times he'd grabbed her like this. It was a reflex, usually a protective one, but there was always a fleeting expression of panic. He thought about her father and felt like an asshole.

"I'm sorry," he said softly, opening his hand but letting his thumb rub over her wrist. "That's a bad habit. Just be still for a minute so I can talk to you."

She sank beside him, eyes settling on his face. "Ross, if we wait too long it'll be dangerous. You'll risk us all. You might kill him, and then we're as good as dead too. You understand that, don't you?"

"I do. But I think you know that trying to keep us both alive will probably kill him too."

Tess nodded. "I know. We have to go home as soon as possible. But until I can figure it out, we need to alt—"

"You're the one we have to keep strong."

She frowned. "I won't let you fade."

"If it comes to that, that's exactly what you're going to do. Don't fight with me about this. You've risked enough for me al—"

"I didn't throw myself at that drug dealer so you could throw your life away!"

The furies howled in his ears. His chest tightened until he couldn't breathe. "You don't need to punish me. I've done enough of that for both of us."

"I'm not trying to punish you, you pigheaded son of a bitch! I'm trying to keep you alive."

Her anger flamed out hot and fast, and a tear slipped onto her cheek. Ross slid his thumb up to meet it. "You can't save us all, Tess."

Her brow creased with pain and confusion. Her lips parted, but before she could say anything Jake had moved to stand over them.

"Do you ever get tired of telling other people what to do?" He reached down and clamped his hand on Ross's shoulder.

The contact jolted through Ross like a gunshot. His hands flew to Jake's arms. He meant to shove him away, but Jake's energy flowed through him, and Ross's fingers dug into his flesh. He heard Jake groan, and Tess shouted something in his ear.

Ross leaned forward, pressing Jake into the ground. Even as he rode the swell and surge of regenerative current, he remembered: *I have to stop.*

But Ross found himself caught up in the flood of images firing through his connection with Jake. They were almost all of Tess—a catalog of lust and tender longing. They were harder to break from than the energy transfer itself.

Ross knew Jake had fallen for Tess, but now he was looking at Tess through Jake's eyes. Jake's physical longing was a bleak and desperate thing, but it was her heart that had won him. Her smile. The warmth and generosity she'd shown the man who'd almost killed her. Even the pain she kept hidden, and her visceral loneliness—something Jake understood far better than Ross.

"Try not to fight it, Jake," Tess's voice broke through Ross's trance. "I don't think he can slow it down, so you're going to have to."

Ross felt Jake's tension begin to slough off.

The cascade of energy tapered. Ross took a few deep, controlled breaths, and he flexed his fingers.

The recoil of the release shoved him against Tess. He rolled onto the tarp, body tingling from the slap of energy.

"Are you crazy?" Ross rasped.

"Not half as crazy as you!"

"Don't you dare do that again."

Jake snorted. "I did it for her, not for you, asshole."

Ross clenched his jaws, nostrils flaring, biting back a retort.

Jake shoved himself to his feet. His legs folded, and he swore as he stumbled to his knees. He reached toward the pile of camping gear and pulled out a sleeping bag. Wrapping it around his shoulders, he stood again and stumbled toward the door.

Ross's gaze fell on Tess's back. Her chin rested on her arms, shoulders and neck rising tightly with every breath.

"Tess, look at me."

She buried her face in the crook of her arm, hugging her knees closer. Shutting him out.

Jake was right; he was an idiot. And an asshole. He didn't know how to both protect her and be what she needed.

He was no longer sure which was more important.

NOTHINGMAN

> Love is a better master than duty.
> —Albert Einstein

Electron boy was too tired to range far from the nucleus. Hooking the top of the mummy bag over his head, he shuffled around the outside of the building and hunched against the west-facing wall. The cold of the stones seeped right through the bag.

The haze was thicker above the horizon, and the sinking sun tinged the sky a brilliant mango orange. He pulled the bag like a cape around him as a breeze swept through the valley.

Still simmering with anger—and smarting from unfulfilled desire—he decided right then and there that when Tess figured out a way to go back, he was staying behind. He didn't want to part with her. He could live with the fact she wanted someone else, but he wasn't going to cling to her like a parasite for the rest of her life, or his.

He could be comfortable here, he thought. Sitting by the fire every night, using the wine stash to keep himself pleasantly medicated, he wouldn't notice the bleak surroundings so much. He could think of far worse ways to go. There was a bottle of pain pills in the first aid kit, so he'd always have an out for when he could no longer stand his own company. He wondered if there were any books down in that hole.

"I am legend," he said, then laughed at his own stupid joke. If only he had a few bloodthirsty zombie vampires for company.

His heart ached in anticipation of losing Tess. He'd known her for what, three days now? Spending so much time in her head made it feel like longer. She felt like family. She felt like sunshine on blighted landscapes. She felt like the missing jigsaw piece of his jumbled-up life. He hoped for her sake that Ross could sort his shit out. Had they all been from the same Earth, Jake would have gleefully taken advantage of Ross's hesitation, but as things were, it was better this way.

Jake's head jerked up as a silhouette inserted itself between him and the sunset.

"Odd man out?"

Tess felt Ross's eyes on her back, but she couldn't bring herself to speak to him. She wanted to apologize for what Jake had done, but the words felt insincere on her tongue. She was *grateful* for what Jake had done.

She heard the tarp crinkle and then felt hands at her waist, lifting her, turning her. He pulled her close, cradling her in his arms, his nose nuzzling hers. His lips lowered, softly caressing.

She sighed against his mouth, relieved and bewildered. Her fingertips pressed into his chest. Ross traced the line of her shoulder until his hand came to rest gently against her throat, where her pulse hammered. He circled the spot with the tip of one finger, and she shivered in his arms.

He parted her lips, and she let her head fall back. He bent over her, tongue pulsing and probing against hers, driving her body into spasms of longing. His hand glided up and cradled her cheek, tongue withdrawing just enough to trace her lips. No one kissed like Ross. No one.

"Tess," he murmured, drawing back to look into her eyes. His thumb brushed her cheek and one corner of her lips. "I'm not very good at this."

"Oh you are," she murmured. "Better than anyone."

The corners of his lips lifted. "Is that why you put up with me?"

She traced the curve of his breast with the pads of her fingers. "That, plus you have the most beautiful chest I've ever seen."

His smile deepened. "Oh yeah?"

"Oh yeah."

His arm tightened around her, and she snuggled closer, cheek against chest. He smoothed a strand of hair back from her face. His voice dropped low, vibrating with emotion as he said, "You scare the shit out of me, do you know that?"

She swallowed, fingers gripping his upper arm and the tensed muscles there. "Why?"

His eyelids fluttered, and he looked away. "The risks you take—with Jake, with Mac." She felt the shudder run through him. "Your past. Your scars. But mostly because when you're close to me I can't think straight—I can't make decisions. It makes me feel . . ."

"Out of control."

He lifted his eyebrows in an expression of outright surprise. "You know?"

"Of course I know."

"*How* do you understand me so well when I feel like I only understand you well enough to get myself into trouble?"

A quiet chuckle escaped her lips.

"Now you're laughing at me?"

"Sorry." She chuckled again.

"I don't think you are." He touched his prickly chin to her forehead. "It's good to see you smile."

She reached up and cradled his jaw in her hand.

"I don't know what's going to happen to us," he said, "but there's something else I want you to know. Maybe you know it already."

She rubbed her fingers over the stubble on his cheek, waiting.

He closed his eyes. "The tension between us . . . it makes me feel sick."

Her breath caught, and she nodded. "Me too."

"I don't want to fight with you anymore." His hand slid down her back, resting between her shoulder blades. "But I don't know what's going to happen when—"

There was a sudden scuffling near the doorway, and Ross's head lifted.

"Here's my favorite couple."

Ross and Tess jumped up. "Jake!" she cried.

Mac stood in the doorway—holding a knife to Jake's throat.

"Stay where you are or he's dead."

Two others came in behind Mac—a man and a woman, both thin and grimy and carrying crude handmade spears. They moved over to the stack of canned food Ross had salvaged and pawed through it with enthusiastic grunts.

"Wow, he was right," muttered the man. He darted a glance at Tess. "There more of this somewhere?"

"Do that *later*," snapped Mac. "I need you to keep an eye on them."

Ross took a step toward Mac.

"You're not listening, asshole." Mac dug the knife tip into the soft skin below the line of Jake's beard, drawing a trickle of blood.

"What do you want?" cried Tess.

Weak from the transfer, Jake couldn't do more than pluck at Mac's arm. Mac was supporting most of his weight.

Mac's new companions moved between the two groups, spears raised in threat. They looked scared and hungry.

"I want you to get me out of this shithole," answered Mac. "I want to go back."

"Do you think we'd still be here if we knew how to go back?" demanded Ross.

"Don't play games with me."

"It's true," said Tess. "Why don't you let him go, and we'll tell you what we know."

"You have one minute to do what I asked, Doctor. And in case it occurs to you to try and hurt me, we're going to recruit your friend here as a traveling companion."

She shot a panicked look at Ross.

"Just take it easy," Ross said evenly. "We're not likely to figure this out with you standing there threatening us."

"Now see, I don't agree. With the right motivation, I think she'll figure it out." Mac narrowed his eyes at Ross. "You try to jump me, and he's dead."

Tess's pulse raced. She knew they weren't going to talk their way out of this, but what could she do? She didn't have the control he seemed to think she did.

Mac cupped Jake's chin, and the blade rose from his throat to his ear, slipping between earlobe and jaw. Jake shouted and squirmed as blood ran down his neck.

"Okay!" she cried. "Just stop it!"

Jake vanished, and Mac stumbled backward.

Instinct launched Tess at Mac, and she landed across his chest.

It had been hours since the last transfer, and his energy poured into her, musky and brackish.

Mac let his body go limp. He smiled at her.

Take me home, Tess.

"Shut up," she snapped.

When Mac went down, his new friends fled, most of the cans they'd tried to pilfer spilling onto the ground.

Ross dropped beside Mac and Tess. Mac appeared helpless under Tess's gentle weight, subdued by the transfer. But the asshole was smiling, and Ross didn't like it.

"Do you think he can hurt her?"

Ross jerked his head at the sound of Jake's voice behind him. "Where the hell did you come from? Did you dislocate?"

"There was a bright light, and a tunnel thing. I felt like my guts were falling out. But then I was back."

Ross's eyes moved back to Tess. "I'm going to pull her off."

"I don't care much for that smirk on his ugly face—no offense, G—but she's feeding. Besides that we don't exactly know what's going to happen if *you* grab her while they're linked."

Jake was right, on both counts. Ross moved closer, studying Tess's face. She frowned in concentration, completely focused on Mac, but showed no signs of distress. As for his twin—he looked like he was enjoying himself, and that was almost more than Ross could take. It was bad enough Mac had put his hands all over Tess, but he was also a reminder of someone else Ross had failed—his brother, Jamie. Mac dealt the drug that had destroyed and almost taken Jamie's life.

Ross's muscles twitched. He quaked with anger at his own impotence. He pressed his folded hands against his mouth as he watched Tess, alert for signs that she was in trouble.

Mac couldn't escape Tess—his life was draining into her—yet he was in control. He modulated the flow by remaining calm, and he used the current to sail his thoughts right into her head.

See how easy it is to control? I can teach you. Help you with your research— help you save the others. I can be more to you than he can. We can be partners. Equals. We can connect on a level you never could with him.

You and I define connection a little differently.

You must realize you can't be with him. She felt Mac's hands clench slightly, squeezing her thighs. *You'll destroy everything that's important to him. Is that what you want?*

Tess's fingers dug into his throat, as if it could silence him. His breaths rasped through her hands, but she couldn't keep consistent enough pressure to stop them completely.

Take him home and see what happens. He'll be pulled back into his world. His job and his obligations. You'll be the woman who defied orders and had to be tracked down. Unreliable. Unstable. What do you think he'll do? Rise to your defense? Think, Tess. What will happen to you then?

Worms of doubt bored into her heart. What *would* happen to her? Would Ross throw away ten years of service in a job he loved? Of course he wouldn't. She wouldn't *want* him to. She'd be off the task force for sure. Ross would be called back to D.C. Would Abby let her keep her job, at least?

You can still save Echoes. I can help you. You need what I've learned, Tess. I need what you've learned. You've gotten so wrapped up in this pointless drama you're not seeing the big picture. Have you thought about how the transfers and dislocations could be used to help survivors?

The man and his energy were toxic. She wasn't confused about the fact he was trying to manipulate her. But also he had a point. And she had committed herself to help these people. It was the reason behind every risk she'd taken in the last three days.

You can't afford to lose sight of that, Tess. And by now you must know that Ross is always going to get in your way.

"Enough, Tess!" Ross's voice cut sharply between them. "Break it off!"

Like her first transfer, letting go wasn't as easy as willing it to happen. When it did, she wasn't sure it hadn't been more Mac's doing than hers. The connection released suddenly, and she sprang backward against Ross.

Mac started crawling for the doorway, and suddenly Jake was on him with the knife. He jerked the blade sharply along Mac's cheek, drawing blood. Then he shoved the tip against the back of his neck. Tess held her breath, wanting it over, yet not wanting to see Jake kill the man.

"Do it, Jake," called Ross. He let go of Tess and scrambled toward them.

Mac took advantage of Jake's doubt, flipping over and tossing Jake against Ross. While Ross fought to free himself from the energy transfer, Mac scooped up the knife and staggered to his feet, fleeing the ruins.

Ross untangled from Jake and ran after him, but Tess cried, "Ross, don't! It's too risky."

He froze in the doorway, and she got up and walked over to their box of supplies. Mac's friends had made a mess of things, but she was relieved to find the first aid kit had not been filched.

"Let's look at your ear, Jake."

They sat down on the tarp, and Tess examined him as best she could without touching him. Mac had cut his left earlobe away from his jaw. It was a bloody mess, and he needed medical attention.

Fishing bandages out of the kit, she asked, "So you dislocated?"

"Sort of. I didn't go back to your Earth. I was in the light tunnel, like when we came here with you, but only for a second, and then suddenly I was back."

"It seems to have had the same type of trigger. It happened right after he cut you."

"Yeah. Though I was more pissed than scared."

She paused in the act of opening a bottle of water. "A 'fight' rather than a 'flight' reaction. Maybe that's why you came right back."

She had him bend forward and tilt his head while she poured water over the wound, wincing sympathetically at his grunted protests.

"So how come we're taking all the rides?" he grumbled. "Ross has done transfers too."

Ross had joined them by the fire, and her gaze flickered his direction. "I have a theory about that," she said carefully.

"You do?" asked Ross.

Jake sat up, and she said, "Smear it with antiseptic. Tape some gauze over it. We'll see if we can fix it up properly when we get home."

She turned to Ross. "You said it yourself: You're very controlled."

He frowned. "That's not exactly what I said."

"Well that can be *inferred* from what you said. I don't mean it as an insult. You're trained to control your emotions."

"I'm pretty sure he comes by that naturally."

"Jake," scolded Tess, and he gave her a sulky look. "It helps you keep your head clear to do your job. It helps you make choices without emotion interfering. It keeps you out of danger. It's probably become like breathing at this point."

Ross's expression relaxed to neutral. "That's true."

She was reminded uncomfortably of the warnings Mac had given about him.

She continued. "But Jake is . . ."

"I can't wait to hear this," muttered Jake.

". . . more like me."

Ross's gaze moved between them. "So if your lack of control is causing dislocation, and my abundance of control is preventing it, does that mean we're stuck until the next time someone tries to kill us?"

Jake gave a snorting laugh. "Who knew there was a sense of humor in there?"

But Ross wasn't laughing. Tess replied, "Actually I think you're our best hope. Once you've made up your mind that the dislocation is safer than us staying *here*, we'll go home."

Ross frowned. "I made up my mind about that five minutes after we got here."

"Then what are you waiting for?"

Ross blinked at her, and he turned to stare into the fire.

Tess returned her attention to Jake, giving him some space. Jake tossed her the ointment and bandages, and she placed them back in the box.

"Can I talk to you outside, Doc?" he asked.

She glanced at Ross, but he was still lost in thought. She followed Jake through the doorway, and he sank down against the wall near the entrance. She did the same, leaving about a foot between them.

"What's on your mind?"

"I've decided I'm not going back with you."

She gaped at him. "What?"

"You heard me."

"I assume you're joking."

He let out a sigh. "A hazard of always playing the fool."

She shook her head, incredulous. "You can't stay here by yourself."

"I belong here. As much as I belong anywhere. And I make a sucky vampire." He shuddered. "Sorry."

Her chest felt tight, and her face hot. He was serious, like he had been when he'd told her he was falling for her. "But how will you survive?"

He laughed. "Considering how hard I've worked to off myself, I'd say my survival is a foregone conclusion."

"Please don't joke about this."

"I'm completely serious. But don't get the idea it was an easy decision for me." He gave her a wistful smile. "No more Tess-flavored transfusions."

She closed her eyes. After the first dislocation, she'd speculated about the possibility of Jake going home. *Someday.* When they'd evaluated his chances for survival. Found a habitable location, and other survivors. But this—she didn't know if she could do it. Leave him here alone to fend for himself. What would happen when his supplies ran out? What if Mac came back?

"Look at me, Doc."

She opened her eyes, choking on the tightness that had spread from her chest to her throat.

"I'll be okay. And so will you."

She swallowed hard, shifting her gaze to the hillside, and the line of charred trees.

"Hey," he continued, "can I ask you something?"

Ross crossed to the doorway, but stopped when he heard Tess's voice. They were sitting near the section of wall that remained around the front door.

"What is it?" she asked. She sounded upset.

"Do you think you'll miss me?"

She sniffled. "Don't be an idiot."

"You can always come back to me, you know that, right? I mean if things don't go so well back in the real world, or if anyone ever hurts you."

So Jake wanted to stay. Ross doubted he'd be shedding any tears, but he could imagine how Tess felt about it. He could also imagine what Garcia was going to say. It would ease relations between him and Tess when they got back, but that would be temporary—until they found another Echo.

"I don't want you to feel like I'm abandoning you," Jake

continued. "Because I've never known anyone who would do for me what you've done. No one but Emily. No one but Emily has ever meant to me what you do."

More sniffling and silence.

"Hey, don't be mad at me, okay?"

"I'm not mad, Jake."

"No, I mean for this."

Ross heard scuffling, and Tess gave a little cry. He darted around the wall—in time to see Jake's hand slipping behind her head.

He's kissing her?

Though it looked like she had started out struggling—her hands were pressed flat against his chest—at the moment she appeared to be kissing him back.

It's not a real kiss, he told himself. The energy transfer would have started immediately. Tess was very still.

But then her shoulders inched down, and he could see her chest rising and falling.

"Breathe slower," Jake said against her mouth.

Ross's heart thundered in his ears. It tried to crawl out of his chest. He was afraid if he didn't go over there and punch Jake, his heart might just do it for him.

Jake's arms twined around her and he hugged her against him, moaning softly.

What must it feel like? For Jake, there would be pain—on multiple levels. But for Tess . . . well, he'd watched Jake feed on *her*. It was like witnessing a religious experience.

Ross pressed a fist against his thigh.

Then suddenly he was moving, and his arms were around Tess. He tugged her backward, separating her from Jake.

Light blossomed behind his eyelids. The ground dropped from under him.

He clutched at her as they tumbled into the light tunnel, keeping her close. But as they plummeted through cellophane layers of space and time, he lost her. He shouted her name, but the light was a tangible thing. Thick and liquid, it seeped into his throat, coating his vocal cords.

But their bodies came back together, tangling again as they dropped into the bed—Mac's bed on the *Kalakala*.

Not here! Pushing back the vertigo, he shot up, reaching for his absent weapon.

He rolled onto his feet just as two men burst through the doorway at the top of the stairs. They raised their guns, and Ross threw his hands in the air, Tess mirroring him.

"Both of you, freeze!"

PSI GAMES

The United States Federal Bureau of Investigation (FBI) and Central Intelligence Agency (CIA) have endorsed a procedure for neutralization of individual Echoes. The procedure, though effective, is considered extremely high risk and should be conducted only by approved personnel. The FBI is in the process of acquiring a secure facility for the housing of captive Echoes and has agreed to take on maintenance responsibilities until such time as the UN Echo Coalition is able to agree upon a longer-term solution. Please see the attached document for further details and instructions.

—Official Memo from the Office of Ann Green,
U.S. Director of National Intelligence

WE'RE UNARMED!" Ross shouted, dropping one arm partway, shielding Tess.

Tess studied the two men—dark suits, government-issue weapons. *Not Echoes.*

One man cautiously lowered his gun. "Agent McGinnis?"

"That's right."

The man's gaze shifted to Tess.

"This is Dr. Caufield," said Ross, "from Seattle Psi. You are?"

"Kendrick, from the Seattle Field Office. We were mobilized to find you after your car was towed from a no-parking zone."

The other agent lowered his gun, and Ross dropped his hands.

"You should warn your men there are Echoes on this boat," Ross told them.

Kendrick nodded. "We found the bodies belowdecks. We're still sweeping the other levels, but it looks like they've all fled." He holstered his gun. "Come on. I'll drive you back to Seattle Psi. Director Garcia is waiting to talk to you."

Tess eyed Ross uneasily. The short nod he gave her wasn't enough to answer her unspoken question.

Who am I now? Lover? Echo expert? Recovered fugitive?

It was a long, silent ride back to the institute. Tess watched the last dregs of blood-orange light drain from the sky to the west. As good as it was to be warm again, it was hard to feel much relief about being home. She'd come back to the same problems she'd left. And she could only guess at the consequences of running from the Bureau and freeing Jake.

Mac's words replayed in her mind. *Unreliable. Unstable.*

She wished she'd had a chance to talk about everything with Ross before the sudden dislocation. She especially wished she'd had the chance to explain about that kiss. Though what could she really say? It had been such a Jake thing to do. And she didn't regret it. They'd been through so much together, and she might never see him again.

But now she was returning to the institute with her only potential ally, not knowing what he felt about her, how the kiss might have changed that, or whether he intended to go along with Garcia's schemes.

Why would he do anything else? It sickened her how much her thoughts sounded like Mac since the transfer.

As Kendrick parked the car in the visitor lot, she resolved not to run again. Her whole life was here at the institute. She had to give Ross a chance. She had to give *herself* a chance. And she had to show them both she was strong enough to face her problems.

Inside they met Garcia in the lobby. "I'm glad you're safe, Dr. Caufield." His gaze took in their muddy, disheveled state.

"Director." She nodded.

"Good work, Agent McGinnis."

Were they going to politely ignore the fact she had intentionally fled the institute? That was fine by her.

"Echo 8 is at large?" asked Garcia.

Tess winced inwardly. *Here it comes.*

"No, sir. Echo 8 faded out."

She stared at him. Was he covering her ass or his own?

"That's a shame." Garcia's gaze shifted to Tess. "Fortunately we've found you a replacement subject, Doctor."

"What?" She exchanged a glance with Ross, who didn't appear any more pleased about the news than she was. "Where?"

"Here, in your lab. I think it's someone you'll be glad to see."

Someone she *knew*?

Her heart thumped in anticipation, but Garcia turned his attention to Ross. "I want you both to shower and change. I've ordered food. I'll send it up when it gets here."

"Yes, sir," said Ross.

"Who is it, Director?" asked Tess, too tired for games.

"When you've eaten, come back down to the cafeteria for debriefing. After that we'll look in on Echo 9."

She reminded herself she'd decided to play along for the time being, and when Agent Perez appeared to escort her she went without a fight.

But she whispered a prayer to the universe: *Please don't let it be anyone I love.*

She started up the stairs, Ross following unescorted behind her. One of them was still trusted, at least. She couldn't help wishing they could go to the same apartment, as they had several times in the days before the director's arrival. She wanted to crawl into bed with him and sleep for a week.

————

By the time she'd showered and eaten the Thai takeout the director had sent up, it was after 10 P.M. She felt wrecked, and unequal to whatever "debriefing" entailed, but she knew the director wasn't going to let her see who he had in the lab unless she complied with his order.

When she arrived at the cafeteria, Garcia and Ross were already seated at the table where they'd all had breakfast earlier that day. *Surely it was more like a week ago?*

Both men rose as she entered.

"Please, Doctor," said Garcia, pulling out a chair for her. The unexpected courtesy scared her more than if he'd started right off with berating her.

She sat down, and Ross—his expression pressed as crisply as his Bureau uniform—poured her a glass of water. It was cold and helped to sharpen her senses, which had gone tepid with fatigue.

"I'm not going to sugarcoat the situation, Doctor. Your decision to fly out of here, flouting the Bureau's authority over a dangerous captive, has obliged me to view you as a very serious security risk."

It was on the tip of her tongue to remind him Jake had been *her* subject, and no one's captive, until the *Bureau* had come in uninvited and started bullying everyone. But she pressed her lips together and waited for him to continue. *Pick your battles.*

"However, Agent McGinnis has indicated that you've expressed remorse about your precipitous departure, and I'm inclined to view the fault as partly my own for not giving you the opportunity to ask questions about the information I'd given you."

Again she stuffed down her first response: Anger, that Ross had believed himself qualified to speak for her. She wasn't at all sorry for rescuing Jake from forced participation in Garcia's death squad. But a calmer internal voice suggested that it could be that Ross was trying to help her.

"As Echo 8 departed this world without killing any innocent

bystanders, I'm also inclined to let bygones be bygones, assuming future cooperation."

Tess swallowed, allowed her lips to part, and spoke carefully. Her brain was barely keeping ahead of her mouth, and she couldn't afford to say anything stupid right now.

"I'd like to point out, Director, that Echo 8 never killed anyone, even while he was 'at large,' due to the work the two of us"—she glanced at Ross—"the *three* of us did together here at Seattle Psi."

Garcia nodded. "Acknowledged, Doctor. And that's why I consider you an asset to our team." He poured himself a glass of water and continued. "Ross has also told me about the most recent dislocation."

Her eyes rolled Ross's direction and back. How she wished she had even a fraction of his control. What exactly had he told Garcia? And why?

Did you expect him to lie to his superior for you? Tess clenched her fists in her lap, trying to flush the Mac residue out of her head.

"He explained to me how he used the dislocation to transport the two of you out of danger on the *Kalakala*."

Tess opened and closed her mouth. She let her gaze rest on Ross. What possible motive could he have for that particular lie? She knew him better than to suspect he wanted to impress the director with his ability. Most likely he was trying to protect her, but she was pretty sure his taking all the credit for the dislocation wasn't going to be enough to make Garcia forget about her.

"Yes, he's very resourceful," she said lamely.

"His disclosure has led to a change in plans. While Echoes continue to be essential to our operation, we no longer plan to use them as assassins. Your role will remain the same, however. You'll work with Ross and the other agents on energy transfers, and you'll conduct Ross's psi training."

"I'm glad to hear that, Director." But the surge of relief was neutralized by her sense that all was not right with this picture. The Bureau would not have so easily given up its objective. "How do you intend to eliminate your targets without them?"

"Echoes are necessary to enable the dislocations. Trained agents will use dislocation to eliminate the targets. The risk of collateral damage is reduced to practically nil."

They're turning Ross into an assassin instead. Ross had done one dislocation; he didn't have that kind of control. But she had no doubt he was capable of it.

Her heart went down like the *Titanic*.

"I understand that you're a scientist and not an operative," continued the director, his gaze flickering briefly at Ross. "And my early mistake was not giving that fact the consideration it deserves. So from this point on we'll draw a line between preparation and end objectives, and will confine your involvement to the former."

And I can go happily about my work, repressing the fact I'm training Ross to track and kill people.

Again she found herself trying to read an unreadable Ross.

"Now, do you have questions, Doctor?"

She folded her hands on the table, asking in a subdued voice, "Will I be able to continue my work with the task force?"

The director frowned. "In a more limited capacity."

"What does that mean exactly?"

"For one, we expect your new responsibilities to consume most of your time. But also we've discontinued your access to task force members until we're reassured of your commitment to preserving the classified nature of this project."

So much for bygones.

"I see."

"The task force will of course be kept apprised of your progress and any new discoveries you make."

"May I request to continue to receive their updates, as well?"

"I don't see why not."

"How about Dr. Carmichael and the institute?"

"We'll continue here until we can locate a more secure facility. Your director is understandably eager to return to her own facility, so we will make that happen as soon as possible."

The first thing Tess read into this was that Abby was raising hell about the Bureau coup. Good for her. The second thing she read into it was that *she* would soon be leaving the institute.

The director rose from the table. "And now if you're ready, we'll take you to meet Echo 9."

She rose quickly. Awkwardly. Still trying to assimilate all the new information, she had all but forgotten the new Echo.

She watched Ross rise from the table, again looking for messages he wasn't transmitting. She followed the director into the lobby, and Ross drew up beside her, cupping her elbow with his hand. A feather-light touch. Nothing suggestive. Reasonable contact between a bodyguard and the woman he was protecting.

Or a man escorting a woman in custody.

They stopped outside the lab door, and Ross squeezed and released her elbow. She peered through the window, afraid of what waited inside.

The man on the floor was transparent. But she still recognized him in an instant.

"Professor Goff!" she cried, stepping close to the door, pressing a hand to the glass. "He needs a transfer!"

She reached for the lock, but Ross's hand moved to cover it.

"All energy transfers will be conducted by Bureau personnel," said Garcia. "It's for your own safety, Doctor."

She almost laughed in his face. *You don't want anyone dislocating that you can't control.*

"He's too weak to come to the door," she protested.

"I'll take care of it," Ross said softly. His hand closed over the knob.

"Can you . . . ?" She resented having to make such a personal request in front of Garcia. But she had to know. "Can you find out if he knows me?"

He exchanged a quick glance with the director before replying, "I'll try, Doctor."

Ross opened the door and slipped inside, closing it behind him. He crossed to Goff, crouching beside him, and Tess switched on the intercom.

". . . to help you, Professor Goff. When I touch you, you're going to feel desperate for a few moments. Both of us are going to try to relax, and everything's going to be fine. Are you ready?"

Tess's throat tightened as she watched them. Ross gave a grunt of pain, and Goff latched onto him.

"Is this typical?" asked the director.

She nodded. "He'll be fine. He knows what he's doing."

After ten minutes Ross rose to his feet and returned to the door. Goff met her gaze through the glass, eyes bright with curiosity. He was a little grayer then her Goff and possibly a little thinner.

"We've all had a very long day," said Garcia. "Let's get some sleep and start fresh tomorrow."

He called Perez over to escort her and said goodnight. Perez followed as she and Ross headed for the stairs together.

"He didn't know you on his Earth, Doctor," said Ross as he was exiting at his floor. "But he does now."

He held her gaze for long enough it seemed significant, and then he turned into the hallway.

She didn't understand it at first. Ross hadn't asked Goff about her. Then she remembered the transfer allowed communication without words.

Shortly after sunrise someone knocked on her door. She'd just finished dressing but was still tying her shoes and called, "Come in."

Ross stepped inside with coffee and bagels from Espresso Noir.

His transformation was complete. In addition to resuming the uniform, he was freshly shaved, and he'd gelled his dark hair into submission. Special Agent McGinnis was as handsome as the day she'd met him, but her heart ached for the loss of the scruffy version with the warm smile and soft lips.

She felt underdressed in her jeans and sneakers—and it wasn't usually how she dressed on the job—but there was still the possibility of her dislocating, and this time she chose practicality over professionalism.

He set the food on the dining table. "Okay if I join you?"

"Of course." Her gaze darted to the door he'd left open, and back to his face.

He was staring at her, hard. He shook his head a fraction of an inch, and she understood. *We're not alone.*

Would they ever be? Was the whole place bugged? How would she find out where he stood with all this?

Maybe you'll have to trust him.

But that too was problematic. Trust him to do what? What Garcia was asking of him . . . was it really all that different from the work Ross had always done? Maybe he'd never used his psi ability to locate and execute targets, but would he second-guess such an order? She liked to think he would, but it was not his job to question the morality of decisions made by his superiors. Tess realized she knew nothing about his politics, and very little about his personal ethics.

Regardless of the choices Ross made for himself, she believed that he would try to help *her*. He had already risked himself by choosing to mislead Garcia, and both lies had made her position more tolerable.

At any rate, Tess sensed that for now she would gain nothing by resisting Garcia. The Bureau had taken possession of Seattle Psi, body and soul, and she knew that whether or not she agreed to help them, she wouldn't be allowed to return to her former life.

She was the possessor of damning state secrets, and she'd been labeled a security risk.

She determined to watch and wait, and hope for an opportunity to talk to Ross. It could be that if she kept her head down and stayed out of trouble they would ease up on monitoring her.

"How is Goff?" she asked after they'd sat for a good five minutes in silence.

He drank the last of his coffee and set the cup down. "Doing well. We did a second transfer last night—Garcia doesn't want any more of them walking through walls—but this morning I thought we'd train a couple more agents."

"Has the director prepared them for what may happen? It took awhile for me to dislocate, but Jake did right away."

Ross nodded. "They understand the risks. But we definitely need to cover all that with them. As well as explain how we believe it's controlled."

She held his gaze. "The director understands we're still learning? We may lose some of them. They may disappear and not come back."

"They're field agents. Dangerous assignments come with the territory."

She sank against the chair back with a sigh. More potential casualties.

"In the afternoon I thought we could work on the training," added Ross, returning his gaze to his bagel.

It was the one aspect of her new assignment she was actually anticipating. This was the work she loved, and she was curious about Ross's abilities. Would he be able to relax his control enough to let them develop?

Also, she had limited experience with remote viewing. Though at various times of great interest to the U.S. military and government, remote viewing had become a source of scientific scorn, and with diminished government interest there was little funding for research. But it was really just an amalgam of less complex abilities, such as precognition and clairvoyance, with which she was well versed.

"I'm looking forward to it," she replied.

Garcia asked Ross to join him offsite for lunch. By the time they came back, she had assembled her materials and equipment in the conference room across from the lab.

"Are you ready, Doctor?" he asked as he took the chair on the opposite side of the table from her. He swung his jacket over the back.

"I am. How about you?"

He smiled, and the sexy eyelids lowered as his eyes moved over her face.

Cocky bastard. He's flirting with me. She knew him well enough to chalk it up to his feeling unsure about the training and uncomfortable with someone else being in control. But it didn't keep the warmth out of her cheeks. Or her gaze from slipping down to his lips.

Clearing her throat, she picked up the pen in front of her, and she tried to pretend he was just another research subject.

"Do you understand what remote viewing is?"

"I think so. It's what I did to find you."

She frowned. "On the *Kalakala*, you mean?"

He nodded.

"Why don't you tell me how you did that?"

He picked up a paperclip holder, turning it in his fingers. "At first I tried focusing on you and Jake. That didn't work. But once I let that go, I started getting visuals. They didn't seem relevant, but eventually they led me right to you."

"Okay, that was an important lesson. Agitated states of mind are not hospitable to psi. Rather than concentrating too hard, it's better to set an intention, and then try to keep your mind open and relaxed."

"What if I've never met the person before? I mean, I assume I was able to find you because of our"—his gaze drifted up from the paperclips, and her stomach fluttered—"connection. Will this really work with someone I've never met?"

"Good question. And oddly enough, yes. As you discovered, a connection with a person *can* be a hindrance. It can generate interference. And most remote viewing tests involve unknown targets. There was a remote viewer involved in a U.S. Army project who could successfully locate targets he'd never met. He didn't even need a name."

Ross frowned. "That's pretty hard to believe."

"Nonetheless true. I'm sure you have clearance to access the particulars, if you'd like to look it up." She smiled archly, and he raised an eyebrow.

"Why don't we get started?" She pushed a pen and pad of paper across the table and picked up a stack of photographs.

"I don't want you to focus too much on how you're feeling, but again, be aware that relaxed states tend to produce the best results. At some point I'll want to monitor your heart rate and brainwaves, but let's just see how we do for now."

"So what do I do?"

"In a minute I'll show you a photo. Before I do, I want you to use the pen and paper to record your impressions of the photo. You can use words or images. You can describe shapes, colors, smells, feelings. Whatever comes to you. Put everything down, even if it doesn't seem important."

Ross looked dubious. "You're not going to tell me anything about the photo?"

"No. You're going to tell me."

He picked up the pen and frowned at the paper. He clicked the pen open and closed several times.

"What's wrong?"

"When I did this with you, I had a real motivation. I was concerned for your safety."

His eyes came back to her face, and she shivered. Despite their early animosity, she realized she was feeling nostalgic about the time they'd spent together after Jake's arrival. In the quiet moments between arguments and energy transfers, she'd enjoyed their exchanges. Ross was bright and funny, and he was no Bureau robot.

Not to mention he has a damn sexy mouth.

"This feels . . . meaningless," he continued, frustration coming through in his tone. "How can I guess at a picture when I have no context? No need or motive? That's all it *will* be . . . guessing."

"You do have a motive. You've been asked to sharpen your remote viewing skills. This exercise will help you do that."

He glowered. "You know that's not the same thing."

"Just take it easy," she said, breathing deeply and modeling a relaxed posture. "There's no pressure. We're just getting started. I don't have any expectations for these first rounds. We're getting used to working together. You're getting used to the process. Why don't we do the first one, just to get it out of the way?"

Ross exhaled audibly, and he dropped the tip of the pen to the paper. He scooted his chair back and rested his fist on the paper, then his chin on his fist. Suddenly he looked about twenty years younger.

"Did you look at the picture?" he asked.

"Not yet."

"Why not?"

"I want to control what we're measuring. If I look at the picture and you describe it accurately, you could be reading *me*. I won't know if you're using telepathy or precognition. There's also a possibility I would subtly react to what you draw and give you cues that guide you."

"Hmph."

Tess couldn't help smiling. And she badly wanted to reach out and muss his gelled hair.

He pushed the pen across the paper in a quick, abstract sketch of . . . the Washington Monument? He tossed the pen down and glared at her.

She turned up the first card, and her breath caught. Not the Washington Monument. But she laid the card down next to his drawing so he could see for himself. The similarity was so striking his eyes widened as he looked at it. The image on the card was the Eiffel Tower.

And so it went for the entire afternoon and well into evening. With each close match his confidence increased to the point he was missing no more than two out of ten. She'd never seen anything like it—his success rate was off the charts.

When they broke for dinner, Garcia joined them and stayed to watch the next session. Tess forced Ross to take more time now, rather than dashing out quick sketches. She had him write descriptions and include details like smells and textures. She used graduated stacks of images, each more complex than the last, and by the third stack his drawings resembled the target almost every time. He pinpointed the geography more than 75 percent of the time, and he identified the feel of the photo—happy or somber, calm or dynamic, hot or cold—more than half the time.

This was good, and this was bad. Her scientist's heart was thrilled and proud as a parent over her subject's success. But there were consequences. If his performance remained consistent, there would be nothing to stop Garcia from carrying his plan to the next phase.

By 8 P.M. they were both bleary-eyed, and she suggested they call it a night.

"Good work today, Doctor," said Ross.

She shook her head. "You did all the work. I don't mind telling you I'm completely dumbfounded. I've never seen results like this. But let's see how we do tomorrow."

"Beginner's luck?"

"Something like that. The novelty of the testing can have a beneficial effect in the beginning. That wears off pretty fast." Tess rubbed her sore neck. "Don't tell Garcia. You'll give the man a stroke."

Ross's lips parted to reply, but he seemed to think better of it and turned for the door. "Have a good night, Doctor."

Tess sank back down in her chair with a sigh. She nibbled a piece of pizza left over from their dinner. If they didn't stop eating takeout she was going to gain twenty pounds.

She wanted to organize and file Ross's drawings, but she got caught up in reading back through them. Trying to hold on to their time together.

But they'd be back at it soon enough. She had to try to figure out a safe way to talk to him. Since that morning she'd assumed they were being monitored everywhere in the building. It wouldn't even take that much effort—Seattle Psi had installed cameras in every room that could potentially be used for training or trials. Garcia seemed to trust Ross. Maybe he'd let him take her offsite for lunch.

Not going to happen.

She groaned, resting her head on her folded arms.

"Doctor?"

Her head jerked up, and pain shot between her shoulder blades. Why couldn't she open her eyes? Her eyes *were* open. Why couldn't she see? Darkness had swallowed her.

"Ross?" she breathed, frightened.

She heard a faint rustling. His voice was closer this time. "Someone cranked up an old window unit, and the power went out."

Typical Seattle Psi poltergeist activity. So she hadn't dislocated in her sleep.

Her chair creaked as she rose from the table. "This building has a geriatric nervous system. We'll have to go down to the breaker box."

"Someone has gone down already. I came to check on you."

"Thanks." She moved along the table, cursing as she stumbled over a chair. She couldn't see a damn thing. How could he?

"Just sit tight. The lights will be up in a minute."

"Okay."

A heartbeat later she felt a hand close gently over her shoulder, and a finger press against her lips.

Ross drew her into his arms and kissed her deeply with no preliminaries. His hands clutched her back, and she wrapped her arms around his neck. After only a moment he broke the kiss, burrowing in her hair, blowing a puff of warm air against her ear.

Then he stepped back, straightening as the lights came up. He gave her a gentle smile. "You should get some sleep, Doctor. Come on. I'll walk you up."

Her heart hammered, and all she could do was nod. She'd needed that moment of connection, of physical reassurance. But what did it mean?

As they walked to the lobby together, she thought about the look on his face. And the desperate quality of that kiss.

He's saying good-bye.

GRADUATION DAY

Three days later

I WANT to see Jake Parker perform."

Ross raised his eyebrows, a warning in his eyes. "I'm sorry, Doctor?"

"You heard me. Jake Parker is a local musician. I don't know where or when he's playing next. I want you to figure it out." She shoved the pad of paper across the table at him.

Garcia had insisted it was time for real scenarios. This was a real scenario, with her own personal touch.

"This is no different from what we've done before."

Ross's face relaxed, and he picked up the pen. "Do you know the answer?"

"Nope. Like I said, just like before."

Tess was snapping at him. She couldn't help it. Because in the last three days there'd been no explanation of the kiss, no *further* kisses, and in fact no physical contact of any kind. He'd given her no information. They hadn't spoken on any topic other than Garcia's project. And Tess was scared. Ross's training had reached the point he hardly needed her anymore. What would happen to them now?

Tess breathed slowly and softened her tone. "Think about dates and locations. Do what you've done before. Draw pictures, scribble notes. Take your time. Breathe and relax."

Ross rubbed his forehead. He stared at the paper. At the wall. At the ceiling. At her.

He bent and wrote three neat lines and handed the paper back to her.

Tabitha North w/guest Jake Parker
The Tractor Tavern, Old Ballard, Seattle
Thursday, Aug. 30, 8:30 P.M.

"Hmm." She glanced up at him. "Check it with your phone. I don't have one anymore." It had been missing since her return to Seattle Psi. She doubted she'd misplaced it.

She folded her arms, waiting while Ross carried on a private conversation with his mobile device. Thirty seconds later he glanced up at her and nodded. He turned the phone so she could see.

"How did you do it so fast? You just wrote it down."

He shrugged. "While I sat there thinking about it, I saw this." He waved his phone at her.

"Your phone? I don't understand."

"The search result on my phone. I didn't have to figure it out because I saw the readout . . . before I actually *saw* the readout."

"Wow," repeated Tess, shaking her head. "A person could go crazy thinking about that too hard."

Ross smirked. "Are you telling me I've actually managed to shock the parapsychologist?"

"That's what I'm telling you."

The door opened and Garcia stuck his head in. "Ross, I need to talk to you."

"Director," said Tess, "I was hoping to—"

"This can't wait. You can work with the other agents."

The other two agents she was working with were already pros at energy transfers, though neither of them had dislocated yet. She was glad for that, but doubted Garcia felt the same. She suspected they had the same control issues Ross did. She hadn't brought that up with them, and was surprised Ross hadn't either. In the meantime she'd started working with one of the others on remote location. There were some promising initial results, but nothing like Ross.

She didn't see Ross again that day or the following morning. She worked with the others until lunchtime and then set out to look for him. But upstairs she ran into Kendrick looking for her, and he told her Garcia was waiting to talk to her in the cafeteria.

As she joined him at the table, he opened a bottle of Scotch and poured a little into two glasses.

She stared at him in wonder, and he smiled. "Sorry, no ice."

"What's the occasion?"

"You've done good work, Doctor." He raised his glass, and she clinked hers against it. "Better than I could have hoped."

"I'm only as good as my subjects. Is Ross going to join us?"

He shook his head as his lips peeled back slightly from his teeth, airing the Scotch. "Ross has gone back to Washington."

A stone grated over her heart, leaving deep ruts in its wake. He hadn't even said good-bye.

"Is he coming back?"

Garcia shook his head like it was the most routine question in the world. "He's on assignment."

Oh God.

"And eventually we'll all be joining him there. I've tasked him with finding a building. We're relocating our operation to the D.C. area. I intend to turn over day-to-day management to him."

Tess raised the glass to her lips. She gulped the whisky, grateful for the slow amber burn that caressed her throat and stomach. Her hand trembled as she set down the glass.

"Are you all right, Doctor?"

"Yes, just a headache."

"Why don't you take the afternoon off? You've earned it."

Tess lay across her bed staring at the ceiling. Ross was an assassin now, and she was leaving Seattle Psi. She wondered if they'd let her see Abby before she went.

She thought about her options, and then stopped because really, she didn't have any.

She could go back to Jake. Help him look for other survivors. Try living as an Echo. But then she could do nothing to help the Echoes caught in the Bureau's web. Eventually she'd have to face this.

She could try to run from the Bureau on *her* Earth. But she couldn't leave Goff with Garcia, and seriously? Run from the FBI? Dislocation might help, but eventually Garcia was going to have his own army of dimensional travelers. At that point he'd no longer need her anyway, so he'd probably just send Ross to kill her.

Groaning in despair, she pulled a pillow over her face. Over the course of the last couple of weeks she'd lost all of her most trusted advisers—first Goff, then Abby, now Ross. She wondered at what point she had started thinking of Ross that way. Had it been the night he'd forced her to take a closer look at herself and her motivations? Or maybe all the discussions they'd had about the dislocations. They worked well together.

She wondered if he could really pull off the assassination. She hadn't been privy to the particulars, but she assumed he would

230 / SHARON LYNN FISHER

have to dislocate to the proper location, take care of business, and dislocate out. As far as she knew he'd only done the one disloca-tion, from Jake's ruin back to the *Kalakala*—between the *two* Earths. Alternately he could dislocate to Jake's world and back on each leg of the journey, but that was a lot of connections to line up, not to mention the dangerous assumption that nothing would go wrong on Post-Apocalypse World.

This all got her thinking again about Jake's dislocation—how he'd vanished and come right back, but in a different part of the room. If Jake could do it, Ross should be able to.

If Jake could do it, *she* should be able to.

She sat up.

She closed her eyes, deepening her breaths, offering herself to the tentacles of light. She thought she felt tingling in her finger-tips, and she gave herself to the sensation, real or wished for.

The tingling traveled up her arms to her chest. White light edged her peripheral vision.

She fell out of the light and crashed to the floor. She stood up quickly, glancing around her. She'd landed in the observation room—and it was empty. It had been a pretty big gamble. The building was crawling with agents, and she wouldn't have been surprised to find them here. But considering there were two watching the lab door and two in each corridor, she had thought it might just be possible they hadn't bothered. An agent in the observation room wasn't much use if Goff escaped.

Her gaze fell on the window as she reached for the sound switch, and her heart leapt right out of her chest. Not *one*, but *four* people in the lab, and one of them looked like Ross.

Only it wasn't Ross.

". . . warm and dry in here," he was saying, "and they won't let you starve, so I really think you should be thanking me for the considerable improvement to your situation."

Her stomach twisted as she wondered if he knew he could walk through walls here. *Only when he's faded. Keep your head!*

She recognized the people he was arguing with—the man and woman who'd been with him when he threatened Jake. She listened to more complaints, waiting for something that might help her understand why they were here. And why hadn't the agents outside done anything? Did they know there were new occupants? Her eyes sought Goff, and she found him hesitating in a corner, eyeing the others warily.

"Now if you'll excuse me," Mac said, "I'm due to be compensated."

It clicked together. *Mac's rounding up Echoes for Garcia.* The son of a bitch. *Which one? Exactly.*

Tess reached for the light almost without thought. An instant later she found herself in the lab, close to Goff.

She grabbed his arm, jerking him toward Mac, and caught Mac's sleeve just as he was blinking out.

He gave a shout of surprise as they fell together into the light tunnel.

Hold on to me! she called to Goff. As she released him to reach for Mac, he seemed to slip away, but she felt his hand catch her ankle.

She grabbed a handful of Mac's hair and held on tight. *This time I'll suck you dry, asshole.*

I can hardly wait. . . .

ERRANT

GlobeWatch's investigative team has discovered that the recent upswing in missing persons is not just a national phenomenon. Internet research and interviews with anonymous investigative personnel have revealed similar statistics in at least six other countries. Furthermore we've obtained photos and autopsy reports for three people who appear to have died of "supernatural" causes within the same time frame. Repeated requests to speak with officials in the Department of Homeland Security, the FBI, and the CIA have been ignored.
—"Unexplained Disappearances on the Rise Worldwide,"
August 17, 2018, GlobeWatch News Service

The previous day

ROSS SCANNED the dimly lit interior of Espresso Noir. Just blocks from Seattle Psi at the end of a quiet residential street, the café was a favorite with the staff. The sign in the window bore the silhouette of a man wearing a fedora.

He hadn't even bothered to question his gut this time. One, he was in too much of a hurry. Two, Tess had told him that 8.6222 times out of 10, his gut was right. *Why* Abby would be hanging around so close to the building she'd been banished from was another question altogether.

When he found her sitting alone with her laptop at a small corner table, the answer came to him: The Bureau people came here too. She was waiting for an opportunity to hold someone accountable. And he didn't have time for that.

"Ross!" she cried, rising to her feet.

She was talking before he even made it to her table. "What the hell is going on? Where is Tess?"

He sank down across from her and leaned close, gesturing for her to sit down. "I'll get to that, Doctor. Just give me a minute."

She gave him a scorching look. He noted that despite her distress, she was as flawlessly put together as ever. Not a hair out of place. Tess's reddish, neither-long-nor-short waves were always pulling out of hair bands and falling over her eyes. From the first day he'd met her he was continually fighting the urge to tuck the loose strands behind her ear. Mainly because he wanted to know if they were as soft as they looked.

"Ross?" hissed Abby.

He knew he was exhausted and drifting. The transfers and the training had taken their toll. Not to mention the fact he'd been aimlessly dislocating for the past two days while he tried to untangle the mess that had become his life. He felt thin and frayed at the edges. He had to sharpen up.

As if on cue, a waitress stopped beside their table—a girl with heavy eyeliner who'd waited on him before.

"Drip coffee. Black," he told her.

"You got it," she said with a wink. "I like the shadow."

Ross whipped around, almost upsetting the flimsy table.

"The beard!" The waitress laughed. "I like it. You sure you don't want decaf?"

Ross dropped his head in his hands as the waitress moved away.

"Where is Tess?" Abby repeated.

He took a deep breath and raised his head. Then he rattled off an account of everything that had happened since Abby had left for her board meeting, omitting nothing but the physical intimacy between him and her employee. He also skirted all the classified information, less for his own protection than for Abby's.

She studied him for a long moment while he rubbed at his stubbly jaw.

"What is it you want from me, Ross?"

Good question. The waitress appeared with his coffee. The tension at their table was palpable, and she set the cup down without comment and moved away.

He drained half the cup before answering. "I honestly don't know. I thought talking to you might help me sort it out."

She sighed, resting her elbows on the table. "You haven't really told me what it is that needs sorting out. I assume whatever this operation is that the Bureau has undertaken is questionable, and you're concerned about the ethics. As for why you've come to *me*, I assume that has something to do with Tess."

He nodded slowly. "That's it, more or less. Although I don't think I would have questioned my assignment a couple of weeks ago."

Abby raised an eyebrow. "*That* suggests to me this is *mostly* about Tess."

He stared at his coffee cup. "I think that could be true."

Abby sank back in her chair. Ross's eyes darted to the café's entrance and around the room. He noted the position of the entrance to the kitchen, which he knew had an exit to the alley behind the building. He pulled the hood of his jacket over his head.

"Then figure out a way to extract her, and go back to your job." Her tone was devoid of warmth. "After that, forget about her."

He closed his eyes. "That's exactly the advice I gave myself. But . . . even if I could go through with it, they're not going to let her go. They'll send someone after her. They might kill her."

"Ah, Ross." Abby's sigh was mournful. She shook her head at him. "I hated her taking this job. She had such a bright future—I knew it was a mistake to let her get tangled up in this."

He gave a humorless laugh. "There's no *letting* her do anything, Doctor. You of all people should know that. She's doing it because she thinks these people deserve a better option than the ones we've given them, and she's determined to make it happen."

Abby smiled. But the smile was for Tess. "What do *you* think?"

He swallowed the last of his coffee and scrubbed his hand through his hair. "I think she's right."

She gave a slight sideways nod, watching him closely.

He rose from the table.

"Help her, Ross. And find a way to let me know. She's like a daughter to me."

He nodded, and he headed for the kitchen. The cook flung a curse at him as he jogged through to the alley. As his shoes hit the asphalt he vanished.

When the capital came up in conversation, it usually deteriorated into a diatribe on corruption and politics. People who'd never been to the city were eloquent with regard to the high crime rate, poverty, and drug problems.

But the monuments were beautiful in the pink-orange light of the setting sun.

"In this temple, as in the hearts of the people for whom he saved the union, the memory of Abraham Lincoln is enshrined forever." Jamie was standing Lilliputian-like at the feet of President Lincoln. He turned as Ross approached. "Hey, Bro."

"Thanks for coming, Jamie."

"Want to take a walk?"

A dozen people milled around on the steps and at the base of the statue.

"Yeah. Let's go."

They headed down the steps toward the reflection pool.

"I was surprised to hear from you, Bro."

"I know. I'm sorry for that."

"I have to admit I might not have answered if I'd recognized the number. To what do I owe the honor?"

"You're still working for GlobeWatch?"

Jamie nodded. Pride blossomed on his acne-scarred face. "I proofread, mostly. But occasionally I write up briefs." He shrugged. "I'm not a real writer or anything."

"It sounds like a good start. I'm proud of you."

Jamie gave a snort of disbelief. "So why are we here?"

"I have some information I think your employer will be interested in."

"Yeah?" His voice rose with interest. "Secret agent stuff?"

"Yes."

"Can't you get in trouble for that?"

"Yes. I'll lose my job."

Jamie stared at him. "Seriously?"

"Seriously."

Jamie ran his tongue over his lips. "Shit."

Ross fished a pin drive from his pocket. "There are classified files on this drive, along with a letter that explains everything. Make sure your editor reads the letter. This needs to be handled carefully, or there will be panic. It's going to sound crazy, and if your employer talks to the Bureau they're going to deny it, but it's all backed up with documentation."

Jamie stared at the drive, wide-eyed. "Whoa, are you sure the crankhead can be trusted with this?"

"I'm counting on it, James."

His brother shot him a look of surprise. "No lecture? You must be in deep donkey shit, coming to me for help. That's ironic, right? I'm never sure if I'm using that word right."

Guilt and regret sank into Ross's bones. He had done everything he could to help his brother, or so he'd believed at the time.

Hired a good lawyer, served as a character witness, helped him navigate the complexities of the legal system. But Ross had been helpless against his brother's addiction, and instead of supporting him, he'd fallen back on his favorite coping mechanism.

"I'm sorry about the lectures," Ross said. "It's not my job to tell you how to live."

"Confessions like that are a little suspect at the moment, Bro."

"I know. But I mean it."

Jamie let out a long breath, and he held out his hand. Ross dropped the pin drive on his palm. Jamie turned it over a couple of times, and he slipped it into his pocket.

"Hang on to it until tomorrow afternoon. Unless I call with other instructions, give it to your editor before you leave for the day. And for God's sake, don't *you* look at any of it. I don't want you involved."

Jamie eyed him, and Ross could feel the shift in his intentions.

"I mean it, James," said Ross, stern as only an older brother can be. "This has already ruined the life of one person I care about. Do you hear me?"

Jamie swallowed. "Yeah, I got it. What's going to happen to *you?*"

Ross stared at the mirror surface of the water, awash in orange light. "I don't know."

"You going to disappear on us?"

"Probably for a while." He met his brother's worried gaze. "Will you let Mom and Dad know everything's okay? That I know what I'm doing?"

"*Do* you?"

"Yeah, I do."

Jamie sighed. "Okay, Bro. Take care of yourself." Then he grinned. "Try to be less of an asshole."

"I'm working on that."

"Ha," Jamie snorted. He nudged Ross with his elbow. "I'll believe it when I see it."

———————

Ross materialized in Tess's apartment just after lunchtime the following day, but she wasn't there. He hadn't really expected she would be, but it would have made things easier.

Next he dislocated to the lab. Not finding her there either, he ran out into the corridor, followed by the curious gazes of the other agents. He bumped into Garcia in the lobby.

"Ross," he said, startled. "I've been waiting for confirmation about your assignment. Report."

"Where's Tess?"

The older man frowned. "Report, Ross. Did you complete your assignment?"

"Almost. I need to talk to you."

Garcia's expression of disapproval deepened. "Almost? What does that mean?"

Perez passed them on her way to the stairs. "Where is Dr. Caufield?" Ross asked her.

The agent's eyes flickered between Ross and Garcia, but she kept walking.

"Ross," said Garcia, "Dr. Caufield has left the institute again. She took Goff with her, as well as an important contact from his Earth."

Having only absorbed the first sentence of this, Ross asked, "Do you know where she went?"

"I'll defer to you on that, but my guess would be the other Earth. I want you to go after her and bring her back."

Calm down and let it come to you. She's probably with Jake. He felt a pang about the fact she'd run to Jake instead of him, but he had no right to expect otherwise. He'd delayed while he was figuring things out, and she'd probably interpreted that as him falling back into step with the Bureau. Then he'd disappeared without a warning.

Besides that, Jake's Earth was probably the safest place for her.

Especially if Goff was with her. During the energy transfers he'd filled in the older scientist about almost everything that had happened to them, and, interestingly, Goff had already seemed to develop protective feelings about her. It reminded Ross of the stuff in Tess's thesis about quantum entanglement between people.

As he thought about this, the rest of Garcia's explanation finally sank in. Goff wasn't the only one who'd gone with her. "Who is your new contact?"

"Ross, I fully intend to fill you in, but I'm still waiting for your report."

He wanted to shout in frustration. Instead he scrubbed his face with his hand. "I came here to tell you I've had second thoughts about the assignment. I don't feel that I can carry it out in good conscience."

Garcia's expression went dark. "You're not paid to have a conscience, Ross."

"It's not just the assassinations. I know what some of those people are, and I agree the world would be a better place without them. But the way we're using the Echoes—Dr. Caufield is right. We can do better."

Garcia reached out suddenly, yanking Ross's weapon from his shoulder holster. "You're relieved, Agent McGinnis."

"Yes, sir. I am."

The director's frown deepened, showing disappointment as well as anger. "It's a good thing we've got two of you."

Ross's heart froze. "What?"

"Your double on the other Earth sought us out. We're working with him now. We can only hope he shares your abilities."

"The contact—the one Tess took with her?"

Garcia nodded. "He's resourceful. He'll be back."

The director opened his mouth to speak again, but Ross had already blinked out.

SURVIVORS

> May the forces of evil become confused on the way to your house.
> —George Carlin

IN THE moments of free fall before touchdown, Mac managed to land a fist in Tess's stomach. Gasping from the impact, she lost the handful of hair, and Mac slipped off into a forking tunnel.

Damn damn damn!

She'd just managed to restart her breathing when the ground knocked it out of her again. She rolled hard away from Goff to prevent the energy transfer from initiating. He groaned beside her.

"Are you okay, Professor?"

"Aye, lass. Have I come home?"

"Yes, sir. What's left of it. And I'm an Echo here, so you'll want to keep your distance."

"Tess?"

She glanced up to find Jake in the entry to the ruin.

Smiling, she rose and joined him. "God, I'm glad you're still alive."

"I didn't expect to see you again. I've sure missed you."

"What's it been?" she said with a weary laugh. "Like two days?"

"Long enough for me to start feeling sorry for myself and get pissing drunk."

That explained the thickness in his voice. "Do you have any of that left?" she asked.

"You're joking, right? I have to pour out three bad bottles for every good one, but I'll still probably starve before I dry out." His eyes moved to Goff. "Who's your friend?"

"Jake, this is my mentor—or at least the version of him on your world—Professor Alexi Goff."

Jake held out his hand. "Echo 8."

Goff smiled and shook his hand. "Echo 9."

"I had Mac too." She frowned. "I lost him in the tunnel."

"Mac! The asshole found a way to get back?"

"Assholes always do," she said with a groan. "I gave him a transfer, remember? He's made some kind of deal with the FBI. I think he's delivering Echoes for money."

"His mother would be so proud." Jake frowned in disgust. "Come on; let's go inside. It's too damn cold today."

As they settled around the fire Jake picked up a half-empty bottle, offering it to her. "Where's the other twin?"

"I don't know," she said quietly, sipping the cold wine. Considering what it had been through, it wasn't bad. "On assignment, I think. He left without saying."

Jake was eyeing her a little too keenly. "Listen, what happened before you left . . . I'm really sorry if it messed things up for you with him."

"That didn't have anything to do with it." She frowned. "Or at least not much."

"So you're not mad at me?"

"I'm not mad."

There was a heartbeat of silence before he said, "Can I do it again?"

She rolled her eyes. "Will you be serious?"

"I was serious," he grumbled. "But fine. What's your plan, Doc? Have you decided to build a summer home here?"

"Yes, actually."

"I was joking."

"I know, right after I told you not to."

He shrugged. "I can't help it. It's why you love me. But what exactly are you talking about?"

"I want to set up a camp for survivors."

Jake glanced around. "Hmm. Which ones did you mean?"

"Mac found some. There must be others. And there are Echoes on Earth who might want to come back."

"Cuz I'm sure they're homesick for all *this*."

"The ones who end up in Garcia's new maximum security prison for Echoes probably will be."

"Good point."

"How would you fund it, Dr. Caufield?" asked Goff. Jake offered him the wine bottle, but he shook his head.

"I don't know yet," she admitted. "I just thought of it. I got the idea from Mac, actually."

"The great philanthropist," muttered Jake.

"If he can make deals between worlds, why can't we? Only better ones. *Humane* ones. If people understood what happened here, I'm sure they'd want to help. I can coordinate on this end, since if I go home Garcia will probably have me killed. Maybe Abby, Seattle Psi's director, could coordinate on the other side."

"Where would you put your camp?" asked Goff.

"I was thinking right here. It seems to be geologically stable. It's not as cold as it's bound to be farther inland. We also might be able to rebuild on this foundation, reusing the materials that didn't burn. I'm sure there are more suitable locations, but this will work until we can figure out a way to assess that."

"And transporting the materials?"

"That's the part I'm not sure about. Can we dislocate *stuff* as well as people? Since we arrive with our clothes and the stuff in our pockets, I don't see why not. I'll have to try it."

"You're forgetting one thing, Doc," said Jake.

"What?"

"Nobody knows about this. The whole Echo thing. How will you get people to believe you, much less want to help you? They'll have you committed."

She frowned, staring into the fire. "I'll have to expose it. Go to the press."

He raised an eyebrow. "Am I talking to myself here? *Who's going to believe you?* You think the Bureau's going to back you up?"

She sighed and accepted another sip from the bottle. "You're right. I'll have to think about that part. Abby at least will believe me."

And Ross. She wondered where he was now and whether he'd completed his assignment. She wondered how he'd feel when he learned she'd gone. Probably relieved. She believed he would have gotten her out of there if he could. Now he wouldn't have to.

She didn't blame him for anything. He was just doing his job. But she did miss him.

Miss him? You think? She covered her face with her hands. Denial had served her well so far. Why stop now?

Jake scooted close to her, and he raised his arm to put it around her. She flinched away. But it was only a reflex. They were controlling the transfers so well now there was very little pain or risk.

"It'll make you feel better," he insisted, lowering his arm over her shoulder.

She rested her head against him, and he was right: The gentle flow was soothing. The pulse of information coming from him was faint, but she could feel the loneliness that had settled over him in the last few days. It intensified her own.

"Am I hurting you?" she asked, just to be sure.

"Only when I laugh, Doc. Now if you're referring to my broken heart, I hardly notice that anymore."

"Very funny."

He gave a dry chuckle. "Who's joking?"

Goff cleared his throat and turned his gaze toward the fire.

"He let you down," said Jake. "I know."

"I'm fine."

"Don't be ridiculous. But remember who he is. I would have ridden in there on a white horse and carried you out of there. Then they would have shot us both. Probably the horse too. Ross thinks things through. He always has a plan. I wouldn't be surprised if you haven't heard the last of him."

She nodded but was afraid to hope. "I don't need rescuing anymore. He can go on with his life."

Jake was quiet a moment and then asked, "You have a hard time trusting people, don't you?"

She gave a brittle laugh. "I trust you."

Jake smiled, but it was the kind of smile that hurt her heart.

"That's how I know you and I will never be more than friends. You don't trust him because he has the power to hurt you." He bent his head so his chin touched her forehead. "I dare you to tell me I'm wrong."

Ross watched them, and he couldn't help wondering whether he should leave it alone. Maybe Jake was what she needed. They seemed so good together—any time Ross wasn't around. True they were from different worlds, literally, and that made things complicated. But there he was, snuggling her by the fire like any normal boyfriend. Just a few days ago he'd kissed her like any normal boyfriend. He adored her. He made her laugh. What did Ross have to offer beyond that?

Only himself. And he had to try.

"I wish you *would* trust me."

Tess jumped to her feet, almost toppling Jake.

She ran straight into his arms.

She landed against him hard, and he grunted and pulled her so close her feet lifted off the ground. "You about gave me a heart attack, woman," he whispered into her hair.

"I'm sorry," she murmured. "I promised myself I wouldn't run like that again. Then you left, and I was confused. Mac showed up at the institute and I—"

He tilted her face back and stopped her lips with his. She gave a little moan, fingers slipping into his hair. Then suddenly she pulled back, looking into his eyes.

"You're not here to kill me are you?"

"Are you seriously asking me that?"

"Sort of?"

Ross laughed out loud, pulling her against his chest. "Jesus, Doctor."

"Come on, Professor," Jake said quietly to Goff. "Let's take a walk on the estate. Maybe we can find Tess some refugees. Some little tiny ones we've overlooked so far."

Jake glared at Ross as he stood up. He tossed the professor a blanket, and they exited the ruin.

Ross led Tess over to the fire. "Here, sit down." He tossed on a couple of barrel staves. Jake had stacked up teepees of them near the fire so they'd dry. Which was pretty forward-looking for a suicidal songwriter. He'd also erected the tent they'd found in the camping gear. Ross wondered if Jake had been nesting in hopes Tess would come back. His gaze fell on the collection of empty wine bottles next to the fire.

"I'm glad you're not here to kill me," said Tess. "But I can't go back there. If Garcia sent you to try and—"

"Why *is* it so hard for you to trust me?" He shot her a look of puzzled frustration.

"It's not personal, Ross."

"That's great." He laughed darkly. *What am I doing here again?*

She shook her head. "I mean it's not that I don't believe you're trustworthy. I just know your job is important to you. I know that our interests don't align. It's not your fault. It's not anyone's fault."

Sighing, he sank down next to her. "That was true yesterday. Or maybe the day before that. Actually I'm not sure when it stopped being true."

She looked at him, and he reached a hand to her cheek. "What are you talking about?" she asked.

"I've given the Bureau's confidential Echo files to a news service. In the past week they've run a couple of investigative pieces on the spate of missing persons. They're going to eat it up."

Tess froze, her eyes wide. He didn't think she was breathing.

"I no longer *have* a job. And our interests, as far as I can see, are in perfect alignment. Except for one thing."

"What?" she whispered.

"I don't think I'm okay with you kissing Jake."

Tess threw her arms around him, pulling his mouth to hers. He cradled her neck, thumbs brushing along her jaw, as her tongue met his. She sighed against him, shifting her body until she was sitting in his lap.

Then she released his lips and nuzzled his cheek. "You came for me," she whispered. "You yourself. Without the Bureau."

"I did."

"Ross, I can't believe . . . Are you sure about this?"

"I'm sure." He pulled her head to his chest so he wouldn't have to watch the effect of his words on her. "I did it because of you. Because I believe you're right that they deserve better treatment from us. But I made my own decision. There are no strings or obligations. The Bureau will come after me for this, and you didn't sign up for that. Also, I know you care about Jake, and if you'd rather stay with him, I'll deal with it. I'll be okay."

She shook against his chest, and at first he thought she was crying. Then he realized she was chuckling softly. "Ross, don't be an idiot."

He raised his eyebrows as she pulled back to look at him. "Okay."

"First of all, you may be number one on the Bureau's most wanted list, but I'm right behind you. As for Jake . . ."

She took a deep breath and tried to organize her thoughts. "You're right that I care about him. I care about him a lot. Under different circumstances I might even fall in love with him. He understands me, and I think in a lot of ways he would be good for me."

Ross began to nod, and she took his face in her hands. "This kind of thing is hard for me. You're right that I haven't trusted you. Something happened to me when I was a kid—"

"I know." His arms tightened around her. "You don't have to say this."

She placed her fingers over his lips. "Something happened to me when I was a kid. The people who were supposed to take care of me let me down. After that I didn't trust anyone."

It was the first time she'd admitted, to herself or anyone, that her mother hadn't been blameless. It gave her a feeling like the beginning of the dislocations. Like the ground was dropping out from under her.

A tear escaped and started down her cheek. Ross followed it with his eyes, looking wretched.

"Jake was right about what he said. The people who can hurt me the most are the ones I trust the least. When I dislocated that first time, I was terrified of you. Because I knew I was falling for you, and I could see all the traps on the road we were traveling. I believed there was very little chance we'd be together at the end of it. Jake said we were imagining problems, and it was him and me who had real obstacles between us. He was wrong about that. But he was right about something else."

She ran her thumb over his bottom lip, and he waited for her to continue.

"That's love, and that's life. And you have to start living sometime."

"Tess," he hissed, pulling her close. She felt the tension trip along his muscles.

She wrapped her arms around his neck, brushing her lips against his earlobe. A shock of desire shot through her, and she whispered, "You'll never know how happy I was to see you in that doorway."

He squeezed the breath out of her chest and then drew back to kiss her. Moving slowly from her mouth to her neck, he traced the curve of her throat with kisses.

A shiver teased along her spine, and she squirmed against him. She tucked her head against his neck and whispered, "Do you want me?"

"Do I ever."

"Are we in danger?"

"Aren't we always?" He laughed. "But no one's coming after us, if that's what you mean. I didn't tell Garcia the truth about where we'd dislocated."

She pulled his head down to her mouth. "How clever of you. Agent McGinnis?"

"That's ex Agent McGinnis to you."

"Ross?"

"Hmm?"

"If you're not inside me in thirty seconds I'm going to find Jake."

In one fluid motion he rose with her in his arms. He glanced around, and his gaze fell on the tent. He carried her over, set her inside, and crawled in after her. She lay back on the blanket while he zipped the flap closed.

He crawled over, planting a knee on either side of her thighs as he tugged off his shirt.

Oh Jesus. Her eyes moved over the pale ridges and curves. Her legs opened against his knees without her willing it.

"They may be back soon," he said.

"Then let's not waste time."

He reached for her and pulled her shirt over her head. Then he tugged off her jeans and pushed her legs farther apart.

"I'm sorry I kissed Jake," she said, fixing him with her gaze. There was a taunt in her words, and he heard it.

He dropped onto her, moving his lips to her ear. "We're not going to talk anymore about Jake, or I'm going to turn into a jealous asshole."

He took hold of her hand and pulled it down between them. She closed her fingers around him, and he sucked in a breath. "After everything you've been through, you deserve gentle. I *want* to be gentle. But honestly, Doctor, I don't know if I can."

Tess squeezed him and guided him toward her, whispering, "I won't break."

She felt his teeth against her throat as he pushed inside her. He moved with slow, fierce thrusts—bone-rattling and deep—claiming her with his body. She had been aching for him for days, and there was no pain, only her own fierce need.

He touched her mouth, slipping two fingers between her lips. She nibbled and sucked them into her mouth, and he groaned from deep in his chest.

Tess unwound her legs from his waist, murmuring, "I need to move."

Ross held her close and rose to his knees. Her legs folded

beside his as he settled her onto his lap. His mouth locked over one erect nipple and flicked it with his tongue . . . charging every one of her nerve endings. She gave a hiss of excitement.

He flicked again, and the contraction that answered from low in her belly sucked the breath out of her and threatened to bring it all to a rapid conclusion.

"Don't come yet," he insisted, cupping her face in his hands.

"Then stop that," she gasped, rolling hard against his hips.

"Shh, no, be still."

Groaning, she let her body go quiet.

He held her still a moment, and then his hands stroked her cheeks and neck, moving down to massage her shoulders and arms. Her upper and middle back. The deliciously sensitive well at the base of her spine.

"Mmm." She brushed the tip of her nose up the bridge of his. "This feels like gentle to me."

"I underestimated myself," he said quietly, rubbing her thighs. Tracing the curve of her waist. "We've had no time for this. Last time you made me explode, and then you went hurtling away like a rocket. You gave me a gift, but you didn't really let me have it."

She tried to swallow the tight place in her throat. "What do you mean?" she creaked.

He ran a hand through her hair. "You're so sexy, so beautiful. I want to fuck you." He kissed her, gently biting her lower lip. "But I want *more*. I want to look at you. Touch your soft skin. Will you let me have that?"

Tears started in Tess's eyes and she leaned forward, needing to feel his warm lips again. Just his lips, soft and wet, working against hers.

"Ross," she whispered, shuddering. "Talking to me like that will get you anything you want."

He grinned, and she felt him throb inside her. "So I'm getting better at this?"

"Can't remember at the moment how you were deficient before."

"Well, for one, most of the stuff that comes out of my mouth seems to either piss you off or make you cry."

"Uh . . ." She let her shoulders fall back as his thumbs rubbed slow circles over her breasts. "I think you're exaggerating."

"Maybe. But I do like these purring noises you're making much better."

She smiled as he settled her onto her back, eyes sweeping from her face to where they were joined.

"Do what you like with me, ex Agent McGinnis." She rested her hands on his chest. "Just don't pull out."

"I don't think I could." He laughed. "But tell me why."

She hesitated. He bent and kissed the rounded tip of her chin.

"When you're inside me I feel . . . I don't know, anchored." She bit her lip, knowing that was thin. Insufficient. "Just now when you said what you said, and I could feel the pulse and surge of your blood inside me . . . I thought I could feel . . . your soul touching mine."

Her face flushed hot, and she turned her head. "It's not a very scientific thing to say, is it?"

Ross pulled her back and kissed her, his tongue slipping into her mouth as his hand lifted her thigh so he could work deeper. She could feel him in that close, dark space—the whole warm, probing length of him. She concentrated all her senses on that depthless exchange, and her climax stole upon her without any warning.

She arched her hips, and sensing the sudden loosening at her core, he made fast, tight circles that opened her and let him push deeper still. He reached down and raised her other leg, locking her tight against him.

There was an explosion of stillness. Motionless and locked

together, she came like an earthquake that rumbles from so deep in the ground only a fraction of its violence reaches the surface. A low moan vibrated through her and out of Ross.

They sank together as one body in a breathless heap. She bore much of his weight, but she didn't care. She wanted him buried inside her. It made her feel safe from the forces that always swept in and tore her away from the people she loved.

"I'm sorry, kids, but it's too fucking cold."

Jake listened to the rustling inside the tent—*his* tent—and tried not to picture the reunion that had just taken place.

Too late.

Goff was still wandering around in the grape graveyard, scribbling science-y things on a tiny pad of paper, so Jake didn't even have the distraction of other company.

Tess came spilling out of the tent, tucking overstimulated curls behind her ears. Her face was red as an apple, whether from embarrassment or exertion it was impossible to be sure.

"Hey," she said, and her expression told him she knew that it was a lame thing to say. "I'm sorry," she added.

"Don't apologize for taking what you want, sweetheart. I never do."

Ross came out behind her, and the Fed pressed a hand against her backside, nudging her aside so he could close and zip the tent flap.

Jake picked up his most recently opened bottle and gulped.

Ross had exited the tent with his shirt in his hands—intentionally, no doubt, as a challenge to any other primate in the vicinity—and now he clasped the woman Jake loved against his bare chest. Jake saw her tense for a moment—weakly fighting the embrace out of consideration for him, he imagined—before going soft in Ross's arms.

"Come *on*," Jake grumbled, feeling the wine buzzing in his brain. "It's bad enough you had to use my tent."

Ross looked at him. "Since I'm the one who went down in that hole for it, I'd say it's a community tent."

"Ross," warned Tess.

"What do you need a tent for? You can go home and fuck in a bed. Hell, you could probably have your choice of beds. First yours, then hers. You could go down to the lab and use mine."

"Always with the pity party," groaned Ross. "Give it a rest."

Jake took an unsteady step toward them. "Listen, *dick*. You got the girl. You got the Earth that still has smart phones and Chinese takeout. Don't you fucking sit there in your . . . postcoital superiority . . . and tell me what to do or how to feel."

Ross snorted. "God, you are one pathetic asshole."

"Yeah? Fuck you."

Jake launched at Ross, and the two men collided.

The energy transfer triggered like a shovel to the back of his head, and Ross wrestled him to the ground. Jake roared and squeezed his hands around Ross's throat.

"Let him go, Ross!" cried Tess.

Ross jammed the heel of his hand under Jake's chin and forced him back. Jake's rage had opened the floodgates, and his energy poured into Ross. His hands fell away from Ross's throat, but as Ross was withdrawing, Jake jerked up and bashed his head against Ross's face.

"Jesus!" growled Ross, kicking Jake away.

Jake threw everything he had left into a final surge—which was stopped by Ross's fist cracking against his jaw.

"Ross, stop it!" Tess shouted as Jake slouched to the ground, moaning.

The Fed shot her a look of disbelief. "I'm not supposed to defend myself?" He got up, wiping blood from his nose. "You're a psychology Ph.D., Tess. Why do you always let him play you?"

Ross stalked out the door, and Tess's eyes followed.

Jake felt a stab of guilt at the pain and confusion in her expression. "Go on, Doc," he mumbled. "I'm okay."

She gave him a dubious look. "Are you sure about that?"

Jake rubbed his jaw, grinning. "Sure I am. Who's bleeding?"

Tess frowned.

"Hey, he could have killed me if he wanted to. Probably a hundred different ways. We're just blowing off steam. Go on and tell him you're sorry for taking my side. He'll get over it."

Ross stomped out of the ruined building furious with himself. Why did he always let Jake bait him? It was easy work for Jake; he had nothing to lose. But Ross had Tess, and he was always walking a tightrope with her.

The worst part was he knew what had happened in there had more to do with jealousy than anything else. Ross had never been jealous. It was the worst kind of petty insecurity. But he'd never been with a woman in love with two men. Before Tess, he would have considered it a waste of his time.

A cool hand came down on his arm, and he jerked away so violently she stumbled.

Ross swore and threw an arm out to catch her. Her fall pulled him off-balance, and they sank together to the ground. She pressed her forehead into his chest, and her breaths made warm puffs against his shirt.

Sighing, he wrapped his arms around her and kissed the top of her head. How could he be angry with her? Loving them both—trying to keep the peace between them as they cycled in and out of resentment—was tearing her apart. It was the reason he'd fallen for her in the first place. . . . She had a heart the size of Jupiter.

———

Jake propped himself in the doorway, watching a makeup kiss that was beginning to look like a prelude to more screwing. He'd been selfishly relieved to hear Tess talk about staying in Camp Desolation. He'd thought maybe he'd stick around after all. See if she could really pull it off. But if the Fed was going to stay with her . . . he couldn't take it. He'd end up shooting himself. Again.

Knowing they were having sex was one thing; observing it was another. It didn't help that he'd encouraged her. The question was, if he'd known it would become possible for him to touch Tess himself, would he have pushed her at Ross?

No way.

Jake's gaze shifted to Goff, who was heading across the vineyard toward them, still scribbling on his pad. As he watched Goff's approach, wondering how he was keeping his footing when he wasn't even looking at the ground, he noticed movement on the blighted hillside in the distance.

"Hey," he called, "we've got company."

Ross and Tess broke apart and followed his gaze.

Four figures moved down the hillside, two of them dragging something behind them.

Goff joined Ross and Tess, and Jake walked over to stand with them.

"Friends of yours?" asked Goff.

Jake shook his head.

As they drew closer, he saw the thing they were dragging was a tarp loaded with belongings—they were using it like a sled. Once they were down the hill they progressed slowly, navigating the muddy, uneven ground.

"Could be your doppelgänger again, G-man," said Jake. "Maybe you and the doctor should scoot back home."

"If he comes to mess with us again it'll be the last thing he does."

"I'll kill him," muttered Tess, and Ross gave her a startled look. It was a very un-Tess-like thing to say.

"You'll both have to beat me to it," said Jake, touching his bandaged ear.

But as the visitors drew closer they ruled out Mac. One of the figures was hooded, but too slight to be Ross's twin.

They released the tarp and continued until they were about five yards away, and Jake realized he was shaking. These were people from his world. *Survivors.* Maybe Tess had been right. Maybe he didn't have to die alone on this cold, barren rock.

Two of the figures wore Seattle-style all-weather jackets, while two were wrapped in layers of blankets. Three of them had scraggly beards. He couldn't see anything but the chin of the smaller one in the hood. But the shape and texture of that one feature was enough to identify her as a woman or an adolescent boy.

A man with a dark beard and haggard expression stepped in front of the others.

"We saw your smoke," he said simply.

Jake took a few steps forward as well, so they were no more than six feet apart. He felt connected across centuries with other men and women who'd found themselves in this same position. Greeting strangers in front of their homes, trying to read intention in tone and demeanor.

"We have a fire," answered Jake. *God, what an idiot.*

The bearded man studied him, arms hanging stiffly at his sides. Jake noticed the other members of his group all held a hand to their waists. They had weapons of some kind. Or wanted Jake to think they did.

"We came down from southeastern Washington," the man continued, "along the Hood River. Thought we might find warmer weather closer to the coast."

Jake pulled his sleeping bag tighter, chuckling. "Welcome to paradise. Sorry to disappoint you."

The man raised his eyebrows, and the smaller figure stepped forward. She pushed back her hood, and two auburn braids flopped onto her chest.

"We left ten feet of snow," said the woman.

Jake's eyes locked onto her face. His heart tried to escape through his throat, and he gulped it back down.

"Somebody please shoot me."

Tess gasped as the woman's hood fell back.

She was a little shorter. Had more color in her complexion. Longer hair. Hardship had worn her thinner. Otherwise, she was Tess's twin.

Entanglement strikes again.

Tess tried to move closer, but Ross gripped her hand. "It's not safe," he reminded her.

The woman's gaze flickered at Tess. She froze, and her gaze swung back.

Tess moistened her lips with her tongue. She said, "Tess?"

The woman blinked at her, and she shot an uneasy glance at the bearded man. He gave a helpless shrug. Finally she said, "No, I'm Eva."

Tess smiled. "Named after your mother."

Eva stared at her, surprised and wary. "That's right. How did you—?"

"Is she alive?" Tess swallowed. "Your mother—is she still alive?"

Eva shook her head slowly. "Who *are* you?"

"Why don't we take this party inside?" suggested Jake.

Eva studied the ruin, hesitating.

"It's comfier than it looks."

"Okay," she said skeptically, bumping her pack higher.

"Here," said Jake, reaching for it.

"I got it," she replied flatly.

"I see that," he muttered, leading the way to the ruin.

The others dragged their tarp close to the doorway. They had an assortment of canned food, blankets, outdoor gear, and extra clothing. Inside they dumped their packs and huddled next to the fire.

"You should save your wood for cooking," said Eva, despite the fact she was warming her hands close the flames. One of the men grunted agreement.

After that, silence settled into the empty spaces around the crackling fire, and finally Eva's gaze shifted back to Tess. Her eyes moved over her slowly.

"Who are you, and why are you so clean?"

Tess shot an uncertain glance at Ross, and he shrugged. "Your call, Doc."

So she told them. Everything. And naturally they didn't believe it, until Jake suddenly dislocated and rematerialized on the other side of the fire. Which Tess was pretty sure he did mainly to impress Eva.

"Can I have some of that?" asked Eva, glancing at Jake's corked bottle.

He picked it up and handed it to her. She took a long pull, closing her eyes as it traveled to her stomach. Then she gave it to Tom, the man behind the darkest beard, who drank and passed it on to the others.

"You three have been through hell," she observed.

Tess raised an eyebrow at her twin. "So have you."

"What's going to happen when you go back?"

Parched from all the talking, Tess emptied a water bottle before answering. "I don't know. If the story does go public, at some point I would think the government will have bigger problems than chasing us down. But between now and then, I'd like to start organizing a relief effort."

She explained the plan she'd hatched earlier that afternoon, while talking to Jake and Goff.

Eva gave her a funny little half smile that Tess couldn't help wondering if she'd ever used herself. "Why would you want to do that? Sounds like aside from a few unwanted visitors, things are all right on your world. Why not forget about us?"

Jake chuckled. "It's what she *does*."

Eva gave a slow nod, seeming to need no further explanation. "Well, I might be able to help you. Pre-apocalypse, I ran a shelter for battered women."

Their eyes met, and what passed between them required no words for understanding.

"I'm sure you could," replied Tess. "I'd be grateful."

"How will you convince the people with the resources to help?" asked Eva. "That's always the hardest part."

"I agree. It's going to be an uphill battle, since our leaders currently view Echoes as enemies. The general public will view them that way too, once the story gets out."

"I emphasized in the letter I gave to my press contact that Echoes are a threat that can be managed," said Ross, "with the right people in charge. I also included instructions for surviving contact. But for a while, people are going to be afraid."

"It seems like the best thing we can do for now," said Tess, "other than obtaining supplies, is track them and bring them back here, so no one gets hurt."

"It just so happens that I'm looking for a job, Doctor," Ross said with a grin.

"I understand you're highly qualified."

"I learned from the best."

"Do you have time for an interview this evening?"

"I'll *make* time."

Jake gave a long-suffering groan, and Tess returned her attention to Eva. A faint smile rested on the lips of her twin.

"I'm sorry," said Tess, flushing. "It's been an incredibly long week. But the difficulties we're facing are trivial compared to yours."

"I don't know about that. At least we're not fighting hidden agendas. If I had to name one benefit of this catastrophe, that has to be it. It's erased all the bullshit. We are what you see."

Tess nodded. "We're glad you're here. I don't know if you're hungry, but it's getting late. Maybe we could open a few cans of ravioli and talk over what you've been through and what you've seen out there."

Eva laughed. "The only thing you need to know about us is we're *always* hungry."

They sat up talking late into the night, and after everyone else had bedded down, Ross and Tess stayed up even later discussing what would happen in the morning. They'd both done short transfers with Jake, so they wouldn't subject anyone else to the dislocations. (As Jake pointed out, "Not all of us got the fling-yourself-into-the-void gene.") That meant they'd have to do it again first thing, or they'd have to leave.

"Maybe you can find Abby," said Tess. They'd wrapped up together in the blankets so Jake and Goff could use the sleeping bags. She felt safe pressed up against him, his warm breath in her ear. "I know she'll help us."

"The Bureau will be watching her," Ross reminded her. The low voice directly in her ear threw kindling on a fire that had never fully gone out. She squirmed her backside closer, and he gave a quiet groan.

"They may be too busy if the story's been broken. We have to start somewhere."

"I'm thinking I want to start right here." His hand slipped around to press between her legs.

"Ross!" She laughed. "We're not alone. And besides that we have to conserve energy."

"I have an idea. Stop talking. Stop squirming. Problem solved."

"Hey, G, I think you better come out here."

Ross and Tess were the last out of bed. They untangled themselves from the blankets, mumbling a greeting to Goff and two of the men from Eva's party. Ross grabbed a bottle of water, and they all went outside to see what Jake wanted.

He and Eva were standing together, eyes on the hillside to the north, watching half a dozen figures descending toward them. About a dozen more crested the hill and started down after the others.

"More survivors?" suggested Eva.

"Maybe," said Ross. Tess didn't like the doubt in his voice. Sometimes he knew things she didn't. "Could be trouble," he continued. "Do you have weapons?"

"We like to try talking first." Tess noted the disapproval in Eva's tone and flashed back to the conversation she'd had with Ross on the patio at Seattle Psi, when he'd suggested she learn to use a gun.

"They're coming fast," warned Tom.

Despite Eva's scolding, blades appeared in the hands of her companions.

Tess's heart gave a thump of warning as one figure moved out ahead of the others.

"Just like a bad fucking penny," muttered Jake.

New Friends, Old Foes

Over the years, *Kalakala* workers say, they have heard footsteps aboard the famous, rusty ferry berthed on Lake Union and given chase in search of intruders—only to find the boat locked and vacant. Recently, a team of amateur ghost hunters boarded the boat with electromagnetic field probes and infrared cameras. They say they found . . . something.

—*"Kalakala's Table Set for Unseen Guest,"*
Seattle Post-Intelligencer, February 13, 2002

G O INSIDE," said Ross, knowing it was a waste of breath but hoping it would earn him compliance on the more critical request.

"Not a chance," Tess replied. "They may need us."

"Fine. But promise me you won't touch him. Not for any reason." He fixed his gaze on her and added, "Please, Tess."

Her eyes moved over his face. "I promise."

"Is he one of yours?" asked Eva.

"One of *yours*," said Ross. "But he's dangerous. He can dislocate."

"But mostly he's just a psychopath," added Jake. "Don't believe anything he says."

"Everybody just stay calm and stay put," Mac called as he approached. Maggie, the redhead from the *Kalakala*, had drawn up beside him.

They were a ragged bunch, but here and there Ross caught the glint of something shiny and new—like the *knives* most of them seemed to be carrying.

Eva and the dark-bearded man had taken a few steps toward the newcomers. Mac stopped in front of them, holding a pistol in plain view.

"What do you want?" Eva bristled.

Mac sized her up with a surprised chuckle. "You're not who I thought you were."

His gaze ran over the rest of her group, eyes coming to rest on Tess and Ross.

"You don't belong here," he said, raising the pistol. "You can go home or I can shoot you. Your choice."

"I hear you made it back to our Earth after all," said Ross.

"Thanks to the doctor," said Mac. "We had a few disappear like that on the *Kalakala*, but they never came back. A dozen feet above the pre-asteroid sea level probably wasn't an ideal spot for dislocation. It took me some time to piece it together. Doubt I ever would have if it hadn't been for all the quality time with your girlfriend."

Ross's stomach wrenched. *This is what he's good at. Don't let him get to you.*

"That's handy," said Ross. "A man who disappears and reappears with goodies for the kids probably makes lots of friends. Do they know about the deal you made with Garcia?"

"You're not as stupid as I thought," replied Mac. But he turned his focus to Tess. "You're welcome to stay, Doctor. I'd like to know you better. But I don't want to be watching my back all the time, so the asshole has to go."

Tess moved closer to Ross, pressing against his side.

"I wonder what makes you so afraid of me," said Ross. "Worried your new friends will find out the truth about you?"

Mac nodded at Maggie, and she directed his followers to spread out and surround them.

"This is your last chance, Agent McGinnis."

Ross pressed a hand against Tess's back to shift her to one side, and he could feel her trembling. Tess had never been afraid of Jake, had dismissed the risks of the transfers, had thumbed her nose at both Ross and the FBI director, but she was afraid of this man.

Ross was glad Jake hadn't killed Mac, because he was going to do it.

"I'm not sure what all this is about," Eva interrupted, "but it's a dangerous mistake not to work together. We need each other if we're going to survive."

"I agree completely," replied Mac. "But you also need a leader who can look out for your interests. That ruin behind you is full of supplies. Food, first aid kits, flashlights. Had your new friends gotten around to telling you about that?"

"Yeah, actually. And frankly, considering they haven't waved any guns at us, or threatened to kill anyone, I'm feeling more inclined to trust *them*."

"You expect me to believe if you had a gun you wouldn't use it to protect your people?" Mac tucked the pistol into his waistband. It was no longer necessary now that his followers had surrounded them.

"Everyone will be migrating toward the coast, where it's warmer," he continued. "It's hard to know who you can trust. But there's no reason we can't work together. Share resources. I have access to tools, seeds, medicine . . . lots of stuff no longer available here. We can build a community together. Protect ourselves from outside threats." Mac stared pointedly at Ross.

"As long as we do what *you* say, you mean." Eva was quick, with a hard edge that had probably been an advantage in surviving here.

"Without a strong leader, there's going to be inequity," said Mac.

"And bickering over resources. But it's your decision. You're free to go if you like."

"However, Mr. Strong Leader will be helping himself to our shelter and our resources," observed Jake. "And yours."

Ross leaned and whispered in Tess's ear, "Stay close to Jake."

She eyed him with alarm. "What are you going to do?"

"For once will you just do what I say?" His fingers rubbed her back, making up for the sting of his words.

Ross stepped away from her and said in a loud voice, "Maybe you should tell them a little more about yourself, so they know what they're getting. I think your previous job was . . . ?"

Mac crossed the distance between them in three short strides and shoved the gun in Ross's face. "You had your chance, asshole."

Mac pulled the trigger, and Tess screamed.

Ross felt a strange crawling sensation as the bullet passed through his head. He touched the spot with his fingers and looked at them. The hand was clean—and transparent. He'd felt himself fading, but he hadn't been sure the bullet wouldn't kill him. He'd placed his faith in the instincts that had always served him well, and in the little glimpses of the future that Tess had taught him not to fear.

"Mac's qualifications for leadership include five years overseeing a huge meth operation," Ross continued. "He was a drug dealer. And a loan shark. He has almost as much blood on his hands as your asteroid."

Mac fired the gun again, and Ross smiled. "You *are* as stupid as I thought."

Ross lunged, and they crashed together to the ground.

Tess rushed toward them, and Ross shouted at her to stay back. Mac's consciousness overlapped with his own.

———

"Get that out of my face," barked Eva.

Jake watched Tess Number 2 land a right hook against the jaw of a spear-wielding man easily a foot taller than her.

The man swung the spear at her, growling with pain, but his aim was way off and she easily bent away from the swipe. She brought her fist down on his extended elbow, and he dropped the spear but managed to land a solid swat against her cheek with the other hand, knocking her down.

Jake snatched up the spear from the ground, shoving it against the man's chest. But someone kicked Jake's knee from behind, and he staggered to the ground. Turning to face his attacker, he found the *Kalakala* redhead drawing a knife.

The blade arced out, toward Jake's face. But another body collided suddenly with Maggie, and the blade swung short.

Tess's arms coiled around Maggie, and she wrestled her to the ground. Maggie screeched and flailed against Tess, fighting hard to free herself. Tess's body, in contrast, was nearly motionless. Maggie wouldn't escape unless Tess decided to release her—Jake knew only too well.

"She's feeding on her?" asked Eva, helping Jake to his feet.

Professor Goff moved to stand beside them. "Draining her energy."

Maggie's body quieted, the noises in her throat sounding strangled now. Before his eyes—and Eva's, and those of twenty or so mesmerized onlookers—color, breath, and life drained from her.

Suddenly Tess broke free, letting Maggie's wasted body fall away.

"Is she alive?" asked Eva.

"Yes," said Jake, comparing what was left of the redhead to the husks he'd seen. "Though probably not very." Then louder he added, "If you idiots will disarm and back off, we can take care of her. She might just live."

All the observers but Jake, Eva, and Goff backed away until there was a wide buffer of space around Tess.

Tess's eyes raked over the crowd. "Forget about Mac," she said. "He's a survivor, but he'll use you. What he's selling isn't worth the price. He pays for those supplies and shiny knives with bodies—*your* bodies. I saw him transport two of you back to my Earth and abandon them there."

No one moved or breathed, and Tess's chin lifted. A breeze teased the ends of her hair, causing that single strand of white to dance around her face.

"I didn't have to let her live," said Tess. "I'll do the same to any one of you who raises a hand or a weapon against another. If you want to survive, you'll settle your differences."

Tess moved silently away. Bodies parted, making way for her to return to Ross.

Jake followed with Eva and Goff. The others pressed in around them.

Mac and Ross were locked in a wrestling hold, rolling over the ground like men had been doing in barrooms and barns for centuries.

Except these men were bathed in a creepy blue light, and sometimes it looked like it was one man fighting himself.

Tess felt a disturbance in the air beside her, and a man materialized—Patterson, one of the other agents she'd trained in dislocation and remote viewing. He grabbed her arm, and she gave a cry of protest.

Jake spun toward her, but it was too late. They were already plummeting down the rabbit hole. She struggled against her captor in the tunnel, but he worked an arm around her throat, paralyzing her until her feet struck something harder than earth.

"We've got Dr. Carmichael."

The words reached her before her vision had reoriented. Seattle Psi, she assumed, since there was no mistaking Garcia's voice. But as small circular windows swam in her vision, she realized her mistake. Patterson yanked her to her feet, and her eyes moved around the cavernous ferry compartment.

A few yards away, near the stairway to the passenger deck, Garcia stood with his gun pressed to her supervisor's head.

"Abby!" she cried. "What's going on?"

"We're waiting for Ross," growled Garcia.

"We don't have time for this," protested Tess in her confusion. "Ross is in trouble."

"That's convenient, but we'll just wait here for a while to be sure."

Tess stared at the Bureau director. His face was drawn and pale. He looked like he hadn't slept or shaved. "Why don't you tell me what's going on?" she asked.

"I'm sick to death of talking to you, Doctor," replied Garcia in a tone laced with threat. "We're going to stand right here, in silence, and wait for Ross."

"What happens then?"

"He's going to pay for his sins."

Finally her brain steadied enough to hook the missing piece. The files. Ross had betrayed the Bureau. It would probably mean the end of Garcia's career.

"Go warn him if you want to," continued Garcia, shoving at Abby's head with his pistol.

"Okay!" cried Tess, holding up her hands. "Just take it easy."

"Wanted to be sure you're paying attention. Now I don't want to hear another word out of either of you."

Her heart pounded, and she could feel the dislocation trying to take her. Peeling at her edges. *Not yet!* Inside her head the brain gremlins were shouting at her.

You have to get back to Ross!

You have to help Abby first!

"What's that noise?" asked Abby.

Tess stared at her, wondering whether her boss could hear the gremlins too. But then Tess heard murmuring sounds coming from the stairs that led up to the passenger deck.

Not murmuring. A woman crying.

"Who's there?" called Garcia.

The crying abruptly broke off.

"I thought the boat had been cleared," he barked at Patterson.

"It was, sir," said Patterson. "Evers and I did the last sweep, and I secured the door myself."

"Obviously you missed someone." Perspiration beaded on Garcia's forehead. "This damn ship is a catacomb. Go check it out. You'll have to take Caufield with you."

"Yes, sir." Patterson tugged Tess's arm.

"Sounds like Adelaide to me," said Abby.

Adelaide! The hairs on the back of Tess's neck raised. Abby shot her a meaningful look. Unfortunately Tess was unable to decipher the meaning.

"Who?" demanded Garcia.

"A woman who died on this ferry."

"Died? When?"

"In 1940. She shot herself in the women's lounge." Abby glanced at the stairs. "Which is on the passenger deck, almost directly overhead."

Garcia's face puckered into an expression of profound irritation. "Are you trying to tell me this ship is haunted?"

"Few modern parapsychologists believe in ghosts per se," said Abby. "But we do believe in residual energy. Which is actually *more* unsettling."

Abby was exercising one of her more useful leadership

skills—baffling with bullshit. It was true that few scientists in their field believed in literal ghosts, but there was no strong consensus about the cause of ghostly phenomena.

Garcia's gaze had shifted to the stairs. He scooted Abby a couple of degrees to the right, away from the sound. "Okay, we've got some time to kill. Let's have it."

"A ghost presumably has some form of consciousness, which, even if limited, implies malleability."

"Which means . . . ?"

"They can do things like change their minds. They can forgive. But a particle can't change its state. An electron is negative forever."

"What exactly—"

A shot rang out directly overhead. Garcia aimed his pistol at the stairs.

"Watch out!" cried Tess, prompted by instinct.

Her shout drew Garcia's gaze her direction, and a blur of something came flying down the stairs, crashing into Garcia and shoving him aside. Abby and the pistol spilled onto the deck.

The blur had focused and now sprawled across Garcia's chest. "Is somebody down here talking shit about electrons?"

"Jake!"

She felt Patterson's fingers grip her arm, and she reached for the light.

As they swooped together into the tunnel he tried to release her, but she caught hold of his shirt. They shot out at the end, rolling onto a rocky ledge that dug into Tess's back and shoulders. She was disoriented at first—mist rained down over her face, and there seemed to be little rainbows everywhere.

The agent beside her scrambled to his feet. He closed his eyes. *He's going! Stop him!*

She bounded from the ground and gave him a shove. He caught at her sleeve, jerking her toward the edge, and she gave a yelp of fear. But as he dropped away he lost his grip on the damp fleece, and down he went. Into the swirling chaos of Snoqualmie Falls.

Cries of shock drifted down from the observation point.

She turned away from the edge and dislocated back to the *Kalakala*.

"Tess!" cried Abby. "Are you okay?"

She flew at the older woman, throwing her arms around her. "I'm okay."

"Are we saving this for anything?" groaned Jake, still locked in an energy transfer with Garcia. The director struggled against Jake, increasing the flow.

Tess bit her lip. She tried to think if there was any other way. But the man had proved he didn't give up. "You'll have to finish him, Jake," she replied softly. "Otherwise, he's just going to come after us again."

"You're sure, Doc?"

No! But the protest didn't make it any farther than her head. The transfer could enable him to dislocate—it had only taken once for Mac—and they couldn't afford to risk it.

"I'm sorry, Jake."

"It's your call," he replied. "I'm just the walking weapon."

Jake released him, and Tess forced herself to look at the husk. It was hard to imagine it having once been alive.

"God," muttered Abby.

"How did you know we were here?" Tess asked Jake.

"I had no idea, sweetheart. I guess I just came back to the last place I was—that asshole's bed. I didn't know how to do anything else."

"Thank God for that. Thank you for coming after me."

"Wouldn't have done it for anyone but you. Makes me feel like I'm gonna puke."

"We have to do it one more time. I have to get back and help Ross."

"Right. Can you give me a lift?"

"Where are you going?" asked Abby, brow creased with worry.

"I can't explain now. Ross is in trouble. But I promise I'll be back."

"Please try to come back in one piece."

Tess reached out an arm to Jake, and he grasped it. "That ghost thing was brilliant, Jake. How did you find out about Adelaide?"

Light swirled around his head as he gave her a blank look. "What ghost thing?"

Ross fought the merging of their bodies and minds as long as he could, but he and Mac were like magnets held apart by threads. Both men were tiring, and the threads snapped one by one as the magnets strove to assume their natural state.

You're a selfish bastard, aren't you? Taking her away from Jake. Ditching the Bureau so she'll feel obligated to stay with you.

Round Two, psychological warfare. Ross curled his fingers around Mac's throat. But he could feel the fingers digging into his own throat and was forced to ease his grip.

You know it will never work. You'll never give up control, and she'll never be controlled.

Ross growled and tried jamming his thumbs into Mac's eye sockets. Mac shouted and writhed out from under Ross, pain boosting his strength. As he tried scrambling away, Ross tackled him again, locking his arm around Mac's neck.

How sad for you, when you inevitably drive her away. She's all that you have left. But she'll always have Jake.

Ross froze, and Mac dug his fingers into Ross's chest, coiling them around his heart.

Mac had wormed around in Ross's brain and found the thing

that scared him most. Ross had won the fight of his life—the battle for Tess's heart. What if it had been a mistake? What if he couldn't make her happy?

Was it possible for him to change?

Anyone can give up control.

These last words processed through his consciousness, and he realized they hadn't come from Mac.

Mac still groped around in Ross's chest, experimenting, trying to inflict one-way damage. But something in Ross cried out from the depths, trying to tell him something important. He shut Mac out and listened for the new voice.

Anyone can give up control. It's a choice, not a fight.

Meaning penetrated through fissures in Ross's protective shield. *It's a choice, not a fight.* How had he missed something so obvious?

Ross had already made his choice. He chose Tess.

He stopped fighting and stepped away from the cliff.

Mac noted the slackening of Ross's form. He uttered a cry of satisfaction, of triumph, over his opponent's surrender.

Ross let one hand fall to his side, resting the other against Mac's back. He applied no pressure. Used the contact as a focal point only for release.

Mac's body tensed. Ross felt the rush and rumble of the energy transfer, like an airplane gaining speed on the runway. Mac panicked and tried to fight. Ross kept still, watching from a distance as the force of the transfer ripped Mac away from the tarmac.

Ross filled his lungs with cool air and let his body root into the earth. This earth was not his own, but it recognized the life inside him and welcomed him. Ross stretched, fingers and toes tingling with energy.

One of two hearts stopped beating.

Ross opened his eyes and flung the dried-out husk away from him.

"Ross?" Tess's voice, trembling. Tess's face, pale with fear.

"Affirmative, Dr. Caufield."

Her lips curved up in a smile. She collapsed on top of him.

"It's not good-bye, Jake."

He sighed. "So you say. But people come. People go. This place is like Grand Central Station. You just never know."

"I *do* know," she replied, settling the back of her head into the solid warmth of Ross's chest. "We're going to tie up loose ends. Get the latest news. Do some planning with Abby. Next stop, Camp Electron."

He rolled his eyes. "I was too clever for myself with that one. It's going to stick forever."

She grinned. "You know it."

"Be sure to contact the university, lass," said Goff. "You may be able to get some help from the Koestler Unit. Because of their association with your Goff, I might be able to help you talk to them."

"I'll most likely take you up on that, Professor. Thank you."

Eva stepped closer and held out her hand. Then in midair she dropped it, smiling instead. "I look forward to working with you. And getting to know you better. I always wanted a sister."

"So did I," replied Tess.

Jake and Eva exchanged a glance, and Eva turned and walked back toward the ruin. Jake's eyes followed her.

"I guess I can stop worrying about *you*," said Tess. "You're in far more capable hands than mine."

"I don't know, Doc," he replied, rubbing his beard. "I'm a little worried about that situation. I can't mouth off to her like I do with you. She'll kick my ass."

"I think an ass-kicking might do you good."

"You're probably right."

"I'm going to miss you, Jake."

"Hey, Strawberry Swirl," he protested. "I thought we weren't saying good-bye."

"You're right," she said with a nod. She swallowed the lump in her throat. "I'll see you soon."

"Are you ready?" Ross asked, arms tightening around her middle.

She glanced back down to the valley, dotted with tents and cooking fires. The orange light washing over the ruin made it almost look homey. Almost.

"I'm ready."

Tess turned, wrapping her arms around Ross, and pointed her thoughts toward home. They plummeted into the void of space and time. The light-washed emptiness enfolded them.

FOUNDATION

The Earth 2 Relief Foundation has leased Seattle's historic Pacific Tower. The allegedly haunted landmark building, built in 1932 in the art deco style, boasts a diverse history of tenants. Formerly a U.S. Marine Corps hospital, it was also temporarily home to online retail giant Amazon.com.

—"Seattle Landmark Building to House E2R,"
The Seattle Times, January 1, 2019

Five months later

TESS TAPPED on Ross's door with her knuckles. "Hey, you."

He glanced up from a pile of paperwork, offering a weary smile. "Hey, yourself."

"We got another application for dislocation certification," said Tess, handing him a manila envelope.

Ross leaned back in his chair, running a hand through his hair. He looked like he hadn't slept much last night. Well, she *knew* he hadn't slept much. But that particular type of insomnia usually left him invigorated.

"Of course we did," he grumbled. "Everyone wants to be Doctor Who."

"I think that's a time-travel thing, lover."

"Close enough. I thought I was hired to track down Echoes, not push paperwork."

"But you push it so well."

Ross fixed his eyes on her face, raising an eyebrow. Then he laughed out loud. "Don't you have anything better to do than torment me?"

"Nothing as fun." She winked at him. "Want to see off the professor with me? He's going home for good today."

"Sure," he said, rising from his desk. "Anything to delay the inevitable. After that maybe we could . . ." He came close, whispering in her ear, ". . . go home for lunch."

"You're insatiable. And incorrigible."

"It's in my job description. Don't you remember? You wrote it."

"Right. I forgot."

They walked two doors down to Professor Goff's office, which was more decorated with paperwork than Ross's. For the last three months he'd served as liaison between Earth 2 and the newly christened Camp Emily, keeping track of camp requirements and fulfillment. Two weeks ago he'd turned in his resignation, and a job description for his replacement.

Ross's brother, Jamie, met them in the hallway. "You sure you don't want to make a thing of this? There's still time to send out a press release."

Jamie was handling public relations for E2R.

"I know Abby said any little bit of press helps," said Tess. "But he wouldn't like a public sendoff. He'd say it was too much fuss."

"All right, then, boss lady." He smiled and headed down the hall.

Tess knocked on Goff's door, and he called them in.

"Ready, Professor?" she asked.

He gave his cluttered office a long, loving look.

"Still time to change your mind," said Ross.

"I was never qualified for this job," he said with a laugh. "All the to-ing and fro-ing . . . it wants someone younger."

"You know Koestler would be happy to have you," Tess reminded him. "And Abby would poach you from us unapologetically. You'd be doing me a favor, really, as she's still got me analyzing research data."

"I know, I know. But it's time to go home."

"Okay, Professor." Tess picked up his teapot from one corner of the desk and pressed it into his hands. "At least take this with you."

He frowned at the chipped, tea-stained vessel. "There's no tea where I'm going."

Tess emptied a box of his favorite Welsh brew into her hand, slipping the bags in his coat pocket. "There is now. I'll bring you more."

Goff gave her an affectionate smile. "You've a kind heart, lass. I hope the man never forgets how blessed he is."

"Not likely," said Ross, "considering she reminds me on a daily basis."

Ross kissed her protesting mouth before she could make a sound.

"Nice recovery," she murmured.

"Shall all three of us go?" asked Ross. "I've got some business on the other end."

Goff stepped closer, and they each put an arm around him.

"Don't think you're getting rid of me," she said, feeling the buzz of the energy transfer. She smoothed heavy, gray curls back from his forehead. "Jake tried to say good-bye to us five months ago, and we see him all the time."

"You send us some real Scottish shortbread and I'll invite you for tea."

"It's a deal, Professor."

"I thought we could take a long lunch and run up to see the boat. What do you say?"

Ross sighed and stretched back against the passenger seat of her car. "If you insist."

Despite repairs and rust removal, "the boat" still gave him the creeps. He couldn't believe she had developed such a soft spot for it after everything that had happened there. But then she *was* a parapsychologist. It was also hard for him not to think about the fact Garcia had died there, which technically had been Ross's fault. *It was Garcia's fault.* The reminder came in Tess's voice instead of his, since she'd had to say it at least a dozen times.

But Ross was proud of her, so he kept his mouth shut. The high visibility of E2R had allowed Tess to fund-raise for the personal project. The boat was now home to a nonprofit counseling center for the homeless. The ladies lounge, now the Adelaide Room, had been set aside specifically for depression counseling.

It was a gloriously cold and sunny January day, mercifully without wind. Tess wrapped a scarf around her neck and retrieved a bunch of roses from the backseat.

They paused for a moment in the little park between the Space Needle Millennial Memorial and the refurbished ferry, squinting at the glare of sunshine on highly polished aluminum.

"She's . . ." Ross groped for something complimentary and finally settled for, "Mighty bright."

"Ugh," he grunted as Tess whacked him lightly in the stomach with her bouquet. "Good thing those are thornless. More than I can say for you."

"You're channeling a little Jake right now, sweetie."

"I figure that way maybe you'll never leave me for him."

She flashed him a grin. "You can wait for me out here. I know how you feel about ghosts."

"What have I told you about the reverse psychology?"

"I'm offering you an out! I'll be gone five minutes. Then you can buy me lunch at Ray's."

"Sounds more like a bribe to me. But you're on."

———

After more like fifteen minutes of chat with the depression counselor, Tess exited the boat and found Ross stretched on a sunny park bench. She watched herself approach in the mirrored lenses of his sunglasses.

"Hungry?" he asked.

"Starving." She gave him a mischievous smile. "I know we'd be breaking our own rules, but do you want to dislocate to the restaurant? We haven't done it, just the two of us, in ages. What do you say?"

He rose and pressed his lips to her cheek. "Anything for my girl."

He wrapped his arms around her, and she reached into the void, catching at light with the tips of her fingers. Welcoming the familiar tickle and tug.

AUTHOR'S NOTE

You can visit the haunted ferry by listening to "Kalakala: Songs from a Parallel Universe." *Original cello compositions by Serena Tideman, recorded (says the artist)* "on the Kalakala ferry boat late one evening as it was moored in Lake Union and somewhat abandoned."

Listen and/or purchase at
http://serendipitymusik.bandcamp.com/album
/kalakala-songs-from-a-parallel-universe.

ABOUT *Echo 8*'S GHOST

Adelaide "Peggy" Bebb

APRIL 13, 1915–JUNE 23, 1940

Took her life aboard the ferry *Kalakala*
shortly after the deaths of her father and sister

Bureau of Internal Revenue employee,
poetry student, daughter, sister, wife

I found life too beautiful and at once too difficult.

I found it rare and splendid,
but the moments were too few and dearly paid for.

I found even the beauty painful
because I could not speak my bursting heart.

I know the best of life and the worst.

But most of all I know myself to be inadequate
to make my life what I wanted to make it.[*]

[*] *"Kalakala's* Table Set for Unseen Guest,"
Seattle Post-Intelligencer, February 13, 2002;
Bremerton News-Searchlight, June 24, 1940.

About the Author

A Romance Writers of America RITA Award finalist and a three-time Romance Writers of America Golden Heart Award finalist, Sharon Lynn Fisher writes stories for the geeky at heart—meaty mash-ups of sci-fi, suspense, and romance, with no apology for the latter. She lives where it rains nine months out of the year, and she has a strange obsession with gingers (down to her freaky orange cat). Her works include *Ghost Planet* (2012), *The Ophelia Prophecy* (2014), and *Echo 8* (2015).